ALICE ON BOARD

BOOKS BY PHYLLIS REYNOLDS NAYLOR

Shiloh Books
Shiloh
Shiloh Season
Saving Shiloh

The Alice Books
Starting with Alice
Alice in Blunderland
Lovingly Alice
The Agony of Alice
Alice in Rapture, Sort Of
Reluctantly Alice
All But Alice
Alice in April
Alice In-Between
Alice the Brave
Alice in Lace
Outrageously Alice
Achingly Alice
Alice on the Outside
The Grooming of Alice
Alice Alone
Simply Alice
Patiently Alice
Including Alice
Alice on Her Way
Alice in the Know
Dangerously Alice
Almost Alice
Intensely Alice
Alice in Charge
Incredibly Alice
Alice on Board

Alice Collections
I Like Him, He Likes Her
*It's Not Like I Planned It
    This Way*
Please Don't Be True

The Bernie Magruder Books
*Bernie Magruder and the Case
    of the Big Stink*
*Bernie Magruder and the
    Disappearing Bodies*
*Bernie Magruder and the
    Haunted Hotel*
*Bernie Magruder and the
    Drive-thru Funeral Parlor*
*Bernie Magruder and the Bus
    Station Blowup*
*Bernie Magruder and the
    Pirate's Treasure*
*Bernie Magruder and the
    Parachute Peril*
*Bernie Magruder and the Bats
    in the Belfry*

The Cat Pack Books
The Grand Escape
The Healing of Texas Jake
Carlotta's Kittens
Polo's Mother

The York Trilogy
Shadows on the Wall
Faces in the Water
Footprints at the Window

The Witch Books
Witch's Sister
Witch Water
The Witch Herself
The Witch's Eye
Witch Weed
The Witch Returns

Picture Books

King of the Playground
The Boy with the Helium Head
*Old Sadie and the Christmas
    Bear*
Keeping a Christmas Secret
Ducks Disappearing
I Can't Take You Anywhere
Sweet Strawberries
Please DO Feed the Bears

Books for Young Readers

Josie's Troubles
How Lazy Can You Get?
All Because I'm Older
Maudie in the Middle
*One of the Third-Grade
    Thonkers*
Roxie and the Hooligans

Books for Middle Readers

Walking Through the Dark
How I Came to Be a Writer
Eddie, Incorporated
The Solomon System
Night Cry
The Keeper
Beetles, Lightly Toasted
The Fear Place
Being Danny's Dog
Danny's Desert Rats
Walker's Crossing

Books for Older Readers

A String of Chances
The Dark of the Tunnel
The Year of the Gopher
Send No Blessings
Ice
Sang Spell
Jade Green
Blizzard's Wake
Cricket Man

ALICE ON BOARD

PHYLLIS REYNOLDS NAYLOR

Atheneum Books for Young Readers
New York • London • Toronto • Sydney • New Delhi

For Grace and Tess Meis,
who love books

✳   ✳   ✳

With special thanks to Drew Godfrey
for his help and nautical knowledge

✳   ✳   ✳

ATHENEUM BOOKS FOR YOUNG READERS
An imprint of Simon & Schuster Children's Publishing Division
1230 Avenue of the Americas, New York, New York 10020
This book is a work of fiction. Any references to historical events, real people, or real locales are used
fictitiously. Other names, characters, places, and incidents are products of the author's imagination,
and any resemblance to actual events or locales or persons, living or dead, is entirely coincidental.
Copyright © 2012 by Phyllis Reynolds Naylor
All rights reserved, including the right of reproduction in whole or in part in any form.
ATHENEUM BOOKS FOR YOUNG READERS is a registered trademark of Simon & Schuster, Inc.
For information about special discounts for bulk purchases, please contact Simon & Schuster
Special Sales at 1-866-506-1949 or business@simonandschuster.com.
The Simon & Schuster Speakers Bureau can bring authors to your live event.
For more information or to book an event, contact the Simon & Schuster Speakers Bureau
at 1-866-248-3049 or visit our website at www.simonspeakers.com.
The text for this book is set in Berkeley Oldstyle Book.
Manufactured in the United States of America
First Edition
2 4 6 8 10 9 7 5 3 1
CIP data for this book is available from the Library of Congress.
ISBN 978-1-4424-4588-8 (hardcover)
ISBN 978-1-4424-6160-4 (eBook)

Contents

1

THE *SEASCAPE* AND THE *SPELLBOUND*

The ship was beautiful.

Of course, since none of us had been on one before, almost any ship would do. But this one, three stories of white against the blue of a Baltimore sky, practically had our names on it. And since it would be our home for the next ten weeks, we stood mesmerized for a moment before we walked on down toward the gangway, duffel bags over our shoulders. The early June breeze tossed our hair and fluttered the flags on the boats that dotted the waterfront.

This might possibly be our last summer together, but no one said that aloud. We were so excited, we almost sizzled. Like if we put out a finger and touched each other, we'd spark. We needed this calm before college, this adventure at sea.

Pamela had received a half-scholarship to a theater school in New York; Liz was officially accepted at Bennington; Yolanda was undecided; and Gwen and I would be going to Maryland. But right now the only future we were thinking about was that wide span of open water ahead of us.

"Which deck do you suppose we'll be on?" asked Liz in her whites. She looked like a sailor already.

"Ha!" said Gwen, the only one of us whose feet remotely touched the ground. "Dream on. I don't think we'll even have portholes. We're probably down next to the engine room."

"What?" exclaimed Yolanda, coming to a dead stop.

"Relax," Gwen said, giving her arm a tug. "We're not paying customers, remember. Besides, the only thing you do in crew quarters is sleep. The rest of the time you're working or hanging out with the gang."

"With *guys!*" said Pamela, and that got Yolanda moving again.

It's a wonder we were still breathing. Five hours earlier, four of us had been marching down an aisle at Constitutional Hall for graduation. And when picture-taking was over afterward, we had stripped off our slinky dresses and heels and caps and gowns, pulled on our shorts and T-shirts, and piled into Yolanda's uncle's minivan, which had been prepacked that morning for the mad dash to Baltimore Harbor. The deadline for sign-in was three o'clock. Yolanda had graduated the day before from a different school, so she was in charge of logistics.

It wasn't a new ship. *Completely refurbished*, our printout had read. But it was a new cruise line with two ships—the *Seascape* and the *Spellbound*, though the *Spellbound* wouldn't be ready till fall. The line sailed from Baltimore to Norfolk, with ports in between. The only reason all five of us were hired, we figured, was that we got our applications in early. That, and the fact that when we compared the pay to other small cruise lines along the East Coast, this line offered absolutely the lowest of the low. But, hey! Ten weeks on a cruise ship—a pretty glamorous end to our high school years!

A guy in a white uniform was standing with legs apart on the pier, twirling a pen in the fingers of his left hand. A clipboard rested on the folding chair beside him. The frames of his sunglasses curled around his head so that it was impossible to see either his eyes or eyebrows, but he smiled when he saw us coming.

"Heeeeey!" he called.

Pamela gave him a smart salute, clicking her heels together, and he laughed. "Pamela Jones reporting for duty, sir," she said as we neared the water. Flirting already.

"I'm just one of the deckhands," he told us, and checked off our names on his clipboard. JOSH, his name tag read. "Where you guys from?"

We told him.

"Silver Springs?"

"Singular. There was only one," Gwen corrected.

He scanned our luggage. "Alcohol? Drugs? Inflammables? Explosives?"

"No . . . no . . . no . . . and no," I told him.

"No smoking on board for crew. They tell you that?"

"Got it," said Liz, then glanced at Yolanda. We're never quite sure of anything with Yolanda.

"Okay. Take the port—that's left—side stairs down to crew quarters, then meet in the dining room for a late lunch. Follow the signs. You'll get a tour of the ship later."

We went up the gangplank, and even that was a thrill—looking down at the gray-green water in the space between ship and dock. Now I could *really* believe it was happening.

On the wall inside, past the mahogany cabinet with the ornate drawer knobs, was a large diagram of the ship, naming the major locations—pilothouse, purser's office, dining room, lounge—as well as each of the four decks: observation deck, at the very top; then Chesapeake deck; lounge deck below that, and main deck, where we were now. Crew quarters weren't even on the map.

A heavyset guy in a T-shirt and faded jeans, carrying a stack of chairs, called to us from a connecting hallway, "Crew? Take the stairs over here," and disappeared.

"How do you know what's port side if the ship's not moving?" I asked, confused already.

Nobody bothered to answer because we'd reached the metal stairway, and we hustled our bags on down.

Gwen was right; we had no porthole.

There were five bunk beds in the large cabin—large by shipboard standards, they told us. Ten berths in all, and other girls had already taken three of the lower berths. We claimed the remaining two bunk beds, top and bottom, and Gwen volunteered to sleep in the empty top bunk of an unknown companion.

"Ah! The graduates!" said a tall girl with freckles covering her face and arms and legs. She looked like a speckled egg—a pretty egg, actually. "I'm Emily." She nodded toward her companions. "Rachel and Shannon," she said, and we introduced ourselves.

"First cruise?" Rachel asked us. She was a small, elflike person, but strong for her size—the way she tossed her bags around—and was probably older than the rest of us, mid-twenties, maybe.

"We're green as they come," Liz answered.

"Same here," said Shannon. "I'm here because I'm a smoker."

We stared. "I thought there was a rule . . . ," Pamela began.

"There is. I know. I'm trying to kick the habit. Compulsory detox. I figure it will either cure me or kill me."

"Or drive the rest of us mad," said Rachel. And to us, "She's a dragon when she doesn't have a cig." She looked at Shannon. "Just don't let Quinton catch you if you backslide."

"Who's Quinton?" I asked.

"The Man. The Boss. You'll see him at lunch"—Emily checked her watch—"in about three minutes. I worked under him on another cruise line a couple of years back, so I know some of the people on this one."

"What's he like?" asked Gwen.

"Pretty nice. He's fair, anyway."

The last two girls arrived. The younger, Natalie, had almost white-blond hair, which she wore in a French braid halfway down her back, and then there was Lauren, with the body of an athlete—well-toned arms and legs. Only three of the girls had worked as stewards before—Rachel, Emily, and Lauren. And out of the ten of us, Lauren and Rachel seemed to know the most. Rachel, in fact, was a wellspring of information, the kind of stuff you never find in the rule books. Like Quinton's favorite drink when he was onshore—bourbon on the rocks—and how to keep your hair from frizzing up when you were at sea. She chattered all the while we put our stuff away, cramming our clothes in the three dressers provided. We'd been warned about lack of space, and I'd managed to bring only my duffel, my cloth bag, and the new laptop I got for graduation.

So here we were—ten women in a single room with a couch, a TV, and a communal bathroom next door. The walls were bare except for notices about safety regulations, fire equipment, the dress code, and various prohibitions: no smoking aboard the ship; no food or alcohol in crew quarters; no pets of any kind; no cell phones when on duty; no men in the women's cabin and vice versa. . . .

Welcome aboard.

The first thing we did was eat—on crew schedule, as I'd come to learn—and we were starved. I guess they figured that "stews," as we were called, would pay more attention in training later if we were fed. There were thirty of us in the dining room, counting the chef and his assistant—ten female stewards, ten male stewards, and eight male deckhands. We sat down to platters of hamburgers, potato salad, fries, and every other fattening food you could think of.

"Don't worry," Rachel told us. "You'll work it off. That's a promise."

But we weren't doing calorie counts as much as we were working out the male-to-female ratio. All the ice cream we could eat, guaranteed not to settle on our thighs, and two guys to every girl? Was this the ideal summer job or what, lowest salary on the Chesapeake be damned!

The guys, who had come in first, were grouped at neighboring tables, and we could tell from their conversation that most of the deckhands were seasoned sailors, older than the rest, who had worked for other cruise lines in the past. They were undoubtedly paid a lot more than we were. A couple wore wedding bands.

"I just decided to ditch my theatrical career and devote the rest of my life to the sea," Pamela breathed, after a muscular guy in a blue T-shirt grinned our way.

"Yeah, and what will you do in the winter months when the ship's in dry dock?" Lauren asked her.

Pamela returned the guy's smile. "Three guesses," she said.

I tried to imagine what this dining room would be like in two days' time when passengers came on board. The large windows spanning both sides would be the same, of course, but I'd seen pictures on the cruise line's website of white-clothed tables with sparkling glassware and candles. It must have been a special photo shoot, because this ship hadn't sailed before—not as the *Seascape*, anyway. Still, I bet it would be grand.

Quinton came in just as the tub of peanut butter ice cream was going around for the second time. We'd met Dianne, his wife, when we'd picked up our name tags. She did double duty as purser and housemother, Rachel told us, but it was Quinton who called the shots.

He looked like a former basketball player—so tall that his head just cleared the doorways. Angular face, with deep lines on either side of his mouth—the sort of person who always played Abraham Lincoln in grade school on Presidents' Day. Dianne was as short as Quinton was tall, and it was hard not to think of her—with her curly hair and the bouncy way she carried herself—as his puppy.

"Welcome, everyone!" Quinton said. He had a deep, pleasant voice and the look of a team player, standing there with his shirtsleeves rolled up to the elbows. "Glad to have all the new men and women on board as well as you old salts who have worked with Dianne and me on other cruises."

He gave a thumbs-up to two more guys who'd just come in, still in their paint clothes.

"This will be a first for all of us, though, as the Chesapeake Bay *Seascape* takes her maiden voyage," Quinton continued, "the first, we hope, of a long and successful run on the bay. This fall her sister ship, the *Spellbound*, will be launched. Dianne and I are from Maine, but we've both worked and played on the Chesapeake and are familiar with all that the bay and the eastern shore have to offer. . . ."

There were lots of handouts—work schedules and tour itineraries, names of officers and crew. There were lists of nautical terms—*abaft, bridge, gangway, starboard;* another list of emergency procedures—*fire, man overboard, abandon ship;* and Quinton and Dianne took turns doing the rundown.

"There are no days off, no vacations," Dianne reminded us, "though you'll get two or three hours of downtime in the afternoons and occasionally an evening out at one of our ports of call. You are going to be asked to work harder, perhaps, than you have ever worked before; you will have more rules regarding your appearance and behavior than you've ever had to follow. . . ."

I thought of all the requirements posted on the wall of women's quarters—*earrings no larger than the earlobe; clear polish on the nails; hair worn back away from the face, especially for servers at mealtime.*

"And for every minute you are in the public eye," Dianne continued, "you are required to be friendly and professional, even though, at times, you may be faced with the appalling conduct of a guest."

We gave each other rueful smiles.

Quinton did the closing remarks: "Remember that you are in a unique situation. You'll be living in close quarters, eating and sleeping on odd schedules, and working ridiculous hours at low wages." General laughter. "But you'll make some good friends here, have some fun, and will, I hope, look back on this summer with pride and say, 'I signed on for the maiden voyage of the *Seascape.*' And now let's get to work."

* * *

The stewards were divided into three groups. The first group went off for a tour of the ship with the first mate, a toothy, good-natured young man named Ken McCoy. The second group was to go with Dianne for a demonstration of cleaning the state-rooms, as the passenger accommodations were called. The third group consisted of the stewards who'd worked on other ships before, and these went with Quinton to tour the galley.

To begin, all the inexperienced people were appointed housecleaners in the mornings, dishwashers and busboys at night. After we proved we were reliable and could get along well with the passengers, we would be able to wait tables at breakfast and lunch, pass out the next day's programs, and turn down beds at night. And after the third or fourth week, we could take turns on the most coveted shift—sleeping in a little in the mornings, going on laundry detail, and serving the evening meal. But even then, Dianne told us, no one would work more than a week at a time in the galley, because with setup before meals and cleanup afterward, it was exhausting.

The staterooms were about the size of small bedrooms—a dormitory room, maybe: twin beds, with a narrow aisle between them; a dresser with four drawers; a small desk and chair; a closet; a picture window; and a bathroom the size of two phone booths. To bathe, a passenger stood in the small space between sink and toilet, pulled the waterproof curtain in front of the closed bathroom door, and turned on the shower—over himself, the sink, the toilet, the works. That was why the toilet paper was in its own closed container.

"Wow!" said Natalie. "I hope this isn't the luxury suite."

We laughed, Dianne included.

"Actually," Dianne said, "all the staterooms are alike on this ship. The *Spellbound* is a larger ship with eight suites, but the Chesapeake line is trying to keep costs down to stay competitive."

Getting down to the nitty-gritty, we learned about cleaning products. How you always wore latex gloves and never used the same cloth or brush on the sink that you'd used on the toilet. You cleaned all the corners. You vacuumed under the beds. And you never, ever, opened a drawer or a bag or the medicine cupboard. Theft called for immediate dismissal. You'd be dropped off at the next port of call. Find your own way home.

We were each assigned a few cabins in a row of staterooms on the lounge deck, where the rooms opened onto a narrow outer walkway that went around the whole of the ship, as it did on the deck above. Only the main deck, where the dining room was located, had cabins with doors that opened onto an inner hallway—no wraparound walkway down there. Dianne went from room to room watching us work, making suggestions, giving her critique.

I knew how to clean a bathroom. You don't grow up in a motherless house with a dad and older brother and not learn how to help with everything there is to do. Even after Dad married again, he and Sylvia and I managed to keep the place clean ourselves, but I had heard Sylvia tell Dad that after I left for college, she was hiring a weekly cleaning service. Fair enough, he said, because she was working full-time too, just like him.

Dianne's only complaint about my work was that I was too slow.

"You'll have fifteen rooms to clean in about five hours, Alice," she said. "You can't take a half hour per room, but your work is excellent."

Great, I thought. If I never get hired as a school counselor, I can always clean the building. I wiped one arm across my sweaty face.

A sandy-haired guy named Mitch was cleaning the room next to mine and gave me a sympathetic look. "It's even slower when the passengers get here, they tell me. Then you've got shoes and bags and shaving stuff in your way." He was making hospital corners on the sheet he'd placed over the bed. No fitted sheets on the Chesapeake line. The flat sheets had to do double duty.

"How you making out?" I asked Pamela as we passed on the deck. She gave a soft moan. There was no time to pause and observe the Baltimore skyline or the two guitarists performing on a sidewalk of the Inner Harbor. If any part of my job in housekeeping was supposed to be fun, I hadn't hit upon it yet. But we were so incredibly lucky to have this job—that all five of us had gotten hired together.

We cleaned up the last remnants of dust and lint and grout that builders and decorators had left behind, and each stateroom would be inspected carefully, possibly cleaned again, when we were through. As the afternoon wore on, we began to find shortcuts, better ways of doing things. Dianne applauded each completed room and gave us a breather when she went to get more towels.

Shannon and I rubbed each other's backs as we leaned over the rail. She was a round-faced girl with blue eyes who reminded me of my friend Molly.

"Tell me I don't need a cigarette," she said as I massaged her shoulders.

"You'd like one, but you don't need it," I said. "How's that?"

"I don't know. I think this might have been a mistake— signing on here. Some people can quit cold turkey, but that's not me."

"Ever tried it before?"

"No."

"Then hold on," I said.

It was around six by the time our group finished the few trial rooms we'd been assigned. We knew that the rest of the cabins had to be cleaned the following day—because passengers arrived on Sunday and the *Seascape* sailed out that evening—but we didn't see how that was possible. We were already sore, muscles stretched from squeezing ourselves into tight places and from twisting to clean behind the toilets. Somehow the promised tour of the ship didn't seem as wonderful as it had before. All we wanted to do was to sit down.

But when we exchanged places with the first group and went back down to the dining room for fruit and cheese and crackers, we found ourselves ready to go ten minutes later. We followed Ken McCoy back to crew quarters on the lowest level and checked out the engine room, storeroom, laundry hold, machine shop. No daylight down there.

Then it was back up to the main deck and a tour of the galley.

The lounge deck, next flight up, where we'd been working, had a lounge at one end—a huge room with a wraparound couch at the bow, game tables, a bar, and a library along one side.

The Chesapeake deck above that was all staterooms, including the pilothouse and the captain's quarters. A row of mops and brushes outside the rooms marked where the first group was now learning the fine art of housekeeping.

But our favorite level was the observation deck at the very top of the ship, with deck chairs, a few exercise bikes, and a shaded area for quiet reading. I stood at the rail listening to the sound of the ship's flag flapping, and as I watched the gulls circling and calling, I thought of Patrick and wished he were here.

Why couldn't we ever do something really fun together— I mean, for more than a day? More than an evening? Why couldn't he have taken the summer off from his studies—just one lousy summer—and spent it with me?

We could sit up here after dark and watch the sky as the ship silently plowed the water; visit the ports of call when we had the chance, our arms around each other, my head on his shoulder. I knew I'd probably watch some of the others pair off—the usual summer romances—before the ten weeks were over. But I'd be alone.

In one more week Patrick would be on his way to Barcelona to help one of his professors finish a book. And he'd be there for the next four quarters, getting in his year of study abroad now instead of later. "After that, I'll be back to stay," he'd told me.

But "back" was the University of Chicago, not Maryland. Meanwhile, he'd be seeing the sights of Barcelona alone. Or not. It wouldn't be me at his side, in any case. We wouldn't be watching a sunset together or walking along a beach or taking day trips into the Spanish countryside.

I was overcome suddenly by a wave of . . . homesickness? . . . that immobilized me momentarily—the same kind of sadness or panic you get when you're on a sleepover for the first time or that sinking stomach-twisting anxiety you feel as a kid when you've wandered away from your parents in a department store.

It lasted only six or seven seconds, then receded, but it left me feeling vulnerable. *What was that all about?* I wondered. Patrick as parent? As home? Security? My breath was coming back, and I inhaled slowly. Gradually I tuned in to the conversation around me, as other stews were pointing out the aquarium, the baseball stadium, and Federal Hill onshore.

I gripped the railing and looked straight up, squinting into the late afternoon brightness, watching one solitary gull fly a huge oval above the ship, its wings barely moving, and wondered if it was enjoying its solitude or missing a mate.

2
PUSHING OFF

It didn't take the five of us long to realize that this wasn't anything like summer camp. As I lay on my bunk that night, my thighs and shoulders aching, the summer we had been assistant counselors at Camp Overlook seemed like kindergarten compared to this.

How could we possibly have thought we'd be staying up half the night, joking around with the guys? That somebody would pull out a guitar or even a banjo, and we'd sing and horse around? Two of the guys had appeared half dead when we took a dinner break at eight, and the rest of us lasted till eleven, with the full knowledge that for some of us, alarm clocks would go off at five thirty the next morning—the next morning and the one after that. Were we insane?

It was Shannon who actually said it: "I was *insane* to think I could go ten weeks without a cigarette. I'm practically clawing at my skin already."

"The first twenty-four hours are the hardest," Emily told her in the dark. "Hang in there."

I was already floating in and out of consciousness. I think I heard Liz say "good night." I think I heard one of the other girls humming along with her iPod. I definitely heard someone tell Shannon to shut up about cigarettes.

And then it was morning. Or the middle of the night. I couldn't tell, because there was no sunlight. Only the sound of our door opening, the glare of the fluorescent light in the hall, and Dianne's cheerful voice: "Everybody up. We've got a lot to do today." And we all wanted to kill her.

"Once you get into the routine, it's easier. Really," Dianne assured us as we took turns in the communal bathroom and pulled on our clothes. We tied our hair back, washed the sleep from our eyes, brushed our teeth, ran some ChapStick over our lips, and sat down with the guys for breakfast.

Dianne insisted we eat a big one. "You start work on a near-empty stomach, and halfway through the morning, you'll eat coffee grounds, you'll be so hungry," she told us.

Liz and I studied the steaming platter of scrambled eggs and sausage that was making the rounds, wanting to opt for half a roll and some orange juice instead. We each took a small spoonful of eggs to make Dianne happy, but she was right: By ten fifteen, I was ravenous. I'd cleaned three more rooms, polished the chrome, brought a load of towels up from the laundry hold, and scraped off a bit of paint that had dried on one of the floors. When Rachel told us there were doughnuts and coffee in the galley if we wanted a break, I felt I needed a doughnut as much as I needed air and headed for the stairs.

"My God, my hair!" Lauren said as we passed the mirrored wall on the lounge deck and stared at our early-morning selves—no makeup, no mousse. . . .

"We look like inmates of a women's prison," Pamela wailed.

Our only consolation was that we all smelled alike, I told her.

When we had our two-hour break that afternoon, we were tempted to go back to bed. Shannon, in fact, did—mostly to take her mind off smoking. But the rest of us showered and washed our hair, applied some blush and mascara, and just that little luxury restored our energy. Then we went up on the top deck, where the guys were gathered in the shade area—all but Barry, who loved the sun. Dianne had left a tall pitcher of iced tea for us, and we sprawled on the vinyl lounge chairs, welcoming the late-afternoon breeze.

It was the first time since we'd come on board that we had a chance to really hang out with the guys, and I found myself studying them one by one. The quiet, broad-shouldered guy who smiled mostly with his eyes was Mitch; the talkative one, Flavian, with his dark good looks, could have been an extra on a movie set; all of us liked Barry, who lay bare-chested, his feet pointed outward, on a chaise longue; Josh, probably a few years older than the others, who had sailed before with Quinton and Dianne and also knew the engineer; and Curtis, who wore a wedding band. They looked great in their black T-shirts and sweat-soaked bandanas, but I couldn't be sure who were deckhands and who were stewards.

We sat around discovering a few connections: One of Lauren's friends was Flavian's ex-girlfriend; Natalie and one of the deckhands had gone to the same high school and had had some of the same teachers. . . . Each connection brought out memories and wisecracks, and we were beginning to feel more relaxed. There's something about letting guys see you at your worst, as we were at breakfast, that makes you feel you can let it all out; you can tell each other anything.

Barry, in fact, was so relaxed—eyes closed, hands folded over his stomach—that he didn't see the gulls that were circling overhead. And when one dropped a load on his chest, a wide splatter of white, he thought one of us had pelted him, and he opened his eyes, frowning around the circle. We broke into laughter.

"What?" Barry kept saying. *"What?"* His hand went automatically to his chest. Then, "Shit!" as he held his hand out in front of him.

"Exactly," said Flavian, and we laughed some more.

Barry's feet came down on either side of the chaise longue, and he grabbed Flavian's shirt from the arm of a chair. With one quick swipe and a satisfied grin, he wiped his chest clean.

"Hey!" Flavian cried. "You moron!"

But Josh was laughing. "You gotta watch that guy. We only did one cruise together, and he was goofing off the whole time."

"Yeah? Who had your back when you went AWOL that time in Savannah?" Barry said, tossing the shirt over to Flavian. "Who got the number of that girl in Martha's Vineyard for you?"

"My buddy!" Josh said. "What would I do without you?"

I wiggled my bare feet and thought how much this reminded me of the banter between Patrick and Mark and Brian back in Silver Spring. Around Mark's swimming pool in the summertime. Back when Mark was still alive.

Josh turned to Mitch. "How early did you sign up for this job, Mitch?"

"Would you believe March?" Mitch said, stretching his long legs out in front of him. "Surprised they were still hiring, but they told me I'd be either a deckhand or a stew, whichever they needed most. Just call me 'Whichever.'"

That got a laugh.

"Man, I applied last November," said Barry.

"Yeah, he heard that Steph was going to be cruise director," Josh told us.

"Stephanie? Stephanie Bowers?" said Rachel. "I heard she got fired from that cruise line down in Jacksonville a couple of years ago."

Josh shrugged. "Just goes to show . . ."

Gwen and Yolanda, Liz and Pam and I sat smiling, just

listening, though we didn't really feel left out. *Must be nice to be part of the "in crowd,"* I thought. Maybe sometime, on some future cruise, Josh and Barry would sit around talking about us. Favorably, of course.

We worked like dogs the rest of the day. Frank, the middle-aged engineer, was aboard now, checking things out. Those of us who had spent all our time cleaning cabins were given a crash course in working the galley—scraping the plates and stacking the dishwasher. And for those assigned to clean tables, Dianne demonstrated carrying a fully loaded tray of dishes, including a pot of coffee, on the flat of her hand, one edge resting on her shoulder.

"I couldn't do that in a million years," I said to Rachel. "I'd drop it on a passenger, first thing."

"Here's a hint," she told us. "If that ever happens, sink to the floor and hold your ankle."

"*What?*" said Pamela.

"Moan a little, and all the sympathy will be on you," she told us. As I said, Rachel knew the most amazing stuff.

Before we turned in that evening, each of us was given two long-sleeved white dress shirts and black bow ties to wear when serving meals, to go with the black pants we'd been required to bring with us; two short-sleeved white shirts for serving breakfast or lunch; and two black T-shirts with SEASCAPE printed on them that we were to wear with shorts when we cleaned the rooms.

And once again, we fell into bed without any midnight party, almost too tired to dream.

I woke to an earsplitting alarm and sat up, startled, confused, my heart pounding, desperately trying to remember the instructions for what to do in an emergency.

"What the heck?" Pamela was saying, as murmurs filled the room.

"What time is it?" asked someone else.

I grabbed whatever clothes were handy, making sure to put on shoes. That much I remembered.

When we emerged on the lounge deck, sleep-befuddled and disheveled, dragging our life jackets behind us, the first vermilion of a sunrise appeared in the sky, and my watch said four fifty-five. I would discover, as the summer wore on, that the Chesapeake had some fantastic sunrises and sets.

Quinton was there timing us, and he frowned at those who forgot their life jackets and had to go back. We sucked in the fresh, cool air of early morning and swayed slightly as we stood in a row and finished waking up.

Ken McCoy and Dianne were also up and dressed, as though their morning had started hours before.

"This is the only emergency drill you'll get, other than the routine muster we do at the start of each new cruise," Ken explained. "So if the alarm rings again at an ungodly hour, you'll know it's the *real* McCoy."

He gave step-by-step instructions for putting on the life

jackets, and Dianne and Quinton went up and down the row, making sure each strap was secure. Dianne made me take mine off and put it on again before I passed inspection.

Next we were each assigned a specific spot on the ship where we were to report. Both Gwen and I got the lounge deck, starboard aft, or "LSA." In case of fire, report and listen for further instructions. If we heard the "Man overboard!" alert, we were to race to our designated places, scan the water for the missing person, and, if spotted, keep pointing to the spot, never taking our eyes off him, while the ship turned around and the passenger or crew member was rescued. If the order was given to abandon ship, we were given the specific staterooms that were in our care during a muster. Our job was to see that all passengers were safely out of their staterooms and had put on their life jackets correctly.

Various possibilities played out in my mind. What if a passenger was in the shower? On the toilet? Were we to go in and drag him out?

"Don't worry," Ken added at the end of his little speech. "One of us—Quinton, Dianne, or I—will be on each deck helping out." And then, before the session was over, we had to take partners, each of us removing our vest and putting it on again, checked by our partner.

This was a different kind of morning. It may have been Sunday in Baltimore—I heard a church bell ringing at seven—but at six thirty the deckhands were pushing carts across the dock and up to the hold of the ship, carts loaded with crates of Florida citrus, boxes of New York cheesecake, grapes from California, pasta and wine and flour and coffee. . . .

Quinton checked off each shipment, each crate, and as the morning wore on, all the activity brought locals and tourists down to the waterfront to watch. I began to feel we were onstage.

Once we had cleaned ourselves up and eaten breakfast, Quinton assigned us a place to stand when passengers began arriving that afternoon. A florist's truck pulled up with a huge bouquet of exotic flowers for the cabinet just inside the entrance on the main deck, and Dianne helped Ken set up a folding table for refreshments in the lounge.

"You'd think we were expecting the queen," I said to Emily as we passed each other in the hall.

"We're waiting for the captain," she said. "That's even more important."

I wondered if there would be sailors flanking the gangway when the captain arrived. Rachel and I were arranging napkins by the punch bowl, and the engineer was tinkering with an air-conditioning unit beneath one of the built-in couches that lined the wall at the bow. Frank had just stood up and slipped his tools in his belt when we saw a taxi unload a passenger on the street and watched the man in the white uniform pay the driver.

Frank walked over to the window and peered down. "What the bloody hell?" he murmured.

* * *

Whatever that was about, we didn't have time to debate. All we got from Josh, who knew Frank from other trips, was that it wasn't the captain we'd been expecting. Meanwhile, the crew was told to eat an early lunch; passengers would start boarding at one.

I put on my short-sleeved dress shirt and took my place just inside the entrance on the main deck. Already I could hear Ken greeting guests who were wheeling their luggage up to the gangplank, welcoming them to the *Seascape*. My job was to check their boarding passes and direct them to their staterooms. There was no elevator, so folks who found stairs difficult had taken rooms on this level, where the dining room was located.

Most of the passengers came aboard smiling broadly, eager for the adventure, and that made the crew even more enthusiastic. It was sort of like being in a school play, the way the audience's reaction can energize a cast.

"This is so exciting!" a woman said to me, clutching her purse tightly under her arm as she came through the gangway. "It's my first cruise."

"Mine too!" I told her. And, checking her name tag, I said, "You're up the stairs and to your left, Mrs. Schield."

"I've never been on a maiden voyage before," a chubby man said, coming up next. "Every woman here a maiden?" And he winked.

Oh, brother! I thought. "Welcome aboard, Mr. Knott," I said cheerfully. "You're on the Chesapeake deck, two flights up, and your bags will be delivered shortly."

This was the day the deckhands dreaded, I could tell.

Though they wore their crisp white shirts and shorts, they were already wet with perspiration. They sprinted through the hallways, a bag in each hand, sometimes two, or another beneath an arm. They were running partly to deliver luggage in a hurry and partly to escape the passengers who stood in their doorways, calling that they were still missing a bag or that they'd been given the wrong luggage.

"Don't worry, we'll sort things out," I assured the man who had come back out of his room at the end of the hall. "We take good care of the bags."

The strap of his camera seemed to pull his neck forward, and he studied me a moment. "There better not be any smoking," he said. "My wife's allergic. They promised us there's no smoking in the dining room."

"That's right, Mr. Jergens," I told him. "She'll be fine."

Slowly the noise level rose as more and more people arrived, and the cartloads of bags coming down from the Renaissance Hotel were higher still. The deckhands worked relentlessly, while passengers were already exploring the ship, peeking in each other's rooms, standing in doorways to chat, and impeding the deckhands' progress.

"Would you like to go up to the lounge?" I kept suggesting. "There are refreshments in the lounge. . . . Would you like to meet the other passengers in the lounge? . . . Perhaps you could continue your conversation in the lounge over refreshments. . . ."

Josh looked at me gratefully as I got a boisterous group of four to head for the stairs.

There weren't any children, and we were glad of that. No pool equals no kids, someone said. And when I heard big-band music wafting from the sound system, I realized we had a ship-load of retirees—empty nesters, anyway. Flavian appeared in the hallway, a monstrous duffel bag in one hand, two smaller bags in the other. His forehead glistened. He grinned as he passed, but I'll bet we were both thinking the same thing: ten one-week cruises, ten embarkings, ten disembarkings, bags up, bags down. . . . Emily had told us that the turnarounds were the worst—the weekends these passengers got off and a new crowd got on—no time at all to ourselves.

Everyone seemed in a friendly, festive mood, though—until, that is, a man in a cowboy hat came down the stairs and faced me: "The letter I got said there would be lunch, and all we can find up there is cheese and crackers," he said.

My mind raced through the day's program. No one was assigned to the dining room until dinnertime. Only Rachel and Barry, the afternoon's lounge attendants, were keeping the refreshment table replenished. Surely the man was mistaken.

"Lunch?" I said. "Oh, I don't think so. But—"

"It says *lunch!*" he insisted, reaching inside his jacket pocket for a piece of paper. He unfolded it and thrust it under my nose.

I took the letter and skimmed the lines: *Welcome aboard the Seascape . . . a thoroughly modern cruise ship . . . Passengers are invited to board from one o'clock on . . . a light lunch will be available in the lounge.*

"I believe there's also fruit and coffee . . . ," I began.

"That's not a lunch," he said. "Where's all that gourmet food they brag about? We got on a plane at eight this morning, and all we've had to eat is one damn bag of pretzels. We were expecting lunch, like the letter says."

"Let me go find out," I said, keeping the letter, and off I went to find Dianne.

I ran into Quinton instead.

"I hate to bother you," I said, "but the man over there says they were promised lunch." And I gave him the letter, signed by the company's president. I could see Quinton's jaw stiffen as he read it.

"I never okayed this," he said. "Never even saw it. You don't say 'lunch' when it's finger food, you say 'refreshments.'" He handed the letter back. "I'll have the chef send sandwiches to his room," he told me.

Everything was different with passengers on board. No slouching through the halls lugging a bucket, no sinking down in a deck chair to catch my breath, no letting my hair fly around my face or simply pulling it back without combing it first.

I was continually aware of my appearance, my posture. Was my shirt tucked in? Were my nails clean? Passengers continued arriving all afternoon. I had barely directed the last couple toward their stateroom when the obligatory muster took place.

A memo to each passenger announced that an emergency drill would be held before dinner, so when the alarm sounded, I raced to crew quarters, grabbed my life jacket, and went up to my assigned emergency post on the lounge deck. Passengers were coming out of their staterooms, orange life jackets dangling awkwardly from their hands. They joked with each other about manning the lifeboats or jumping over the rail.

I saw our cruise director for the first time—a thirty-something woman, forty, maybe. "Please listen carefully to our instructions and remain outside your staterooms, wearing your life jackets, until one of our crew checks you out," Stephanie Bowers said. People paid attention not only because of the megaphone she was using, but also because she was gorgeous. Her brown hair was shoulder length and streaked with gold, her eyebrows delicately arched, her shirt showed just the right amount of cleavage, and she wore a skirt that hugged her hips. "Place the life jacket over your shoulders, like so," she said, demonstrating with her own, "the opening in front. Now thread the black strap through the ring on your left side. . . ."

"Whatever you say, baby," I heard a man murmur.

I walked slowly along the line of passengers, Gwen coming at me from the other direction, assisting where we could. I couldn't begin to fit the puffy orange jacket around the body of an enormous woman who was already embarrassed by the effort, and I congratulated myself that I got the strap through the ring at all, laughing with her when she tried out the attached whistle for distraction.

The men, I discovered, did not want any help but seemed to have more trouble getting the straps right than the women. I was glad when Ken McCoy appeared on the scene and I could bypass the frustrated man with straps all going the wrong way.

Ken gave a two-minute talk on ship safety, then Stephanie took the megaphone again and said she would be making some announcements after dinner regarding the excursion schedule. And finally, when the all-clear signal was given, people gave relieved sighs, yanking off their life jackets and going back inside to stow them under their beds. I was happy too.

"Glad *that's* over," said Gwen, who somehow managed to look as elegantly put together as she had at the beginning of the afternoon. She and Yolanda had done each other's hair in elaborate coils before we'd started the trip, threading beads into them on either side of their faces.

Passengers were gathering at the rail now, and Gwen and I joined them. A crowd had collected on the dock below to watch the gangplank being lifted and swung onto the bow of the ship. Already we could feel the vibration of the engines.

Now two deckhands on the pier were unwinding the lines that held us to pilings—one at the bow of the ship, another at the stern. Looping the lines around their arms like a lasso, they tossed them into the hands of two sailors on deck, then made the leap from shore to ship. The engine noise grew louder still as the bow thrusters in the depths of the ship moved us slowly away from the dock.

People we didn't know waved at us, and we waved back. The wind in our faces grew stronger, the space between us and the dock grew wider. Then I heard Dianne saying, "Girls—galley duty, pronto," and we remembered we were part of the crew.

We headed downstairs to change into T-shirts and shorts, to spend the evening scraping plates and filling the dishwasher—course after course after course.

Pamela and Natalie had it easy that night—shadowing some of the more experienced stews to learn how to turn down the beds when the guests were at dinner; put a chocolate imprinted with an *S* on each pillow and a program of tomorrow's events, plus the weather forecast, beside it. Pull the blinds, turn on the bed-side lamp. . . .

But Gwen and Liz and I were in the galley till ten thirty. I was glad I wouldn't be there every evening—the dishes and all that cleaning up of the dining room afterward. You'd be surprised at how much grown people can spill on the floor. I was wiped.

When we got off at last, smelling of grease and detergent, Gwen opted for a shower and sleep, but Liz and I needed to unwind, so we decided to go up to the top deck for twenty minutes to cool off.

We were climbing the narrow staircase from the Chesapeake deck to the observation deck when we heard Dianne's voice just above us. ". . . too big a hurry," she was saying. "That letter was just an example—people expecting lunch. *We're* the ones who take it on the chin! And not a word to us about what happened to Captain Sawyer. Not even Ken knew about the switch."

"We've put up with worse than this." Quinton's voice.

Liz and I should have left, but we didn't. We just stood there, frozen, on the stairs, our heads below floor level.

"One of the reasons we agreed to take this on was that we got to sail with Sawyer," Dianne persisted.

"Well, it's not in the contract, Dianne. We're here, the ship has sailed, we've got a captain, we *make* it work, that's all. Nothing says we have to sign up for their fall cruises."

Liz and I were already backing down the stairs when the conversation stopped. I don't know if they'd realized someone was listening or not.

3

MITCH

When we woke the next morning, we were already docked in Norfolk, with its huge shipping port and naval base. It was weird to go out on deck and find a completely different landscape from the one you saw the day before.

Another cruise ship, slightly larger than ours, was just leaving port, and a few early risers were already at the rail, watching it move away from the dock. It reminded me that we weren't the only cruise line on the bay. Most of the others, though, added New England and Nova Scotia or the Bahamas to their itineraries. But the *Seascape* and the *Spellbound*, according to Josh, wanted to be Chesapeake Bay exclusives, sailing spring, summer, and fall, and eventually getting the lion's share of the market.

I didn't have to be told to eat a good breakfast, and afterward I reported to the linen hold for clean sheets and towels, then set off for my block of fifteen staterooms. It was hard not to get distracted by the planes flying in now and then and by the submarine one of the guys detected, trolling the water a ways out.

I'd been instructed not to start cleaning until the bell rang for breakfast. Since passengers could go anytime between seven and nine, this meant keeping an eye out to see when people left for the dining room, so we could rush into those staterooms and clean them.

You learn a lot about people when you clean up after them. Some left their quarters immaculate—clothes hung up, toiletries neatly assembled in one place, towels folded, even though we'd replace them with fresh ones. Other people left their towels on the floor, slippers askew, bottles and tubes and jars scattered around the sink, and dirty laundry dumped in a corner.

Those of us who cleaned staterooms would have two hours or so off in the afternoon before beginning our evening stint clearing tables during the dinner hour and scraping dishes in the galley.

"Anybody want to tour a battleship?" Barry asked when Gwen and I returned our buckets later and were heading for the showers. He and Mitch were coming up from crew quarters, obviously ready to leave.

"A battleship's about the last thing on my wish list," Gwen said, "but go for it."

"Actually, it's a submarine," said Mitch, waving a printout from Stephanie.

"Some other time," I told them as we went on by. "There are nine more Norfolks to go. See you guys later."

It was when we were rummaging through the dresser for clean clothes that Gwen dropped the bombshell: "Just thought I ought to mention that Austin and I aren't a couple any longer."

The bra I'd picked up fell out of my hands, and I turned to stare at her. Austin—the big, thoughtful guy we'd met at a soup kitchen one summer when we volunteered, the person we'd all felt was so right for Gwen, maybe on and on into the future—was out?

"You broke up?" I couldn't believe it. "When did *that* happen?"

Gwen knew how we felt about Austin, about them as a couple, and that's probably why she didn't look at me when she answered. "I simply thought we should. I've got a lot of school ahead of me. You know that."

Liz came in just then, all gung ho to go see Norfolk in the little time we had. She reacted the same way I did to the news.

"*Why?*"

"You want us to get engaged? Is that it?" Gwen was beginning to lose patience with us both. She flung a clean shirt over her arm. "Liz, I'm not the same person I was eight years ago when I was going out with Legs. I may not be the same person in eight years that I am now."

Liz looked at her wide-eyed. "Who would you *be?*"

"Who knows? Maybe I'll go through six years of med school

and then decide to dump it all and raise chickens! Maybe I'll want to make up for lost time and see the world. How can I ask someone to wait for me when I don't even know what I'll want?"

We picked up our towels and followed her to the showers.

"So . . . breaking up was your idea?" I asked.

"I suggested it, yes, and finally he agreed. I said I couldn't stand the thought of him waiting for me all those years—didn't want that hanging over my head, going through an internship and residency."

We went in the shower room and put the OCCUPIED sign on the door.

"Well, it wouldn't be like he was just cooling his heels," I reminded her. "He has plans for his life, too."

"Yeah, but before he waits that long for me, or is insane enough to think we could get married when I'm up to my ears in books, he'd better be sure." Gwen took one of the showers, her voice rising above the sound of the spray. "We need to go out with other people, Alice. How else will we ever know?"

I guess I didn't want to hear that because I was thinking of Patrick and me.

When I was dressed, I looked around for Pamela to see if she wanted to go ashore with us. Josh said he'd seen her on the observation deck, so I went up there. She'd finished cleaning before we had, so she was probably ready.

I found her sitting on the side of a lounge chair, arms resting on her knees, holding her cell phone.

"What are you *doing*?" I said. "I thought you wanted to walk into town with us."

She sighed but didn't move. "I do."

I walked over to stand in her line of vision. "Problems?"

"Only one. My mother. What else?"

"I thought things had been going okay for her, Pamela. What's wrong?"

"Her love life."

"That really nice management guy from Nordstrom—the one you liked?"

"Yeah. I thought maybe that was going somewhere, and so did she. But he's pulling back. He's not as serious as she'd hoped."

"And she's dumping on you?" I sat down across from her but leaned forward to show that time was short, we needed to leave. What was this, anyway? Breakup Summer?

"Actually, she's told me very little about that, but she fell recently at her apartment," Pamela said.

"Oh no. Was she hurt?"

"Nothing major—her ankle. But you know what this probably means—she's drinking again." Pamela covered her face with both hands.

"You think so?"

"As sure as I can be without a blood test," she said through her fingers.

"What does she expect you to do? She knows you're on a ship all summer. Why is she telling you this?"

Pamela dropped her hands and gave me a resigned look. "Because I made the mistake of returning her calls. Besides, who else has she got to tell? They're all little asides, actually. She talks about her apartment and the shoes she's trying to find and how things are going at work, and then a sort of P.S., that George hasn't come around much lately, and did she mention she'd somehow missed a step leaving her complex, and even if she'd found the shoes, she couldn't try them on now because her ankle's so swollen? 'Nothing serious,' she adds."

I stood up and gave her shoulder a little tug. "Well, if she says it's nothing serious, then take her at her word and don't worry too much about it," I said. "If you have to worry, concentrate on Gwen. She broke up with Austin."

"What?"

"She doesn't want him to spend eight years waiting for her since she might change her mind by then."

Pamela's reaction was not what I'd expected. "Well, better now than later," she said. "Let's go see Norfolk."

The Captain's Dinner was held that night, beginning with a reception in the lounge. This and the farewell dinner at the end of each cruise were the two occasions when passengers dressed up.

The captain, Joseph Haggerty, and Ken McCoy, in their dress whites, stood at the entrance to the lounge. Frank, the engineer, stood next to Ken, then Quinton and Dianne and Stephanie. Guests came through the door and were greeted by

Stephanie first, who introduced them to the next person as the passengers moved up the line toward the captain. The rest of us, in our starched white dress shirts and bow ties, hustled back and forth, seeing that champagne glasses were returned to the galley.

When the miniature crab cakes and quiches were almost gone, we were instructed to fill the gaps with cherry tomatoes and stuffed mushrooms. When we ran out of these, we took the trays off the table and brought out the celery and carrots. I quickly learned that all the effort went into first presentations, and after that, we filled in with cheaper fare. But after the champagne, few of the guests seemed to notice.

Dianne was in a royal blue cocktail dress with a neckline that plunged just enough to be daring, while Stephanie wore a short black sheath that showed off her tanned arms and legs.

"Wow!" I murmured to Rachel. "The *Seascape* must have been lucky to get her for the cruise."

"It's the other way around," Rachel whispered back. "She comes with a history. Had an affair with a customer on another line and has been out of work for the past two years. All us career sailors know about it."

Hmmm, I thought. This maiden voyage was starting out with both a second-choice captain and cruise director? No wonder Quinton and Dianne were a little upset. I gave Captain Haggerty a good look. It was the first time I'd seen him up close. He was about five foot ten or so, late forties, had a somewhat cocky manner, and looked as neatly pressed himself—perhaps more so—as his uniform. His smile never left his face—just stretched and retracted a little with each handshake.

Ken McCoy made up for it with his toothy grin and infectious laugh, and his eyes searched each name tag as he introduced the guests to the Captain. Frank, bald and bespectacled, did his part patiently, fixing his eyes on each guest and welcoming them to the *Seascape* without overdoing it. Stephanie was too effusive by half, but Quinton and Dianne, a bit more reserved, were a nice counterpart to the others, their faces relaxed and friendly.

If there was any tension among the officers and crew, it didn't show. But those of us helping out at the reception didn't miss the fact that when the last of the guests had passed through the receiving line, the VIPs didn't stand around chatting with each other. Quinton and Dianne moved off immediately to mingle with passengers on the port side of the lounge, and Frank disappeared entirely. Only Ken and Stephanie stood with the captain making small talk until Ken, realizing they were alone in the doorway, touched Haggerty's elbow lightly and guided him over toward the champagne.

When Dianne gave the signal for us to head to the dining room ahead of the guests, we worked our way to the exit and went down a flight.

The menu for dinner each day was placed in the glass case next to the dining room. When I read the menu for that evening, I wished I'd eaten something before I'd reported for work: shrimp bisque with tomato and goat cheese crostini; rack of lamb with fingerling potatoes and asparagus; sea bass with truffles; chocolate lava cake with fresh raspberry sauce.

The bell chimed for dinner. I smiled at a bejeweled woman who was being escorted to her table by a slender man with a thin mustache, and I folded my arms over my stomach to stop the rumblings.

After the main course had been served and eaten and the dishes taken away, Captain Haggerty took the microphone and gave a brief welcome: "Good evening, ladies and gentlemen," he said. "I want to extend an especially warm welcome to all you wonderful people aboard the maiden voyage of the *Spellbound*." I paused at the galley door with a tray full of dishes as a low murmur ran through the crowd, and then the captain added hurriedly, "Well, *that* got your attention!" and he laughed a little. "The *Seascape*, of course."

"Doesn't know his ass from his elbow," Barry whispered as he came in after me, carrying a pot of coffee.

We could still hear the captain through the sound system in the galley: "I'm jumping the gun because the *Spellbound*, too, will be taking her maiden voyage in September, and I'll be piloting that ship as well, so you know how eager I am to get her in the water. But I have the privilege of taking this fine ship out on the bay this summer, and I know we are going to have a terrific cruise."

He went on to introduce the others, who had been standing in the receiving line with him before dinner, and then, on signal, all of the crew—servers, deckhands, and chefs, all in our dress uniforms—came filing in, smiling, to introduce ourselves and tell where we were from. From all over, I discovered—mostly Maryland and Virginia, but New York was represented as well as Delaware, Pennsylvania, and even Hawaii—and after receiving an ovation from the passengers, who were eager for their dessert, we disbanded and went back to our assigned jobs.

This was finals week at the University of Chicago, I knew. Between his tests and my schedule, there was little time for Patrick and me to talk with each other. We couldn't have cell phones with us when we were on duty. No cell phones in our cleaning buckets, in our jeans, no walking along the deck holding cell phones to our ears. We could only use them during our breaks and after we'd finished for the day, but even then, it was sometimes hard—almost impossible—to get a connection down in crew quarters, and no matter where I was calling from, there was no guarantee I'd reach him.

This time, though, late at night with only a few people milling around the observation deck, I tried my luck and Patrick answered.

"You're there!" I said. "Hope you weren't studying."

"Hey! Nope. One more exam tomorrow and I'm done. Just finished a bruiser on international policy and global change."

"Arggghhh! Now, that's a winner," I said. "How are things going?"

"Totally hectic," he said. "Between exams, I'm trying to pack. Figure out what I can leave behind. We fly out on Friday, and I've got to send everything else home."

"Must be crazy."

"It is. But I'm pretty psyched."

"I don't know whether I'm more happy for you or sorry you're leaving," I said honestly.

"Be happy. We waste too much time when we're sad," he told me.

"I know, but Gwen told us this afternoon that she and Austin broke up. I still can't believe it." I realized that Patrick hardly knew the guy. "They just seemed so right for each other."

"She upset?" Patrick asked.

"It was her idea."

"Oh. Any idea why?"

"She's got eight years of medical school ahead of her, and she didn't want him just waiting around for her."

"Maybe he wouldn't."

"She may have worried about that, too," I said.

There were several seconds of silence. I did *not* want this to start a conversation about us and was relieved when Patrick said, "So where are you calling from?"

"I'm sitting here on the top deck, and there's a great breeze. Reception's good up here too, by the way. I can see the lights of a ship way out on the water."

"But where is the ship?"

"Norfolk. We just finished the Captain's Dinner. A lot of sailors here. Some are down on the dock right now, talking to the crew."

"Yeah? And how are the guys on the *Seascape*?"

"Big, bronzed, brawny," I teased.

"Should I worry?"

"Didn't you just say we should be happy?"

"Yeah, but not necessarily about that," said Patrick.

We were docked at Yorktown the following morning for our Yorktown/Williamsburg port of call. I had mixed feelings about going ashore. I remembered my visit to the College of William & Mary in the spring and wondered if I would always think of Williamsburg as the place that turned me down.

A lot of the stewards had been on class visits to Williamsburg back in middle school, but my class had never gone, so I decided to at least take the trolley around Yorktown. But after the Captain's Dinner the night before, passengers had been invited to the lounge for a slide show on Colonial Williamsburg and the Jamestown Settlement. And now a few of those passengers, having stayed up too late or drunk too much at the reception, hadn't come out of their staterooms yet, and those of us on housekeeping detail couldn't go off duty until all of the rooms were done.

"Darn!" said Natalie. "I've never seen Williamsburg or Yorktown or Jamestown, and if it always follows the Captain's Dinner and people sleep in, I'll never get there."

Gwen saved the day. "I went to Williamsburg back in sixth grade, so tell me the room numbers and I'll clean your staterooms for you."

"Really?" said Natalie. "We'll owe you one."

"Big time too!" said Gwen. "But go now while you have the chance."

Natalie, Liz, and I studied the little map of the town and set out along Water Street, looking for an ATM machine and, after that, Ben & Jerry's Green Mountain Coffee Café. When we recognized Mitch sauntering along solo, hands in his pockets, we invited him to come along.

"It's all so different from Silver Spring," Liz said, the York River on one side of us, side streets full of history on the other.

Mitch, with one of those Greek sailor caps perched on his head to shield his eyes, looked down a tree-lined side street and said, "Well, the streets are about as narrow as where I live, and almost as quiet."

"Where's that?" asked Natalie.

"Vienna, Maryland," he said. "You never heard of it. No one ever has. Over in Dorchester County, eastern shore."

"Then this is practically home to you," I said.

He grinned this time. "Well, we've got a couple of historic houses, but not like this."

Mitch was twenty or so, I figured. Large calloused hands. One of those blonds who tans easily. Looked pretty cute the other night in his white dress shirt and black pants, but seemed far more natural now in a T-shirt and khaki shorts.

We found the café and each ordered a different flavor of ice cream so we could share—a spoonful of Chunky Monkey for Cake Batter, a spoonful of Chubby Hubby for Dublin Mudslide. Sitting at a little table for four, we studied the printout we got on the ship. I pointed to the Watermen's Museum. "'The lore, legends, and equipment used by crabbers and oystermen over the past century,'" I read.

"I was there earlier," Mitch told us. "Wanted to see if they had anything about muskrat trapping, but they didn't."

"People trap muskrats? For what?" I asked.

"Their pelts. Women's coats," Mitch said.

"Are you a trapper?" Liz asked.

"Me and my dad and brothers. We trap and do oysters in winter, crab in the summer."

"How come you're not crabbing now?" asked Natalie.

"Just wanted something different for a change. I've watched the cruise ships going around the bay and heard there was a new line looking for deckhands. Dad said he figured he could spare me for a couple of months—at least it would be sure money. Can't count on much of anything from crabbing these days."

"You like it? Working on a ship?" Liz asked.

"Well, I applied for deckhand, but sometimes I'm a steward, too. I like the deckhand part. Hardly got my feet wet so far," Mitch said.

"But isn't it hard, jumping from deck to dock when we're coming in or going out?" I asked.

"Only the experienced guys do that," Mitch said. "Suppose I'll catch on to it before the summer's over." He stretched his legs out alongside the table. The hair on his thighs looked almost white in the sunlight.

"Yeah, but what would happen if a guy fell in that space between ship and dock when we're tying up? He'd be crushed," said Liz.

He shrugged. "So life's risky. You can die trapping muskrats too. My uncle died last year—drowned in the marsh."

"My God!" I said. "I'm sorry. That's awful."

"Yeah. We were all sorry to lose him. I think that's what made my dad say he could spare me this summer, though. Give me a chance to try something else."

We talked a little about families then, but Liz looked at her watch and saw we had only an hour before we had to be back on the ship.

Natalie grabbed the printout again, her fingers following along a street on the map, her French braid dangling over one shoulder.

"Reenergized!" she declared. "I'm off to look for earrings. I'm going to buy a pair in each port of call—mementos of my cruising summer."

"I'll go with you," said Liz.

But I wanted to see more of Yorktown while I had a chance, and so did Mitch, so we located a trolley stop on the printout and went outside to wait.

Emily, Yolanda, and Barry were on the trolley when it came, and we all sat together in the back. As we passed the old Custom House, the church, and an archeological dig, I wondered what it was like to live in a tiny place like this, where most of the people you met each day were tourists. How different it must seem to Mitch, who worked in the marshes with trappers. I was mentally composing an e-mail to Patrick—telling him I was a seeing a little more of life too, even if it wouldn't compare with Barcelona.

When we got off, we caught up with Liz and Natalie and all sauntered back together, not eager to spend the evening scraping plates and stacking the monstrous dishwasher—over and over and over again. As we approached the *Seascape*, I noticed a couple up on the lounge deck, and as we got closer, I saw that it was Flavian and Gwen. He had her cornered, his hands resting on the rail on either side of her, their faces a few inches apart. And Gwen was definitely smiling.

4
SINBAD

The Crisfield port of call, where passengers took a ferry to
Tangier Island, was probably the one I wanted to visit most.
The island sounded faraway and mysterious. Captain John
Smith had once been there, our ship's pamphlet read, and
residents still had traces of the Elizabethan accents of their
ancestors.

But I didn't get to go, and neither did Liz, because this
time Gwen had passengers who decided to sleep in instead of
going ashore. One, in fact, was sick and needed not only the
rug in his room shampooed and dried, but the blankets and
bedspread washed as well. But fair was fair, so Liz and I loyally
told Gwen we'd do the rooms she had left, and she headed for
the ferry without a trace of guilt.

"That was quick," Liz said, peering over the rail as Gwen left the ship with Flavian.

"She's having fun," I said. "She deserves it."

I was glad in a way that I didn't take the tour, because it was a steamy, sticky day, and the only way to get around Tangier Island, Stephanie had told us, was on foot, unless you rented one of the few golf carts available. Consequently, passengers returned to the ship that afternoon tired and hot, and not too interested in evening entertainment. Out in the middle of the bay, or in remote places like Crisfield, we had little or no cell phone service either, though there was wireless Internet access throughout the ship that made us all the more eager to get moving.

When dinner was over, the dining room cleared sooner than it usually did, and after the crew had eaten and the galley was cleaned, some of the stewards started a poker game in air-conditioned comfort, and others sat around to watch. But I opted to go up on the observation deck with Emily and Liz, even though the air was humid and still.

Frank and some of the guys were already up there—Mitch and Josh, Barry and Flavian—all sitting around a big pitcher of iced coffee. We sat off to one side, faces tilted toward the night sky, letting their conversation float our way. We soon learned that the *Seascape* was perhaps not all it was cracked up to be.

"*Sinbad*?" Barry was saying. "This was the old *Sinbad*?"

"You're kidding!" I heard Flavian say.

In the half-light of the moon, I saw Frank wipe one hand

across his face as though to erase his smile. "You didn't hear it from me," he said.

"What was *Sinbad*?" Mitch asked.

Josh looked over at him. "Ever heard of those fantasy cruises? One time it's a pirate ship. Next it's the Wild West or Arabian Nights or something?"

"And?" said Mitch.

"And *Sinbad* had more things wrong with it than you could count," said Josh. "Like it was jinxed." He looked at Frank to see if he should go on, and when the engineer said nothing, Josh continued: "Anything that could break, broke. Anything that could leak, leaked."

"But now it's been refurbished!" said Barry.

Frank smiled and straightened up in his chair. "Yeah," he said. "So they tell us."

Barry propped his feet on the chair next to him. "So that's why Sawyer backed out? He knows something we don't know?"

"Sawyer wouldn't do that without a reason," said Frank. "Maybe he just didn't quite swallow the 'refurbished' bit. The only thing I know about Haggerty is that he hasn't sailed the Chesapeake, but he was available. But the fact they that had to take whatever captain they could get at the last minute—that can't be good."

"But, heck. *You* must feel confident enough to take this ship out," said Flavian.

Frank gave a small shrug and looked over the water once

more, rubbing one shoulder. "Sawyer's going on sixty, got a house on the Severn—he could retire anytime he wants. I haven't got the choice."

"So what is he—some sort of prima donna?" Emily cut in. Her freckles were hardly visible in the moonlight. "A ship's got to be brand-new or he doesn't sail it?"

"No. Prima donna he's not. He just wants a ship without problems," Frank told her.

"Then what would be his objection to the *Seascape*? He suspects we've got a leak?" asked Mitch.

"A leak we might be able to handle," Frank said, laughing a little. And then realizing, perhaps, that we'd all been listening, he reached for his glass. "Well, who's to say we won't have the best season ever?"

"At least we're not out on the ocean," Liz said when we were sacking up.

"I sort of like the idea of *Sinbad*," said Rachel when we told the others what we'd heard. "The curse of *Sinbad*. *Sinbad* strikes again!"

"Gotta have a little excitement," said Yolanda.

"Well, one of us seems to be feeling a little excitement of her own," I said, glancing over at Gwen, who was slipping a T-shirt over her head. "Getting pretty chummy with Flavian, Gwen?"

She grinned mischievously and pulled on her sleep shorts. "He's a fun guy."

"I still liked Austin," Liz said, as though that would change anything.

Lauren glanced over at Gwen as she crawled up into her bunk. "You got somebody back home?"

"I've been going with a guy named Austin," Gwen said. "But our future's up for grabs. I've got eight years of school ahead of me."

"Ouch!" said Shannon. "I couldn't wait to get out of school. What, you haven't had enough of it?"

"Gwen's going to be a doc-tor!" Yolanda warbled.

"What kind of doctor?" Natalie wanted to know.

"Male anatomy," Liz teased, and we laughed.

"I haven't decided," Gwen said. "Obstetrics, maybe. Pediatrics."

"I'd want to start a family before then," said Natalie. "I love kids. I've already decided that if I don't find the right guy by the time I'm thirty-two, I'm looking for a sperm donor."

"No way!" Shannon declared. "Go through all the work of pregnancy and labor and none of the fun? If I ever decided to use a donor, I'd pick him live and conceive the old-fashioned way."

"And if it didn't take the first time?" I asked.

Shannon grinned. "If at first you don't succeed . . . God, there was a guy in my tenth-grade civics class who would have made the most gorgeous kids!"

"*Listen* to her," said Emily. "Don't you people know it's past midnight? Somebody get the light."

We were becoming accustomed to little sleep, I discovered.

After a few days of getting up at five thirty or six, that groggy feeling in mid-afternoon was familiar. But still I lay awake a while longer because I was thinking about Patrick. Had I ever thought of what our children would look like if we married? Had we ever even talked about having children? We liked to watch them on a playground, and we'd laugh at the way babies would stare at us without the least bit of self-consciousness. But had we actually said we wanted to have babies together? No, because we'd never even discussed getting married. We'd been going together longer than most of our friends, but . . .

I was just drifting off to sleep when I heard *scritch, scratch, scratch*. I lay still, listening more intently. Nothing. Then, *scritch, scratch* . . .

I lifted my head from the pillow. "I hear a mouse," I said.

Instantly the room was filled with rustlings and mattress squeaks.

"What? What?" voices cried.

Feet thumped on the floor, the light came on, and Pamela dived back into bed, legs pulled up after her.

"I won't sleep for a minute with a mouse in the room," Liz declared. "Did you know they can climb up walls? That commercial where they're running across the drapes?"

"You don't have mice on a ship, you have rats," said Shannon. "I need a cigarette."

"Listen!" I cautioned as the scratching noise came again.

We all turned toward the smaller of the two dressers that stood in one corner, its bottom drawer opened an inch.

"It's coming from there," said Lauren. "Behind the dresser."

"Or in it," said Emily. "Get the plunger."

"The what?" I said.

"The toilet plunger. Don't we have a plunger? We can trap it under that and—"

"Get one of the guys," said Shannon.

"No! Wait!" Natalie sprang off her bunk and gave us a sheepish look. "Promise you won't tell?" And without waiting for an answer, she padded over to the dresser in her panda-print shorts, opened the bottom drawer, and lifted out a shoe box with a turtle in it, five inches across.

We stared.

"It's a Maryland terrapin," Natalie said proudly as she lifted it by its shell. "A kid was selling it in Crisfield this afternoon, and I bought it for my brother's birthday on Sunday. He'll be ten."

"Natalie!" we said, practically in unison.

"I wanted something really special, and Kevin will love it!"

"It's against regulations," Liz reminded her. "No pets of any kind."

"Just until we get to Baltimore. They're meeting me on the dock."

"That's four days off!" I said.

"Dianne checks our quarters once a day! You know that," Rachel said. "And she's a stickler for cleanliness, especially when it comes to transmitting diseases to the passengers."

We eyed the greenish-brown creature dangling from Natalie's

fingers, its legs flailing. I was only familiar with the small box turtles you find in pet stores. Natalie's turtle had extended its scrawny neck full length, and it slowly turned its head from side to side, as though taking us all in.

"What does it eat?" asked Shannon. "Do you even know?"

"The boy said to feed it chicken, fruit, and worms," Natalie said, stroking the terrapin's head with one finger.

"It needs water," said Liz. "Salt water or fresh?"

Natalie looked helplessly around. "Look. All I want to do is get him to Baltimore Sunday. I'll figure out the rest tomorrow."

"Okay, but keep him quiet," said Emily.

Natalie grabbed a handful of dirty laundry from a heap in the corner and lined the shoe box with underwear and socks. Then she put the terrapin back.

"Death by asphyxiation," Rachel said when the scratching stopped.

I met Captain Haggerty the next morning when I was coming up from the linen hold. We'd docked at Oxford, and when I reached the main deck, he was standing at the entrance to the dining room, drinking coffee and talking with Quinton. There must have been an awkward gap in their conversation, because they both turned and focused on me.

"Alice, I wonder if you've met the captain," Quinton said. The stewards had been introduced to him en masse, but not one by one.

Quinton, as always, was in his short-sleeved shirt and black pants, his head nearly reaching the door frame. Haggerty, a foot shorter, was in a T-shirt, but he still wore his captain's hat. He moved his body in a kind of swagger that said he could handle any ship, at any time.

"Hello," I said, and walked over, shifting the stack of towels into my left arm so I could shake hands. "I'm Alice McKinley."

He had a firm handshake, but he held it only a second. "How's it going?" he asked pleasantly.

"I guess you'd have to ask Quinton," I said. "But I think I'm doing all right. There's a lot to learn."

"First time at sea?"

"Yeah."

"This guy treating you okay?" he joked, nodding toward Quinton.

"A regular slave driver," I said, laughing. "But we're getting used to it."

"Well, if he gives you any trouble, let me know," the captain said, and took another sip of coffee from the black ceramic mug with a captain's insignia on it.

It was all in fun, of course, but there was something about the remark, something cocky, that sounded like showing his rank. Putting Quinton in his place by even *suggesting* that I go over his head and report something.

I shifted the towels again. "Well, nice to meet you," I said. "I'd better get back to work." And I quickly took the stairs two flights up to the Chesapeake deck. Maybe he was just one of those people, like me, who lets things slip out, sometimes the very thing you *don't* mean to say.

My first room for the morning was empty. The Colliers were early risers, and when I was ready for the second stateroom, the Anselminos were just leaving.

"Good morning, Alice," they said, holding the door for me. "You're looking perky today."

"And you look like you're setting off on a new adventure," I said.

"We signed up for the walking tour of Oxford," Mrs. Anselmino told me. She was short and round, with a wreath of dark curls around her face. "I hope you'll get a chance to see the town. Make sure you visit the Robert Morris Inn. We celebrated our thirty-fifth anniversary there."

"I'll put it on my list," I told her. "Have a good time."

I wished all the passengers were like the Anselminos. They wiped down the sink before I even had a chance to get at it, and picked up everything off the floor to make vacuuming easier. They'd only been aboard two days when the dining room servers had figured out that Mr. Anselmino had a great sense of humor, someone they could kid around with.

I finished their stateroom in record time and was about to head to the third when I heard a loud voice out on the walkway saying, "If you don't search her immediately, you won't find it."

I stayed out of sight in the doorway and listened.

"It was there when we went to breakfast—right there on the nightstand," a woman's voice was saying. "I remember it distinctly, and now it's gone. I *thought* she had a strange look on her face when I passed her on the deck a few minutes ago."

"Omigod!" I whispered to myself. Were they talking about me?

"Mrs. Collier, I want to find that watch as much as you do, but let's not jump to conclusions." Dianne's voice.

"What else *can* I think?" the woman continued. "No, you can't want to find it as much as I do, because that diamond watch belonged to my mother-in-law, and Gordon gave it to me when we married."

I set my bucket on the deck, locked the Anselminos' door behind me, and started down the walkway just as Dianne turned in my direction.

"Oh, Alice," she called. "Could you stop here, please?"

"She could have hidden it anywhere by now," came Mrs. Collier's voice from inside her room. When I reached her doorway, Mrs. Collier was sitting on the edge of one of the twin beds. Her cold gray eyes settled fiercely on me as I crossed the threshold, and Dianne closed the door behind us.

"You cleaned the Colliers' stateroom this morning, didn't you?" Dianne asked.

"Yes. It was my first one for the day," I said, and tried to keep my voice neutral, but I was furious inside.

"Well, my watch was—," Mrs. Collier began, but Dianne interrupted.

"Mrs. Collier's watch is missing, and she remembers leaving it there on the nightstand. Did you see it?"

I tried desperately to single out that particular nightstand in my memory. Every two rooms are exactly alike, the bathrooms placed side by side, except that they are mirror images of each other. Lamps are the same, bedspreads the same, even the pictures on the walls, nautical scenes of the Chesapeake Bay.

"No, I don't remember seeing a watch," I answered. "I saw a pair of glasses on a bedside table, but they may have been in the room next door."

The thin brunette sitting on the bed gave an exasperated sigh and turned her face away. She was wearing a sailor top with a wide blue and white collar over her white slacks, and one foot bounced up and down impatiently. "Talk is useless," she said.

My anger was getting the best of me, and I held my arms out at my sides. "Would you like to search me, Mrs. Collier?" I asked.

She startled, a little flustered. "That's not my job, but the watch could be anywhere by now. We need to search crew quarters."

"That won't be necessary, Alice," Dianne said. "Why don't the three of us check the room over again to see if perhaps it's in a drawer or—"

"I *know* what I *know*!" Mrs. Collier said emphatically. "The watch was here on the nightstand when I went to breakfast, and now it's gone."

"If you see or hear anything at all about a watch, Alice, I'm sure you'll let us know," Dianne said. And then, to Mrs. Collier, "I know you must be terribly upset, but I need to remind you that there is a safe in the purser's office, and we encourage people to keep their valuables in it."

"So I have to put my watch in the safe every evening and get it out again each morning?" Mrs. Collier said.

"We encourage that," Dianne repeated, and nodded me toward the door to show I was dismissed. As I went out, Mrs. Collier's voice trailed after me:

"That means you must expect thefts to happen. My husband is going to be extremely angry over this, I can tell you."

I had run out of miniature soap bars, so I went on down to the linen hold but ducked into crew quarters for a few minutes to calm myself. I'd barely sat down on my bunk when Gwen followed.

"I heard some commotion down on your deck. What happened?" she asked, and I told her.

"Mrs. Collier wanted Dianne to search my stuff, but Dianne said no. I'm sure that's not the last of it, though. It's my word against hers," I added. "I'll probably get fired."

"On what grounds?" Gwen asked.

But we knew the answer to that, and Gwen realized it too. The application form we'd signed said that we understood we were being hired "at will" for no definite period and that our employment could be terminated with or without cause at the option of the company.

"How can I go for nine more weeks knowing that Dianne will always wonder about me?" I said. "And if any of the other passengers misplace anything at all, I'll be the first suspect. You should have seen the look on Mrs. Collier's face when I left her room, Gwen. It was as though she were saying, 'You know and I know you're a thief and a liar.'"

Scritch, scratch, scratch came from the bottom dresser drawer.

"Well, if Dianne does search the room, she'll find that," Gwen said, and grabbed my arm. "Come on. Let's finish up our rooms and go see the Robert Morris Inn everyone's talking about. If you sit down here and worry, you'll fry your brain."

We finished our rooms, then showered and changed, but when we started up the stairs to the main deck, we met Dianne coming down.

"Alice, I saw Mrs. Collier in the library, and that little problem is resolved," she said. "Her husband had the watch in his pocket. I was just coming to tell you."

I came to a dead stop. I wasn't sure which I felt more: relief or anger. "Why didn't *she* tell me that?"

"She knew I'd let you know. Evidently, her husband left the breakfast table early for a walk but stopped in their stateroom first and saw the watch on the nightstand. Said he put it in his pocket for safekeeping, then forgot about it till his wife told him it was missing. So that's the end of it."

Not quite, I thought.

"Isn't she going to apologize?" I asked.

"I'm sure she feels embarrassed by the whole thing," Dianne said, and there was a hint of discomfort in her voice. "You girls have a good time in Oxford now. It's a very picturesque town." She turned and went back up the stairs. Gwen and I looked at each other.

"Wait here," I said, and went up to the library on the lounge deck.

Mrs. Collier was sitting at a little table checking things off on a brochure and drinking a Bloody Mary. A diamond watch on a black band glistened on her left wrist. I walked over.

"Hello, Mrs. Collier. Oh, you found your watch!" I said cheerfully. "What good news!"

She looked up and gave a little laugh. "Yes, my husband had it in his pocket, exactly where he should have put it. He took a walk right after breakfast, but I didn't know he'd stopped by our room first."

"Yes, I heard," I said. "I'm so relieved. As you can imagine, I was pretty upset with the accusation, so I thought you'd want the pleasure of telling me the good news yourself."

I was asking for trouble, I knew, but I had to get it out. And I was so sickeningly cheerful and smiley that I couldn't quite see her complaining to Quinton about it. "Well . . . of course," she said. "I didn't mean to imply that anyone here was dishonest, but . . . I was just . . . naturally . . . very worried."

"I accept your apology," I said. "Have a nice afternoon in Oxford."

"Oh, yes, I will, I will," Mrs. Collier said, and lifted her drink again.

I went triumphantly back down to the main deck where Gwen was waiting, through the gangway, and we set off to see the town.

5
A FORGETTABLE FRIDAY

We all wanted shore leave at St. Michaels. I woke Friday morning determined to clean my staterooms faster than ever before. Quinton had told us of a bed-and-breakfast that rented bikes, and I decided that's how I wanted to spend my afternoon, especially when I got up on deck and discovered a beautiful day. The temperature had gone from the low nineties to the mid-eighties, the humidity had dropped, and the passengers in my cabins were all going ashore.

I was ready by 1:30—showered and changed—and left the ship with Lauren, Pamela, and Shannon. Natalie, however, had finished even before us and was walking swiftly toward a grassy area, her large canvas bag slung over one shoulder, and we all knew what was in it. She'd been devoting all her break time for the last two days to that terrapin, her only goal being to keep it alive and kicking till Sunday.

"So what if I miss doing something now? I'll do it later," she'd said, and that became the mantra for all of us: We'd have nine more chances to do everything.

"Do you think things will grow old by the time the ten weeks are over?" Yolanda had asked yesterday.

"*I'll* grow old," Pamela said. "I've never worked so hard in my life."

"It's the hours," Emily told her. "It's the fact that we have so little time to ourselves. You'll toughen up. That's a promise."

Mitch and Barry were already at the bike place when we got there, and they waited till we'd rented ours. Then we all set out together. It wasn't long before Josh caught up with us, riding the last bike they had left—it didn't even have gears. But he didn't need them. The roads were flat, the scenery fantastic.

"Wow! This is the life, huh?" I said as we rode in and out of shade. "We're actually getting paid for this?"

"We're actually not," said Barry. "We're so low on the pay scale, we're practically paying *them* room and board."

We'd left in such a hurry that I'd brought only a comb, lip gloss, and money, so my hands were completely free. How long had it been since I'd ridden a bike?

Off to our right we could see the *Seascape*'s tour group entering the gate of the Maritime Museum—eighteen acres with exhibits, a working boatyard, and a lighthouse. Stephanie was following along behind the group, looking svelte in black pants and a black halter top. I saw Josh and Barry exchange knowing grins.

"Yeah?" I said, questioning.

"There goes trouble," Josh said.

"Who? Stephanie?" Pamela asked, following their gaze.

Lauren overheard and let her bike coast till we caught up with her. "Oh, c'mon, Josh. It takes two. He was as much at fault as she was."

"Hey, he was a passenger. You're not supposed to hit on passengers," said Josh.

"Give her a break. She lost a job over it, and she's probably sorry it happened."

Barry chuckled. "She look sorry to you? Looks like bait to me, not that I'm complaining."

"And they think *girls* are catty!" said Pamela. "Hey, careful, Barry. You almost ran into me."

I looked around to see if Mitch was still with us and saw him riding along with his arms folded over his chest. His bike began to wobble slightly when he saw me watching.

"Wow!" I said. "We've got a stuntman here."

He laughed.

"I can do that!" said Josh, folding his arms across his chest, and immediately his bike lurched and he almost went over. We hooted at him.

Josh made up for it by being our unofficial guide. Nice to have someone along who had been on a Chesapeake Bay tour with another line.

"Ladies and gentlemen," he said, "you are now touring the historic town that fooled the British. In the dark morning hours of August something or other . . ."

"Uh-oh. A dark-and-stormy-night story," said Barry.

"No, no, this is true. Some British barges planned to attack St. Michaels, and the people found out about it. They hoisted lanterns to the tops of trees, and when the British fired, they overshot."

"Cle-ver!" said Pamela.

"And," Josh continued, "if you now look to your left, you'll see the Cannonball House."

It really did begin to feel like we were back in colonial days. Even the names on mailboxes—like Haddaway and Hambleton—sounded historical. When did I ever meet anybody named Haddaway?

The trees opened up once to a particularly beautiful stretch—just water and boats, branches framing the picture. The way the sun glinted on the edge of each ripple, the deep blue of the sky—I couldn't help smiling. Mitch noticed and smiled back, and we didn't have to say anything, just knew we were enjoying the day, the moment, the crew.

We had about an hour and a half left before we had to be back on board, so we returned the bikes and went to the Maritime Museum. Lauren and Pamela and I headed for the lighthouse, but Shannon didn't want to come. When we looked down, we saw her over by the gate, smoking.

"Don't," she said, when we caught up with her later.

"Didn't say a word," I told her.

"You were going to, and I don't want to hear it," she said.

Lauren shrugged but asked anyway. "This your first since the cruise started?"

"No, and it won't be my last. I've decided I'm a smoker and that's that. I like myself better when I'm not so grumpy and nervous."

We couldn't argue much with that.

The boatyard sounded like you'd expect it to—the rasp of a saw, the thud of a padded hammer, the clinks and clunks—all laced with the scent of sawdust, glue, and varnish. We found the guys watching a white-haired man carving a wood canoe. His glasses rested on the end of his nose, and he reminded me of Geppetto, working in his shop in *Pinocchio*.

Leaving the museum, we ran into Gwen and Flavian and two of the deckhands. They were sitting at a table outside a small seafood place, so we grabbed another table, pulled some chairs over, and ordered po'boy sandwiches with fried oysters.

What interested me far more than the oysters, however, was the fact that Flavian, I noticed, was sitting with one arm over the back of Gwen's chair. She was wearing a yellow T-shirt and an intricate long necklace, each loop carved of wood. Flavian was examining the necklace.

"Plastic," he said.

Gwen elbowed him and laughed. "It is not! It's wood. My aunt bought it in Jamaica."

Flavian pretended to read some fine print on the back of one loop. "Made . . . in . . . China," he said.

Gwen smacked his hand, but he fed her the last remaining oyster from his paper plate, and she snapped at his fingers as though she might bite them. And laughed. And then they kissed.

She was out-and-out, full-speed-ahead making out with this gorgeous, olive-skinned, lightly stubbled guy she'd known for only a week. I guess Austin really was history. She and Flavian were looking into each other's eyes and smiling.

As we all headed back to the ship, Shannon lagged behind, smoking one cigarette after another, like she was making up for all the cigarettes she'd missed this week and all the ones she couldn't have till she was off the ship again.

Mitch noticed too.

"She's been trying to quit," I told him.

"Well, the stuff's addictive," he said as some of the smoke drifted our way. "I know, 'cause I was hooked for a while."

"Yeah?"

We were trailing the others, and as a group of passengers merged onto the sidewalk ahead of us, separating us even more from the crew, we were in no hurry to leave St. Michaels.

"Dip," Mitch said. When I looked puzzled, he added, "Dipping tobacco. You know, pinch." He motioned to a spot behind his lower lip.

"Oh. Like baseball players."

"Yeah. One little pleasure while you slog through the marsh in the winter."

I realized I knew not one thing about muskrat trapping. "Do you do this slogging on foot?"

"Yeah, once we get to the marsh by motorboat, usually solo. The dip keeps us company."

I couldn't be sure if Mitch was enjoying telling me about trapping or if he was doing it out of politeness. I'd asked out of politeness, but now I was curious. He was a lot taller than I am—taller than Patrick, even, a lot more solid. Wearing a faded gray T-shirt with a SMITHWICK'S ALE label on it. I was also curious about him.

I tried to picture what he was telling me. "How do you know where the muskrats are if you're in water?"

He walked on, hands in his pockets. "The marsh is a maze of muskrat tunnels, see, and you have to know where they run. You climb out of the boat in your hip boots, sack over your shoulder, and step from one clump of grass to another, checking the spring traps between."

I didn't look at him when I asked the next question: "How did your uncle die, Mitch?"

He was quiet for a moment, and I started to worry that I'd gotten too personal.

"We don't know for sure," he said. "You can be knee-deep in mud before you know it. Maybe he went under and couldn't right himself. Maybe he was so far in that he couldn't get out. He was sixty-eight. Or maybe he froze to death. Hard to think about, but it happens."

We walked on a little farther without speaking. Finally I said, "So trapping's in your family, huh?"

"My dad, my uncles, my grandfather . . . We do a little bit of everything, I guess, but all of it's in the water."

"And now you're *on* the water."

Mitch smiled this time. "Yeah. Imagine that. Nice for a change. Don't know I'd want to do it full-time, though."

Up ahead, we saw some more of the *Seascape*'s tour group coming along the path from the museum and merging with the line of people heading for the dock. Stephanie was walking with one of the male passengers and laughing at something he'd said. He was looking at her appreciatively.

"Careful, buddy," Mitch joked.

It was getting close to five by then, and . . . And suddenly I thought my heart was in seizure. *Patrick!* I glanced down at my watch and automatically reached for my bag before I realized I hadn't brought it. It was Friday afternoon. Late afternoon. Patrick's plane was leaving at . . . ? Was it five or six?

Think! Think! I told myself, fumbling for the cell phone that wasn't there. *Wake up! Wake up! This can't be happening.* It felt as though my whole head was heating up, hot pain behind my eyes, my forehead. I'd wanted to tell him good-bye! He may have been trying to call me!

I guess I'd stopped there on the sidewalk, saliva collecting in my mouth because I couldn't swallow. Mitch was looking at me strangely.

"Something wrong?" he asked.

"Oh my God!" I gasped. "I've got to make a phone call! I'll see you," I said, and began to run.

I was only fifty yards from the ship, but the tour group was already there, ambling one at a time up the gangplank. Dianne was checking off names on her clipboard as they passed, and women were chatting with her and with each other while my head was screaming, *Let me by! Let me by!*

I felt physically ill. How could I have forgotten? *How?* I'd thought about it several times yesterday, about calling Patrick before he left, thinking about the best time to do it. I hadn't wanted to interrupt him while he was packing; didn't want to bother him when he was trying to get a cab. What time was his flight? I couldn't remember his departure time! How could I not remember?

There was a break in the line. A man had gone up the gangplank, and the woman behind him had turned to talk to the person behind her. I edged around her saying, "Oh, sorry! Late for work. Excuse me."

Dianne frowned, but I zipped on ahead and bounded through the gangway, then clattered down the stairs to crew quarters. Grabbing my cell phone from my bag, I checked for messages, but there weren't any. I ran back up to the main deck. Mitch was standing in line on the dock and looked up at me quizzically, but I didn't stop. On up to the lounge deck, then the Chesapeake deck, to the observation deck at the top.

A small group of passengers was standing at the stern, drinks in hand, another in the shade area. I turned toward the shady side of the ship's funnel and punched in Patrick's number, my chest aching. It was 4:57, by my watch, 3:57, central time. I still had time, didn't I? Or were they an hour ahead? *Think!*

Answer, Patrick! Oh, please, please, answer! Eight rings. Nine. And then the voice message: "The party you are trying to reach is not available. Please leave a message . . ."

I pressed END, my mouth dry. If I left a message, I would sound breathless, hurried, anxious, hysterical, even. Did I want Patrick to remember me that way?

Okay, I told myself. *You have time to think. You can leave a message anytime. It doesn't have to be right this minute.* He could be in a taxi on his way to the airport. He could be going through security. *Slow down and breathe normally.*

I let out my breath and took several steps one way, then another, keeping in the shade of the huge exhaust funnel that rose like a giant shark's fin at the top of the ship. *Think!* I ordered myself. Why couldn't I remember his departure time?

Five o'clock kept coming to mind. No . . . six something or other. But I wouldn't have gone off without my cell phone if I thought I'd miss him, would I? Six o'clock Chicago time was seven o'clock here, so maybe he *hadn't* left yet. Or was I supposed to have remembered five o'clock *central* time? All I knew for sure was his flight number, 6739, so I needed to call the airline and find out when that flight was scheduled to leave. I began to feel better.

I dragged one of the deck chairs over and sat down. The plastic was warm beneath my bare thighs. I didn't know the airline's number, so I had to ask for the directory. When I got the number and was connected, I had to listen to the menu.

"Welcome!" said a friendly voice. "This is Susan. I'm an automated clerk, and I can help you. Tell me what you want to do. If you want to make a reservation, press or say, 'one.' If you want to check arrival or departure times, press or say, 'two.' . . ."

"Two," I said loudly.

"Great! You may speak to me in a normal voice. If you want to hear an arrival time, press or say, 'one.' If you want a departure time, press or say, 'two.' . . ."

"Two, damn it!" I said.

"I'm sorry," said the voice. "I believe you said, 'two.' Is this correct?"

"Yes!" I said pleadingly.

"Great!" the voice said again. "Do you have the flight number?"

"Yes!"

"Please tell me the flight number. Say each number distinctly. For example, one . . . two . . . three . . . four . . ."

I gave her the four-digit number.

"Thank you. I believe you said, 'six . . . seven . . . three . . . nine.' Is this correct?"

"Yes!" I said, almost sobbing with exasperation. The people at the end of the deck looked in my direction, then turned away again. It was now three minutes past five.

The automated woman was on again. "Flight six . . . seven . . . three . . . nine departed O'Hare International Airport on time at four . . . oh . . . two. . . ."

I dropped the cell phone in my lap, covered my face with both hands, and cried.

How could this have happened? What was the matter with me? I had gone trotting off to St. Michaels without even checking Patrick's departure time! My mind was still stuck on the number five—that his departure time was five something. That's six o'clock eastern time, so I must have thought I'd still have an hour to reach him after I'd returned to the ship. That he'd be sitting in the boarding area and his cell phone would go off and he'd smile when he saw it was from me.

I leaned my head against the base of the funnel and silently sobbed, my chest heaving. Patrick would be gone for a year, and I hadn't said a real good-bye.

It was only when a sob escaped that I realized someone was watching me. Through my tears, I saw Mitch standing over by the rail, looking at me, concerned.

I wiped one hand over my cheeks and blinked my eyes, but I kept my head down. Then I saw his feet standing beside my chair.

"What's wrong, Alice?" he asked.

I stifled another sob and glanced toward the little cluster of passengers who were looking at me again. Mitch pulled another chair into the shade, his back to the passengers, and sat down beside me.

"I just . . ." I began, "I missed telling my boyfriend good-bye before his plane left for Europe. I don't know *how* I let this happen. . . . I thought it was leaving later . . . and he—he'll be g-g-gone for a whole year!"

"Oh, jeez." I could see Mitch shaking his head. "Rotten luck."

"It's not luck, it's stupidity!" I wept. "How c-c-could I remember the flight number but not the departure time? Sane people don't do that!"

I needed a tissue. Mitch got up, went over to a small table next to the passengers, and returned with a cocktail napkin.

"Was he expecting you to call at a certain time?" he asked, handing it to me.

"Not exactly." I blew my nose. "I didn't tell him I'd call, but we haven't talked for a few days because he's had exams and he's packing—but he'd naturally think I'd want to say good-bye."

I was through crying now, and my hands went limp in my lap.

"Why . . . why didn't he call *you*?" Mitch asked.

"Well, I thought he might have, but there weren't any messages waiting. He knows I can't have a cell phone with me when I'm on duty, so I usually call him in the afternoon on my break when I can reach him. But I *didn't* this time, and I can't understand myself."

"You can't call him now?"

I looked over at Mitch. "You can't use a cell phone on a plane."

"Oh," said Mitch. "I didn't know that." He smiled a little. "Never been on a plane."

"I've only flown a couple of times." I could feel tears rising again, but I checked them. "It's just like . . . like I'm losing my mind. I mean, I've been so upset about his going away for a year, you'd think I'd make *sure* I didn't forget this. I even rehearsed what I was going to say. And then I didn't even check the departure time."

"Well," Mitch said, "you could always text him now, and he'll have a nice surprise waiting for him when he gets to wherever he's going. Where *is* he going, by the way?"

"Spain."

"Oh. Well, since you didn't get a message from him, it probably means he was rushing around like crazy right up to flight time. And if you *had* been able to reach him, you wouldn't have had a decent conversation anyway."

That was amazingly comforting. I smiled a little and blew my nose one last time. "Thanks," I told him. "I didn't mean to bother anyone else with this."

"No bother." He straightened up, hoisting his shoulders back, the T-shirt expanding across his chest. "The one thing I learned when my uncle died was to talk about it. It really helps."

I kept smiling at him a second or two longer, then suddenly looked at my watch.

"I'm late!" I said. "Galley duty."

"They'll survive," he said, and gave me a final once-over. "You okay now?"

"I think so," I said. "Thanks, Mitch."

6
CONNECTIONS

I went through the motions of work in the galley that night. Thankfully, I wasn't assigned to clear tables. I was one of the two "galley slaves" who slide uneaten food off the plates into the trash bags, spray the gunk off the plates, and load them in the huge dishwasher.

Natalie was the other slave on duty, and when I saw her dumping all but one grape off a salad plate and setting it aside, I remembered that the terrapin was still a passenger.

"Where is it?" I whispered as we shared the sink. "I didn't hear it last night."

"The engine room," she told me. "Frank won't say anything if I have it off the ship by Sunday."

"Is it doing okay?"

"I've added grass and water. Gwen donated a little worm this morning, but it's still there. Terrapins can go a week or more without eating, I read. I just hope the noise of the engine room doesn't do him in."

"It's a he?"

"Haven't the faintest idea. But Kevin will love it."

I wondered if there's always the urge to get something really special for a brother. Never having had a sister, I wouldn't know if that's even more special, but I had to smile as I remembered the angst I went through thinking up gifts for Lester over the years: the beer cookbook, the Mickey Mouse boxers, the two half-pound bars of Hershey's chocolate, and—omigod—his twenty-first birthday present!

"What are you smiling about?" Natalie asked curiously.

"A present that Pam and Liz and I cooked up for my own brother's birthday a few years ago," I told her. "They'd had a crush on Lester for as long as I could remember, and they wanted to be in on a surprise. I'd found out from Les that his girlfriend had promised him a surf-and-turf dinner, served by her in the outfit of his choice, which was a leopard-skin bikini and knee-high boots."

"Wow! Now, that's creative!" Natalie said.

"So Pam and Liz and I decided to serve him a surprise breakfast in bed in the outfits of *our* choice."

Natalie was grinning already. "And?"

"Liz was in a long high-necked dress, I was in my bathing suit with a sweatshirt over it because I was cold, and Pamela was in a skintight cat costume with black net stockings she'd worn at a dance recital. I think we blew his mind."

Thinking about Les almost pulled me out of my blue funk, but then I was back to figuring out how long it took to fly from Chicago to Spain. Hadn't Patrick said something about changing planes in New York? If so, this meant he could check his cell phone in New York, and there still wouldn't be a good-bye message from me. I watched an anchovy slide off a plate onto a half-eaten roll, and my stomach turned. But then I realized that Patrick could try *me* from New York, and I might still find a message waiting when I got off work.

I was holding the spray nozzle too close to a plate, and water splattered on my face. I wiped my cheek on my sleeve, set the plate on the rack, and went back to figuring out what time he'd reach Spain.

How many time zones would he cross? Was time going backward or forward? Did I even know that? Seven hours came to mind, but where did that come from? The flight number? I was really losing it. I thought of the way I'd been crying up on the top deck and the way Mitch brought me a napkin to blow my nose. And then I remembered what he'd asked—why hadn't Patrick called me?

And suddenly I thought of all the excuses I'd made for him: He had exams; he was packing; he knew I couldn't have my cell phone with me while I worked. . . . He could have texted me, couldn't he? He could have left a message.

"Alice!" the chef, Carlo, called. "Incoming."

I set to work removing plates and silverware from the trays, but my mind wasn't functioning. Was I just borrowing the seven from the flight number?

The thought that Patrick could have called but didn't bothered me even more, and I felt tears rising in my eyes again, but I checked them. There's a moment or two when you feel you can make tears subside without doing a thing. And, just as quickly, you can lose your chance, and water collects beneath your lower lids and won't go away. Newsflash: They do not evaporate. Either wipe your eyes or wait and wipe your cheeks. I dodged the bullet this time and found myself excusing him once again.

Okay, Patrick's flying across the Atlantic, so he's going east. Time gets later and later, so he's losing time. If it takes seven hours, and he crosses—what? Five, six, seven time zones . . . No. When Dad flew to England to visit Sylvia before they were married, it was a five-hour difference, wasn't it? It doesn't mean that Patrick will get there any later in real time, it just means that it will be later in Spain than it is here. Right?

The fish and garlic smells accumulating in the garbage can as the meal went on were like noxious fumes, and I had to turn my face away when I dumped a plate of food on top of the mess.

Why was I *doing* this? Patrick was the one who was leaving, not me! Why shouldn't *he* be calling *me* to say good-bye? Why was I putting myself through all the agony of "should have, would have," as though the whole relationship depended on me doing the thoughtful thing? What was I so afraid would happen if Patrick didn't get the right kind of farewell?

I didn't like the thought of separation, I knew. From anyone. Anything. I'd been fighting it all year, just thinking about leaving home for college. Maybe when you lose someone close—your mom, in particular—you go your whole life wanting things not to change. Wanting everyone you love to stay right where they are. But what kind of a life was that to wish on Patrick? On myself?

I almost dropped a water goblet that slipped from my soapy gloves. My thoughts seesawed back and forth. If it was a seven-hour flight, then I had seven hours to get a text message to Patrick before he landed and could turn on his cell phone. There was still time. . . .

Carlo came over to check out the uneaten food waiting to be dumped.

"Oyster mousse didn't go over so well, I see," he said.

"You win some, you lose some," his assistant said, and Carlo went back to the broiler, where the Cornish hens were spitting fat.

What would I say to Patrick if I texted? My first thought was to let it all hang out—tell him how much I'd fantasized about sending the perfect good-bye message, how mixed up I'd been about his departure time, and how I'd rushed up the gangplank to get to my cell phone and cried when the automated Susan told me the plane had taken off. Did I want him to think of me like that or as a woman of mystery, excitement, surprises, who lived an interesting life with or without him?

But . . . if two people really truly cared about each other—if you were "soul mates"—why *couldn't* you tell each other all your little troubles as well as your big ones? Talk about your feelings? Wasn't I interested in his? The thing was, I always seemed to be the one with the problems, who worried about everything little thing. Patrick, world traveler, the sophisticate, just knew how to navigate through life without hitting any sandbars.

I reeked when I finished work about ten. Despite the waterproof aprons we wore on galley duty, there were splotches of putrid water on my clothes. I could smell cooking oil on my arms—in my hair, even. But the minute I was off duty, I got my cell phone and sat down at a port-side window. The only other person in the dining room was Curtis, one of the deckhands, the married one, who was vacuuming the floor. How often did he call his wife? I wondered. I propped my feet on the chair beside me to keep out of his way.

> *Patrick—I don't know when or where you're reading this,*
> *but I hope you had a great flight.*

Great? Does anybody have even a *good* flight anymore? I changed it to *uneventful*, but that was too cold, so I settled for *good*, then continued:

> *It's been an insane day, and I missed telling you good-bye,*
> *but maybe this will be the first message you read when*

you get off the plane. If it is, I'm glad it's from me. Tell me everything!

Short and breezy. Interested in him. Fond but not fawning. I pressed SEND.

I sat at the table a long time, staring out over the dark water, not seeing much because of the reflections on the glass. If this had been a letter, I would have signed it, *Hugs, Alice* or something.

Is this the way it would be for the next year—worrying and waiting and wondering, revising my messages and e-mails over and over, working to get things just right, not wanting to depress him or annoy him? To show concern but not cling? If we were a couple, didn't he have a responsibility too? What I really wanted to say in that text message was *Why in hell didn't you call to say good-bye or leave me a message?* Weren't *my* feelings important? Didn't *I* matter?

The thing was, were we really a couple? We hadn't broken up, like Gwen and Austin, but it was understood from the time Patrick went away to college that there were no strings attached—we could, if we wanted, go out with other people.

Patrick and I had said "I love you" only once—the night of the prom in the limo, after our wild ride to the Bay Bridge and back. But I didn't want us to say it again unless we were sure of it. And even if we were sure, I didn't want us to keep on saying it like a mantra at specific times—signing off a phone conversation, for example, or walking to the store to buy fruit. Like if we didn't say it, we didn't love each other, and one of us would get run over by a dump truck.

We'd been careful up to this point to say we were special to each other, and we meant it. But we were thousands of miles apart. Was this even natural? To like—love?—someone for so long and yet so tenuously? Was it a mistake not to have slept together? Not to have that to remember?

I could hear Curtis closing up the galley. A thud, a click, a clank. And then it really was quiet. There was relief in knowing that my message was on Patrick's cell phone, however. I wasn't asking for promises or commitments or maybes. I was just here for him. Interested in him. And living my own life. Just what he wanted me to do.

Still, I longed to connect with *somebody* other than my crewmates. It was probably too late to call home—Dad and Sylvia would be in bed. So I punched in Lester's number and waited.

"Yeah?" came my brother's voice. "Al?"

"Hi, Les. I just wanted to see how things were going back home," I said.

"Not bad. How are you? Where are you right now?" He didn't sound eager to get rid of me, so I guessed he was alone, with time to kill.

"We're docked at St. Michaels, headed for Annapolis in the morning," I told him. "It's been a wild week, but I think I'm getting the hang of it."

"Good for you; build some muscles. Having any fun?"

"Yes. Some. I'm making friends. Have you rented your extra room yet?"

Lester lives with another Maryland graduate on the top floor of an elderly man's house in Takoma Park. They've been trying to find a tenant for the third bedroom since a friend of theirs got married and moved out.

"No, we'll wait till later in the summer to advertise it. Get a grad student."

"Are *you* having any fun, Les?" I asked. Meaning, did he have a new girlfriend? Lester used to have so many girls clinging to him, he practically had to swat them off. Now that he's "matured," you might say, with a steady job, I tease him that he's becoming an old stick-in-the-mud.

"Of course I am," said Les. "But don't expect all the details."

Neither of us said anything for a few moments. I knew I had to say something quick or he'd ask what I really wanted to talk about.

"Les," I said, "I forgot to call Patrick before he left. I mean, I didn't tell him good-bye."

"So why are you telling me? Call him up."

"He was already on the plane, so I sent a text message."

"And? What's the big deal?"

"Did you ever screw up big-time over something you should have remembered?"

"Oh, man. Did I ever!"

"What? Tell me."

"I sent flowers with a Happy Birthday note to a girl when it wasn't her birthday."

"That's not so bad," I said. "The fact that you gave her flowers should have made up for getting the date wrong."

"It was another girl's birthday, and they knew each other," said Les.

"Oh!" That was definitely worse than my forgetting Patrick's departure time.

"And . . . what happened?" I asked.

"They both married someone else," said Les.

I laughed in spite of myself. Marilyn and Crystal, I'll bet. "I feel better already," I told him.

When I woke the next morning, I realized I'd slept all night with my cell phone beside me. I pulled on shorts and a tee, my flip-flops, and ran up four flights of stairs to the sun deck where I could read a text message if there was one. There was:

Got your message. Here at baggage pickup. So far, all I've seen of Barcelona so far are the backsides of fellow passengers waiting for their luggage.
More later. Patrick

It was enough. The "more later" sustained me. Patrick was going to be busier than he'd ever been, trying to help his professor finish his book before fall classes began. It was like a huge load had lifted. We'd set the standard for text messages—for now, anyway. Short, breezy, informative, interesting, funny . . . He'd tell me about Spain, I'd tell him about the bay. Deal.

When I got back to crew quarters, there was a drama going on.

Natalie was standing in the middle of the floor, her long braid undone and dangling carelessly down the front of her T-shirt. Her sneakers had no laces, and her wrinkled shorts advertised the fact that she'd pulled on the first thing she grabbed.

"It's gone," she was saying as the other girls, in various stages of dress, paused, clothes in hand. "The box in the engine room is empty."

7
AWARDS NIGHT

"Did you check around?" Shannon said, reaching for a cigarette, then slowly slipping it back in the pack. "How far can a turtle get, after all?"

"I looked everywhere I could. There are a lot of places I can't get to in there, and the noise in that room is deafening. What will I do? Kevin's birthday's tomorrow, and they'll all be waiting for me on the dock."

"Have you asked Frank?" I put in.

"He's not there." Natalie sank down on one of the bottom bunks, then jumped up again. "The showers! I didn't check the shower room!" She bolted for the door.

We weren't that optimistic and resumed dressing. I changed from one T-shirt to another. "Anything could have happened to that turtle if Frank was the only one who knew about it," I said. "She said she put it in a bigger box with a lid. Someone could have piled stuff on top of it, then mistaken the whole heap for trash."

The door opened and Dianne peered in. "Who else is on galley duty for breakfast?" she asked. "Carlo needs some help up there. A busy day coming up."

"Coming!" said Emily, and followed Dianne into the hallway.

When Dianne had gone, Lauren said, "Natalie can't be *that* attached to a terrapin."

"She's attached to her brother and wanted to give him something really special," I said.

Natalie, of course, came back from the shower room empty-handed.

"Come shopping with me in Annapolis this afternoon," Lauren said. "There are some great shops—"

"I'm going to stay right here and search every inch of this ship," Natalie declared. "I've already told Kevin I've got a surprise for him, and he's so excited."

"Well, at least braid your hair," said Shannon, but she ended up doing it for her.

I don't know how we managed it, but Pamela, Gwen, Liz, and I all got to go visit the Naval Academy together that afternoon. Annapolis was our last port of call on the cruise, and the farewell dinner was that evening, before the whole thing started up all over again with a new set of passengers on Sunday. We had to be back at the ship by four, not five, but there we were, arms linked, walking four abreast around the grounds ("the Yard," they call it) of the Naval Academy.

There's something about all those men in white—well, women, too, but we weren't paying much attention to them. We watched the short video in the Visitor Center, but we missed the noon ceremony we'd heard about, when the Brigade of Midshipmen form for uniform inspection.

We didn't have reservations for a tour, either, so we did our own walking tour, watching the "middies" in racing canoes out on the water, instructors giving orders through a bullhorn from a neighboring canoe.

Another crew was just coming in off the Severn. We watched the way their bodies moved in unison as they rowed, each man falling into the rhythm of his own particular job as they reached the shore, an exercise practiced to perfection.

"I'll take the second guy from the bow," Liz told us, one hand shielding her eyes from the sun's glare on the water.

"I'll settle for number four or five," I said. "Four in particular. Woo! Look at that chest!"

"Yeah. That's the first thing guys notice on us," said Gwen.

When we left the river at last, we ambled through the Yard, around huge buildings with uniformed cadets murmuring a polite "Good afternoon" as they passed.

"Did that guy wink at us?" Pamela said, turning as a copper-haired midshipman passed by.

"He might have. I wasn't watching his face," Gwen said.

We entered a vast courtyard with buildings on all four sides—more like a town square. A place where Caesar might be crowned or something. We felt oddly conspicuous standing there by ourselves, no other visitors around, and suddenly from one of the doorways, a fiftyish man with stripes on his sleeve came walking briskly toward us. There was no "Good afternoon" from him.

"This is a restricted area," he said, and pointed us in the direction we'd come. "Please respect the signs."

All four of us began apologizing at once. He made no reply but stood with his hands on his hips until we were at least ten feet in retreat. Then he strode back out of sight, arms swinging. Sure enough, we'd passed a small sign that told us the courtyard was off-limits, but we were so busy checking out the middies that we'd walked right past it.

We were still giggling about it when we met up with more of our crew, all heading back to the shuttle the ship had provided. Some of our guys were bronze already from the sun, just a week into our season, and looked every bit as good as the midshipman who had winked. When Gwen sat down on Flavian's lap at the back of the bus, Mitch slid onto the seat beside me. Unlike the caps the midshipmen wore, Mitch was wearing an Orioles cap backward.

"Impressed?" he asked me, eyes twinkling. "All those sailors?"

"Aren't you?" I said. "But I don't know how they stand it—all those rules and regulations. I thought we had it bad on the *Seascape*."

"Yeah, I'm just contrary enough that if they said right foot, I'd lead with my left," said Mitch.

I laughed. "Me too." And then, thinking of Patrick, I added, "They see a lot of the world, though."

"But where do you stop?" Mitch seemed thoughtful. "I mean, it's not like you've seen one country, you've seen 'em all. There's always some other place you haven't been."

"But that's no excuse not to see any!"

He folded his large hands over his stomach. "No, it's not. How about you?"

"I guess I'd like to see some of the world, but . . . I don't know." I shrugged.

"Thing is, I like where I live now. The marsh, the bay, the rivers, the ocean. Just like being here, that's all," Mitch said.

"Nothing wrong with that. But . . . if you've never been anywhere else, how do you know you wouldn't like somewhere else better?" Who was I trying to convince? I wondered.

"Well, that's like what I'm saying—maybe I would. But then, how do I know that once I'd moved there, I'd want to try some place after that?"

I laughed out loud. "Mitch, you're hopeless."

"Suppose I am," he said, and smiled. "But then so was my dad and my uncle and my grandpa and his dad before him. We've been crabbers and trappers 'bout as long as anyone knows. But you give me the choice of waking up to geese calling overhead or some officer blowing his whistle in my ear, I'll take the geese any day."

"How do you stand the wake-up call on the *Seascape*, then?" I asked him as we neared the dock and the ship came into view.

"When you know it's temporary, you can take most anything," Mitch said. "The Canada geese and the autumn sky are still going to be here come September."

Natalie was on edge, not only because she now had no great surprise for her kid brother, but because wherever the terrapin turned up, somebody would have some explaining to do.

"I looked everywhere I could think of on this level, and all Frank can offer is that it's probably crawled in some unreachable crevice and won't be discovered till it's decomposed. Oh, man . . . I'd better tell all you guys good-bye now, especially if it's in an air vent."

"Quit worrying, Nat," Emily told her. "And check your nails. Dianne wants top performance tonight."

Pamela was supposed to work with me busing tables for the big farewell dinner—with filet mignon and lobster, baked Alaska and cherries jubilee—but she was nowhere in sight when dinner began.

"Has anyone seen Pamela?" Quinton asked me as I carefully maneuvered a tray of salad plates back to the galley.

"She was getting changed a half hour ago," I said.

Quinton took the tray from my shoulder and balanced it on one hand. "Would you go look for her, Alice? Tell her to get up here double time."

I took the stairs down to crew quarters and checked the

showers, the stalls. When I didn't see her in our cabin, either, I had a hunch she'd be on the top deck, since everybody else was at dinner. And as I emerged from the Chesapeake deck, I saw her perched on the edge of a chair, screaming into her cell phone.

"There's nothing I can *do!*" she was saying. "You've got to figure this out for yourself, Mom! Get a taxi if you have to!"

She saw me motioning to her, and I could read the exasperation in her eyes. "You have *friends*! *Somebody* can go with you! Mom, I'm supposed to be on duty this very minute. They're waiting for me. . . . I know . . . I know . . . I'll call later. Bye."

She stood up and dropped the phone in the pocket of her apron, her cheeks red, the way they get when she's really mad.

I took the cell phone from her pocket. "I'll put it down in our cabin," I said. "You can't have her ringing you during dinner, and you couldn't answer if she did. Quinton's asking for you. You'd better get down there fast."

"Thanks," Pamela said, and ran on ahead of me. But as she descended the stairs, she suddenly stopped, threw back her head, and wailed, "Damn it! Damn it all! I'm *sick* of this, Alice! Sick, sick, sick!"

She scooted on into the galley when we reached the main deck, and I went on down to our cabin. As I put the cell phone on her bunk, it rang again. I put a pillow over it and went back upstairs.

✳ ✳ ✳

The farewell dinner went off without a hitch. There were champagne toasts among the passengers, to one another and to future cruises, and the captain told them—as he'd tell all the ones to come—that they were the best passengers he'd ever had on board. They clapped like they believed him.

It was late when the crew finally got their dinner. Thankfully, the passengers didn't linger after they'd eaten their cherries jubilee because all bags had to be sitting outside staterooms by six in the morning, all passengers out of their rooms by nine. Most people packed up that night.

We did get a good meal, though, in preparation for all the work we'd do on Sunday. Quinton stopped by briefly to thank us for a successful week and to remind the housekeeping crew that we had only a few hours between the departing and the incoming guests tomorrow to get the staterooms in order.

After he left, Josh got up ceremoniously and announced that in celebration of a successful first cruise, the deckhands wanted to present some awards.

"Hear, hear!" somebody said.

"This is tough work," Josh continued, putting on a sober face. "Blood, sweat, toil, and tears. Neither cold nor rain nor dark of night shall—"

"Cut the bull and get on with it," Flavian shouted, and the other deckhands clapped.

"O-kay!" Josh continued. "To the deckhand who snores the loudest, Barry Morris!"

Huge guffaws from the guys. Josh reached into an old

shopping bag and lifted out a harmonica. "We're going to tape it to your mouth, Barry, so at least you'll make sweet music when you snore," he said. More clapping and cheering.

Josh turned back again as the coffeepot went around the tables a second time.

"To the deckhand with the largest bladder." Louder laughter than the first time. "A man who has been known to stay at his post seventeen hours without once unzipping his pants." Josh reached into the bag once more and produced a latex glove that we housekeepers use when cleaning the bathrooms. This one was filled with water. "For you, Curtis Isacoff. In case you ever find yourself in a situation you can't handle, use this as a receptacle and let fly."

Curtis laughed and reached out to accept the artificial bladder, mindful of the leak that had started around the twist tie.

"And our last award," Josh said. "To the deckhand who eats the most and never met a food he didn't like, Mitch Stefans."

Mitch grinned, then looked nonplussed as the door to the galley opened and Carlo came out holding a chafing dish. When he reached Mitch, he leaned down to present it, lifting the silver lid with a flourish, and there lay Natalie's terrapin on its back, legs flailing wildly.

Natalie shrieked and leaped to her feet, not knowing whether to be grateful or furious. "You *guys!*" she sputtered, lifting it gently from Mitch's hands and turning it upright. "I looked *everywhere!*"

She was cradling it in her lap when Dianne stepped into the

room to see what all the laughter was about. When she heard that Josh was giving out deckhand awards, she laughed and said, "Keep it short, guys, because the more bags you can bring down tonight, the less you'll have to do tomorrow."

We had managed to survive the first week of ten, and no one got fired. Yet.

8
STORM

We felt like seasoned employees when we started the second cruise.

All the staterooms were cleaned before the next group got on, and when we'd finished, then showered and put on fresh shirts, we presented the same enthusiastic smiles to the world as we had a week ago, welcoming the newcomers aboard.

Josh and Curtis carted luggage down from the Renaissance Hotel to the ship, and Flavian, Mitch, and Barry ran up and down the three flights of stairs carrying bags as though the ship would sail any minute. This time I was assigned to sit with Stephanie at the activities desk and be her girl Friday, escorting passengers around the ship as she directed.

I started counting the number of times we were asked, "When do we sign up for excursions?"

"I'll be giving a short talk after dinner and passing around sign-up sheets then," Stephanie had answered cheerfully.

"Does this ever get old?" I asked her after the seventh consecutive question.

"Not at all," she said. "Every face is a surprise package— somebody else to know."

It was sort of awkward having a conversation with her, knowing what I did, what I'd heard about her, anyway: three broken marriages to her credit—the first one her own; the second that of a deckhand, a friend of Curtis's, whose wife and kids left him after his affair; and the third, that of the passenger on the Dutch line, which fired her as assistant cruise director when the news got out.

I could see why men were attracted to her, though. Along with her shapely legs and high cheekbones, she had expressive eyes that fastened themselves on every person who stopped by. But her skin seemed older than the rest of her—heavily made-up, with many small lines, like a ceramic plate with finely cracked glaze. Curtis was especially teed off with her because of his friend, as though the deckhand weren't responsible too. But I think for the rest of us, Stephanie was like our job insurance. If they hired someone with her reputation, then our jobs were probably safe.

"I've heard that the big cruise ships are like floating cities," I said, trying to make conversation with her, then desperately wishing I'd kept my mouth shut. I wondered if she thought I was referring to the one that fired her, if she suspected we'd been talking about her.

She knew. When my eyes met her steely look, I tried to change the subject: "Did you always want to be a cruise director?" I chirped. *Arrrggghhhh!*

She gave me a patronizing smile. "I always wanted to work with people," she said, and turned to the woman approaching our desk. "Yes, may we help you? Oh, what a gorgeous necklace!"

"I'm looking for your gift shop," the necklace woman said. "I do my Christmas shopping all year long, and I'd like first pick of whatever you have."

"Actually," Stephanie said, as though divulging a secret and leaving me out, "it's in the alcove behind this desk, but we're only open at certain hours. The thing to remember is that we put out something new every day, so you'll want to check it often." Stephanie was *good*.

The woman scrunched up her face to mimic a disappointed child. "Can't I just peek?"

Stephanie playfully returned the scrunch. "No," she whispered, "but if you tell me your stateroom number, I'll slip a preview list of items under your door."

The necklace woman went off pleased with the deal. Stephanie assembled some price lists and a photo or two, and sent me up to the Chesapeake deck to deliver them. "Then see if you can help out in the lounge," she said, and I knew I had been dismissed for the afternoon.

* * *

I was scheduled for one more week of housekeeping in the morning and busing tables at night before I'd be assigned to breakfast and lunch waitressing in the dining room. But by Sunday evening, I wondered if I'd even make it through the dinner hour, and I groaned as I climbed into my bunk afterward and sprawled out on the mattress.

"Even my blisters have blisters," Yolanda complained. "Why was this Sunday even harder than the first one?"

"Because then we were high on adrenaline," Lauren told her.

"Yeah, but you and Emily and Rachel have worked on cruise ships before," Natalie said.

"New cruise, new boss, whole new experience," Emily said.

It was a whole new experience, all right, because this time the ship didn't sail till later that evening. Something to do with a misunderstanding about a food delivery, or a change in the forecast, or a storm in the Midwest that had delayed the flights of six of our passengers . . . maybe all of these.

In any case, when we got up the next morning, whitecaps were forming on the water. Captain Haggerty announced that we'd arrive in Norfolk later than scheduled, and we might be in for a little rough weather on the way. But, he added cheerfully, it was all part of the adventure, and he was looking forward to seeing us at the Captain's Dinner that night. He suggested we stay inside, but there were already passengers at the railings on the decks above, practically welcoming the storm to come, as we departed the dock.

As the morning wore on, the wind grew stronger, and it rained heavily. At lunchtime Stephanie announced that there would be a game of Trivial Pursuit in the lounge, men versus women, and—just in case—guests could request seasick pills at the activities desk, but she doubted anyone would need them.

"Oh, she goofed there," whispered Lauren. "You never want to use the word 'seasick' on a ship. The power of suggestion, you know."

"This is June, after all," Stephanie continued, "and most of our summer cruises are calm and placid. But we're going to heat things up here with a battle between the sexes, so we invite everyone up to the lounge at two o'clock and let's see how you do."

It sounded like an interesting diversion, but the passengers were more interested in "storm at sea." They talked excitedly among themselves as to whether it was better to be high or low on a rocking ship and how high the waves might get on the Chesapeake.

When I went up to the observation deck to help Mitch and Barry secure the deck chairs—a long line over the row, tied down tightly at the other end—passengers were roaming about, head scarves and jackets flapping in the wind, taking pictures. Waves sloshed against the side of the ship, and the dark clouds moved even faster overhead.

I'll admit, I liked it too—liked listening to the thud as each wave slapped against the hull, sending spray several feet into the air.

The sky itself was like a sea, dark masses of roiling clouds racing above, the wind gusts so strong that passengers staggered backward, grasping the rail for support. Occasionally a wave was so high that the spray reached the floor of the lounge deck, and Ken McCoy made the rounds, ushering passengers inside.

When I checked the lounge at two-thirty, the Trivial Pursuit game didn't have many takers. A few men stood at the bar, drinks in hand, debating a history question, but the small group of women on the opposite side of the lounge were discussing something else entirely, and I saw Stephanie discreetly slip the cue cards back in the box. She checked the library shelves, instead, for books about weather and storms and placed them strategically around the room. But most of the passengers, by now, were in their staterooms.

As I helped straighten up the lounge—plastic cups that had slid off coffee tables, magazines on the floor—I saw the horizon out the windows disappear as the bow of the ship rose in the air, and then suddenly there it was again, disappearing once more as the bow dipped. It was then I began to feel queasy.

I went out in the hall and heard someone vomiting in the men's restroom, and I felt my own jaws tighten. How were we supposed to put on a Captain's Dinner that night with all this? I braced one hand against the wall to steady myself as the ship dipped again.

"Hey," said Josh, coming up the stairs from the main deck. "You don't look so good."

"Why doesn't the captain just dock somewhere?" I asked. "Most of the other boats went in an hour ago. We're the only ship out here."

"You can't dock a big ship like this in a storm," Josh said. "You try that with waves this high, we'd probably bring down half the pier and knock a hole in the hull too. If we're going to get tossed around, you want it to be out here, where we're not going to hit anything. Even if we got the ship docked, it would be too dangerous to try to get anyone off."

I closed my eyes and felt the tightness in my throat again as the ship rocked, the pull at the corners of my mouth.

Josh took my arm. "If you want the sailor's cure, come with me," he said.

"I'm not putting anything in my stomach, Josh."

"Don't have to." He gently pulled me toward the big panoramic window at the bow and positioned me right in front of the glass. "Now," he said, "focus on the horizon. Nothing else. Just focus."

I studied the faint demarcation line between gray sky and gray water.

"Now, no matter what the ship does, keep your eyes on the horizon," Josh said.

Standing at the bow of the ship with the huge picture windows, I could follow the horizon whether it rose or fell. I don't know if I was especially suggestive or whether it really worked. But like a ballerina focusing on one particular spot as she twirled, I guess, keeping an eye on the horizontal line ahead seemed to settle my stomach.

It was even better when Emily invited me to share her mackinaw, and we opened the lounge door to the deck, almost getting blown over by the wind. We went around to stand in front of the windows, the rain lashing our faces, and watched the horizon together from there. She was about six inches taller than me, and only my eyes peeked out from the collar of the rain gear.

"Let's don't tell anyone we're out here," she said, as though they couldn't see us through the window.

"Yes! We'll just stand here like the figurehead of a ship," I said.

"Two Maidens in Mackinaw," said Emily.

The worst of the storm was over by four thirty. The rain grew softer, the waves less forceful against the side of the ship, and though the sun never came out, the tumbling black clouds had floated away, leaving a dull gray sky in their wake.

The dining crew set up the reception in the lounge, and Emily and I went down to change into our dress shirts and black bow ties. When I came back up with Gwen and Pamela, guests were tentatively emerging from their rooms in cocktail attire, with their own story to tell of just how queasy they had been or how expertly they had survived the rock and rolling.

We didn't have a full house, though. A dozen or so passengers didn't show up all evening, and Shannon spent the whole time in the crew bathroom, we found out later. I also learned that none of our summer cruises had sold out completely, a worry for the company, which depended on every stateroom being occupied in order to break even.

But I'd made it through without barfing and had a good story to tell Patrick if I had time to text him later.

There was an e-mail waiting from him that night when I checked my laptop—a long one. In the few days he'd been in Barcelona, he told me, he'd walked along the Rambla, had made paella with his professor out of mussels and squid. He kept rolling off the couch where he slept at night, but he was easily falling into everyday Spanish, trying to strike up conversations with strangers, just to practice.

In turn, I e-mailed him about the bike ride around St. Michaels and the storm on our way to Norfolk.

We didn't have a full day in Norfolk because the storm had put us a few hours behind schedule. So Liz and I walked into town on our break to pick up a few things we needed from a drugstore and do a little window shopping.

A small boutique was advertising a new fragrance called Passion Petal, and Liz was overcome.

"It's the most glorious scent I've ever smelled," she said, and the woman in the purple smock behind the counter offered to spray her neck and shoulders.

"You'll just have to wash it off when you get back to the ship," I reminded her. I prefer a musky scent myself, but one of the rules was no perfume at all.

Liz felt obligated then to buy something, so she purchased a belt, but when we were starting back to the ship, she saw some flip-flops she wanted in a sandal shop. She had turndown duty that evening, but I was busing dinner, so I said I'd see her back on board and set off by myself.

I felt like a flight attendant, walking up the gangplank—one of the crew, not having to show a boarding pass—getting a nod from Ken or Josh or whoever was on duty. I went down to crew quarters and put on my uniform, checked my makeup, combed my hair. . . .

The ship sailed in twenty-five minutes, and people had gathered on the dock to watch us pull away. Deckhands were moving things around to make room for the gangplank when it swung back, but mostly it was showtime—all of us just waiting around, smiling at the children who waved up at us, willing the ship to move, ready for the blast of the horn.

I had just sauntered the length of the walkway when Dianne came hurrying toward me.

"Alice?" she said, and had the harried look she often gets just before we sail. "Where's Elizabeth?"

9

PASSION PETAL

I stared at her blankly. "She's not back?"

"No. And Pamela said she'd gone off with you."

"She did. We were shopping. But she has the late shift, so I came back early. She should be along any minute. Liz is *always* on time."

"Well, today she's not. And crew was supposed to be on board ten minutes ago. We sail in fifteen."

And when Curtis came up the gangplank, asking if it was time to bring it in, Dianne said, "Curtis, get the motor scooter and take Alice to wherever it was she saw Liz last. But be back before we sail. I can't afford to lose all three of you."

I had wondered about the motor scooter. I'd seen it locked to a chain on the *Seascape*'s stern. As Curtis wheeled it down onto the dock, I tried to remember what streets I'd been on with Liz. I hadn't been paying attention to street names.

Curtis handed me a helmet that was too big, but I buckled it under my chin, and when he asked, "Which way?" I could only tell him it was a small shop next to a CVS and I thought it had a blue sign with sort of yellow bubbles on it. I felt like an idiot.

"Hold on," said Curtis after I'd climbed on behind him, and I circled his body with my arms as we sped across the dock and waited for a light at the corner.

"Can you remember the name of the shop?" he yelled over his shoulder.

"No. I think it had the word 'song' in it, but . . . I can't remember."

The motor scooter sprang forward as the light turned green, and I pressed my cheek against his back to keep the wind out of my face. Now I knew why motorcyclists wore goggles.

"Tell me if you see anything familiar," Curtis shouted at the next intersection. "I think the shops begin about here."

He turned down another street, and I frantically surveyed the storefronts on one side, then the other. A nail store, a hair salon . . .

What would Liz do if the ship left without her? It was so unlike her not to be back on time. It was usually Liz who looked at her watch and said, "Let's hurry."

I saw a paint store on a corner and remembered that it had a color wheel in the window. We'd stopped to find teal, because Liz said the color had more blue than green, and I said more green than blue.

"It's down that street, I think," I said. "We're getting close."

But even before we reached the corner, we saw the flashing lights of a rescue squad double-parked outside a CVS and a policeman keeping people from entering the store.

"The drugstore!" I cried, tugging at Curtis's shirt. "And there's the boutique. Let me off."

"We've got about seven minutes," Curtis said.

I jumped off the scooter and ran across the street, looking both ways for the sandal shop. When I spotted it, a woman was standing outside, arms hugging herself.

"My friend Elizabeth was just here," I said. "She was interested in those blue flip-flops with the silver streaks? Do you have any idea where she went next?"

The woman nodded toward the CVS and said, "She bought flip-flops and then went across the street to shop. But about fifteen minutes ago she came back here and said she was feeling sick. She wanted a place to sit down. I told her there were chairs at the pharmacy in the back of the CVS and walked her as far as the entrance to make sure she got in okay. . . . I'm here alone so I can't leave my shop. And five minutes ago the rescue team pulled up."

A little crowd had gathered, but the policeman still wouldn't let anyone enter the store. Inside I could see two men moving about, coming toward the entrance. And then the glass doors of the CVS swung open, and a man backed out, pulling a stretcher, while a second man guided it out the door.

"Liz!" I cried, recognizing the dark hair splayed against the pillow.

She barely moved her head.

"It's Liz!" I called to Curtis.

"You know this girl?" one of the rescue workers asked.

"Yes! We're part of the crew on the *Seascape*. We've been looking all over for her. What happened?"

"You'd better ride along," said the other worker.

The next few minutes were surreal. I walked alongside Liz, holding her hand as they wheeled her toward the truck. One cheek looked puffy and her lips too full—like they'd been enlarged—and I wondered if some shop was offering free samples of collagen.

"Liz?" I kept saying. "I'm here. You okay?" which was stupid, because she obviously wasn't. All I could figure was that she'd fallen on her face or something.

Then they were lifting the stretcher up and sliding it into an ambulance while Curtis was talking to one of the guys. When I tried to climb in after Liz, the other man told me to sit up front.

"You can't ride back here," he said, motioning around to the other door. I ran to the passenger side and had to climb to crawl in. Then the truck was moving forward, and the siren was going, and cars were moving out of our way.

It was a hard, bumpy ride that must have felt even worse to Liz, whatever had happened. And it was so noisy—the engine itself was so loud—that it was hard to hear much of anything. I squirmed around enough under my seat belt to see Liz. She had an oxygen mask over her nose, but I was shocked to see that the man bending over her had turned her on her side and was pulling her shorts down.

"Hey!" I cried. I mean, you read about things like this in the paper, rescue workers and unconscious patients and . . .

But the molester paid no attention; he had pulled on surgical gloves, and then I saw him jab some kind of needle device into her left buttock.

Liz yelped.

"Hey!" I said again, but the worker rolled her onto her other side, picked up another syringe, and injected the right buttock. She yelped again and tried to swat at him, and this time he must have been talking into a radio phone because I heard him say, "Okay, Doc, I've given her one cc of epinephrine and one of Benadryl IM."

The driver glanced at me. "Bee sting. She's having a bad reaction, and we had to get medication into her fast."

I turned forward again and closed my eyes momentarily. Okay, so I overreacted.

If I didn't stop hyperventilating, I'd be the next patient.

I expected Liz to be unconscious, but by the time they had wheeled her into a cubicle at a local hospital and I could stand beside her, she'd turned her face in my direction. She was staring strangely at my head. I realized I was still wearing the helmet and lifted it off.

But I didn't even get a chance to say anything, because a doctor and a woman with a clipboard crowded into the cubicle behind me, and I squeezed out of their way. They rolled her onto another stretcher and attached an IV to her arm. More monitors. More oxygen. I was terrified.

"Elizabeth, do you know where you are?" asked the young doctor in a white coat with the name badge DR. GRINLEY, on it. I couldn't tell if she nodded or not.

"Would you tell me your full name?"

I started to answer for her, but Dr. Grinley shook his head.

It was obviously taking Liz some effort. She rolled her tongue around in her mouth, and finally said, "E-li-a-beh An Pr-i . . ."

"Good enough," Dr. Grinley said, checking the clipboard. "Elizabeth Ann Price, right?"

She nodded.

"You've had an allergic reaction to a bee sting," the doctor told her. "We're going to keep a close watch on you, but I think the medications we've given you are starting to take effect, and you should be fine." He turned toward me. "And you are?"

"Alice McKinley, her friend. We're part of the crew on the *Seascape*, but I think they must have already sailed. . . ."

I don't know if you can call a doctor cute, but Dr. Grinley wore glasses with designer frames that looked really good on him. Maybe he was more than an intern if he could afford those. He had the greenest eyes I'd ever seen. Usually green-eyed people have hazel flecks, but his irises looked more like shamrocks.

"You, uh, work in the engine room or something?" he asked with a trace of a smile, and I realized he was looking at the helmet in my hand.

"We were out looking for Liz on the ship's motor scooter," I said.

Dr. Grinley was watching the monitors hooked up to Liz and began reading off numbers, which the woman with the clipboard wrote down. "Blood pressure, one twenty-six over seventy-seven," he said. "Pulse, eighty-five." Then he said to Liz, "Excuse me," and slipped his stethoscope up under her T-shirt and checked her heart, then asked her to roll over on her side so he could hold it to her back, and checked her lungs.

"Breathing's good, vital signs good," he said, and relaxed a little. "Where's the ship heading?" he asked me.

"Yorktown next," I said.

"Well, I'm glad it's not heading for the Bahamas or the Caribbean, because we've got to keep Elizabeth here for at least another hour to make sure the allergen is out of her system."

At that moment Dr. Grinley got a call over the PA system, and he pulled off his gloves. "The nurse will keep an eye on you, and I'll check you again before you leave," he told Liz. "Would you allow your friend here to find your wallet and give us some information about your insurance?"

She nodded, and whoosh—the doctor was gone. We were left with the woman with the clipboard, who handed me Elizabeth's bag. I fished around for her wallet, found the insurance card, and gave the clerk the information she needed. As soon as she was gone, a nurse came in bringing Liz a glass of Gatorade or something with a bent straw.

"I'll be back in a few minutes. Press this buzzer if you need anything at all," she said.

For the first time Liz and I were alone.

I stared down at her and made a face. She smiled a little but still looked strange.

"Man, when you make a scene, you make a *scene!*" I told her. "Dianne sent Curtis and me out on the motor scooter to see if we could find you. What happened?"

Haltingly, stopping occasionally to roll her tongue around like she was trying to get it back in place, Liz told me how she had bought the flip-flops, done some more window shopping, and then, about the time she decided to head back, she'd felt a sting on her cheek and swatted a bee away.

Now she reached up and gingerly touched her lips. "It flew off, but . . . I don't know . . . my lips felt funny and my cheek was . . . beginning to swell, and I had this sort of panicky feeling. I went back to the shoe store to ask if I could sit down, and the woman told me to go to the CVS . . . and . . . I'm not sure what happened after that. I think the pharmacist called 911. And then you were there with that thing on your head . . . I'm sure the ship's sailed by now, Alice. What are we going to do?"

I hadn't got that far yet, but suddenly I realized I had nothing with me but a helmet that wasn't even mine. No toothbrush, no ID . . .

Liz nodded toward her bag. "Check my messages?" she asked.

I picked up her bag again, set it on my lap, and began rummaging through it. "Can I use your lip gloss and comb if we have to sleep all night on the dock?" I asked.

"Do I have any tampons?" she asked.

I fished around some more. "One. Can I have half?"

"If I get the half with the string," she said, and we were laughing when the nurse came back.

"Well, well, that's a good sign," she said. "We're going to get you up and moving, Elizabeth. We won't release you till we're absolutely sure you're going to be okay, but right now I'd bet on it. We'll give you some epinephrine syringes and Benadryl capsules to take with you."

While Liz stood and walked and turned and sat and performed all the other obedience tricks the nurse asked of her, the IV stand rolling along beside, I checked her messages. There was one from Dianne:

Goodness gracious, Liz! The hospital called with news about your allergic reaction. We do hope you're okay and are glad you got immediate help. We'll be holding the ship for a little while to see if you can make it. Check in with the harbormaster when you get back.

"This is forty minutes old," I said.

Liz looked pleadingly at the nurse. "I really need to leave," she said. "Look! I can stand on one foot!" She tried and almost fell over.

"Or not," the nurse said. "Sorry, but we've got to keep you a while longer. Doctor's orders. We'll call a cab to get you to the dock."

"I've been stung before and this never happened," Liz told her.

"She never wore Passion Petal perfume before either," I commented, and the nurse smiled.

"Bees love anything that smells floral, but I wouldn't press my luck. Especially with you out on a cruise ship where you can't get immediate help. If you're ever alone when this happens again and have to give yourself an epinephrine injection— and this is only if you experience a breathing problem or facial swelling—you can use your thigh. If someone's there with you, they can either inject your buttocks or inject you like this." She squeezed the inside of Elizabeth's upper arm and made a lump. "Right there," she said.

"Then why . . . ?" Liz asked, and flushed slightly.

"Why did the ER guys use your fanny? Well, what other excitement would they have on a slow Tuesday?" the nurse said. "Joke! Joke! Seriously, that's the best place because there's lots of muscle back there, and it's less likely to bother you."

"Less likely than to have a guy she doesn't know holding her down with one hand and pulling her pants down with the other?" I said. "No telling what would have happened if I hadn't been watching. You owe me one, Liz."

I nudged her and we laughed.

"The ER guys are trained to do what they do, and we're glad

to have them," the nurse said. "But I'm going to give you some towels and cleanser to get all that perfume off before you leave here. And if I were you, I'd shampoo my hair as soon as I was back on the ship." She unhooked Liz from the IV and pointed the way to a restroom.

As we went down the hall, Liz said, "I hate needles. I can't stand the thought of injecting myself."

"Not to worry," I said. "We'll get one of the guys to help out."

When Liz was released at last, we sprang out of the hospital entrance like runners at the sound of the starting gun. I guess people who have to work in linoleum-floored places with antiseptic smells and hallways lined with stretchers concentrate on other things, like flowers in the gift shop and coffee machines and sunrooms and the banter of staff in the elevators.

But all we wanted to do was get back on board and forget that this ever happened. Liz had stuffed the syringes and capsules in her bag along with her new flip-flops, and at last the taxi pulled up to the docking area. Liz paid the driver and asked for a receipt, and then we bounded down to the waterfront to face . . . a big empty space.

There's nothing quite like staring far out over the Chesapeake Bay at your cruise ship, sailing slowly out of sight.

10
STATEROOM 303

If ever there was a sinking feeling, this was the sinkiest.

"A-lice!" Liz whimpered. "Should we just jump?"

But somebody was looking out for us. A guy in a cap that made him look official walked over and said, "You wouldn't happen to be Elizabeth and Alice, would you?"

We turned and just stared at him, like he was the angel Gabriel.

"I'm harbormaster here, and I'm supposed to get you to Yorktown, which isn't far as the crow flies but sure is a round-about way by land. And since the *Seascape* left only ten minutes ago, why don't you get in my boat and I'll take you out to your ship? I'll call and let them know we're coming."

And that's how we found ourselves skimming across the

water in a fancy speedboat with a cabin up front, our hair tossed by the wind in an early-evening sky, grins on our faces. The harbormaster invited us to ride in the cabin with him, but we wanted to experience the whole nine yards, and Liz said no bees would bother her at thirty knots or whatever speed we were moving.

We were met by a little welcoming committee of Quinton and Curtis and Ken McCoy. The captain had to drop anchor to get us aboard, but we were so grateful that we kissed the harbormaster and he said he was glad to oblige, we were welcome to miss the ship anytime.

Liz had to sit out her shift that night, but Dianne wanted to keep an eye on her, so she put her to work folding napkins from the laundry. By the time she had recounted her adventure several times over to everyone in the galley, both she and I were sick of hearing it, but it made good material to e-mail home.

The air was super fresh in Yorktown the next day. Since I'd toured Yorktown the last time we were here, I opted to take a towel and lie out on the beach with Natalie and Lauren and Pam in our bikinis, away from the immediate gaze of passengers, but not so far away that no one could find us. I was mentally composing another e-mail to Patrick.

I really do wish you were here, I would say. *Or that I was there with you.* But I would stop just short of saying *I miss you,* like, if I went any further, it would open a whole universe of yearning.

Later I'd tell him my big surprise: I was saving all I earned this summer so I could visit him in Spain at Christmastime.

The ship headed for Crisfield the following morning, and once again, it didn't look as though I was going to be able to make the ferry along with the passengers to visit Tangier Island. There were too many dawdlers, and when Dianne told me I'd need to clean four more staterooms on the main deck as well, I knew for certain I wouldn't make Tangier Island.

"Is one of the crew sick?" I asked, wiping my forehead with my arm.

She gave me a woeful, resigned look. "Not exactly. But Shannon's getting off at Crisfield," she said.

Crisfield? No one would get off at Crisfield to stay unless they were fired, I thought. Dianne didn't stick around to explain, so I kept my questions to myself. All of a sudden I didn't feel so secure. Shannon had been a good worker, I thought. She didn't love her job, exactly, but she was polite to the passengers and reasonably friendly with them. Unless she'd done something horrendous, how could I be sure that Dianne wouldn't tell me or one of my friends to just pack up and get off if we did something inexcusable in her eyes?

I moved to the next stateroom, determined to do everything by the book.

"Housekeeping," I called as I tapped on the door. I glanced at my watch. It was ten. Passengers who were going ashore had already gathered on the main deck near the gangway.

I picked up my bucket and tapped once more, then turned my key in the lock. "Housekeeping," I called again as I opened the door.

As I entered, a man of about forty stepped out of the tiny bathroom buck naked, wiping his armpits with a towel.

"Oh! Sorry!" I said, and backed out so quickly that my bucket clanged against the door frame and clattered onto the deck.

I closed the door after me and felt my face burning. Either I hadn't heard him tell me he was there or he hadn't heard my knock. Dianne would probably get a complaint before the day was over. I went quickly on to the next room, hoping that if I met that man face-to-face, we wouldn't recognize each other.

I did all my other rooms, then went back to number 303. The curtains on the little walkway window were still drawn. I knocked two times and called two times, then opened the door a crack. And when I turned on the light, the room was empty. Only one of two beds had been occupied, so I realized it was a single man traveling alone, probably had to pay extra to occupy the room. I cleaned it hastily and left.

Back in crew quarters that evening, as we changed for dinner, the chief topic of conversation was why Shannon had left. No one had seen her go. She'd just packed her bag and was out of there.

"Her smokes," said Emily. "I think she was fired."

"But she could smoke onshore all she wanted," I said, buttoning my shirt and smoothing out the pocket. We have to share a washing machine with the guys, and if someone finds your stuff in the dryer, they just take it out and drop it, and the wrinkles are up to you.

"I think she was smoking on the ship too, up on the top deck when she thought no one else was there," Emily told us.

"I can't believe they'd let her go over that," Gwen said.

Lauren came in from the bathroom and joined the conversation. "The way I heard it from Josh, Dianne noticed the smell on her breath and thought it pretty offensive. She told Shannon she had the choice of keeping her breath fresh or sticking with housekeeping the whole ten weeks, that she couldn't wait tables because several passengers had complained. And Shannon said, quote, 'Enough of this shit, I'm outta here,' so Dianne told her she was off at Crisfield. Curtis said he didn't think they'd replace her. Which means the rest of us have to work harder."

"But when we divide up the tips at the end of each week, it means we each get a little more," said Rachel.

"Yeah, but, man! That was quick," Yolanda said. "I mean, the work gets you down now and then. Anyone could say something they might be sorry for later. You're out of your summer job, just like that?"

"You are when your employer knows that they could replace any one of us overnight if they wanted to. Just put up a notice at Harborplace when we get back, and I'll bet someone would apply within ten minutes," Rachel told us. "Even at *our* wages."

"Great," I said. "I'll probably be the next to go." And I told them what had happened that morning in room 303. They thought it was hilarious.

"Of course he won't report it," Emily said. "You can bet he won't be anywhere in sight when housekeeping comes around tomorrow."

There was a light tap on the door. Gwen checked to see that we were all dressed, then opened it. Curtis was standing there holding a peach-colored bra in one hand. "Found this in the dryer along with my stuff," he said, handing it over.

"Anybody?" Gwen asked, holding it up.

"The dryer?" Natalie asked. "It was in the dryer? The way I'm eating, I can't afford any shrinkage."

"Bon appétit," said Curtis, and went back to men's quarters at the end of the hall.

I didn't really mind missing Oxford the next day, because that was no biggie on my list. But the addition of four extra rooms to clean was a lot. When I came to room 303, I started to knock, thought better of it, and did two more rooms before I returned. The drapes were still closed, as they had been the day before.

I knocked. Loudly.

"Housekeeping," I called.

No response.

I knocked again. "Housekeeping!"

I turned the key and opened the door a couple of inches, calling again.

When I got inside and turned on the light, the man was lying naked on the bed, hands behind his head, smiling at me strangely.

I went back out without a word and closed the door, my heart pounding, my cheeks flaming once again. Was he *trying* to get me fired? What was his *problem*? What was I supposed to do? But it was his face that bothered me the most. I wouldn't call it seductive or threatening or anything. More . . . tentative? Anxious, even.

I was perspiring all over, and I walked to the fantail at the stern to cool off.

"What's the matter?" Yolanda asked me as I passed. She put down her bucket and followed me back. "That guy again?"

I nodded and told her what happened.

"Was he, you know? Did he have a hard-on?"

"I'm not even sure. Believe it or not, I was looking at his face."

"You going back there? Want me to go with you?"

"No! I'll wait. Last time this happened, he was gone when I got back." I truly didn't know what to do. I hated to tell anyone there was something I couldn't deal with on my own. And, as I'd hoped, when I finally went back to his cabin that afternoon, he was gone. I cleaned it in record time and left. Except for the unmade bed, the room had been neat. There were no suggestive magazines lying around. No condoms. No underwear on the floor.

But the next morning in Annapolis, as I was finishing up on the lounge deck, Dianne asked if I could help her on the main deck. I still hadn't knocked on door 303. I decided to level with her, explaining why I had one more room yet to do.

She listened, her head cocked to one side, then held my arm as we went back to room 303.

"You call, I'll go in," she said.

I clanked my bucket. "Housekeeping!" I called.

No response. If he was dressed now and answered the door, would Dianne ever believe me? If a passenger decided to make trouble for you, he could. What if Mrs. Collier had never found her watch? Would Dianne always wonder if I had taken it? What if I reported this guy and then he denied it?

I knocked again and called louder.

Nothing.

Dianne put her key in the lock. "Wait here," she mouthed, and went inside.

I didn't see what she saw, but I heard her say, matter-of-factly, "Good morning, Mr. Jurgis. We'd appreciate it if you'd get dressed so we can clean your room. I'll be back in a few minutes." She came out, closing the door behind her, and we walked to the stern and waited where we could keep an eye on the door.

"Was he . . . ?"

"Naked as a jaybird," she said.

"Is he dangerous?" I asked.

"Probably not. He likes the shock on women's faces when he exposes himself. He looked embarrassed, frankly, but I doubt it will happen again. Not on this cruise."

"He's sailed with you before?"

"Not him, but there have been a few others." She looked at

me, bemused. "He's just part of the great human swarm, Alice. We all have our eccentricities."

We heard the door of room 303 open, and seconds later Mr. Jurgis left, walking briskly, heading for the stairs.

Later, when I passed him in the lounge, he walked right by me as though he'd never seen me before.

11
HOMEBOY

You don't see much of the captain on a cruise ship. Whenever we spent evenings docked, Captain Haggerty usually went ashore for dinner. Like most pilots, I suppose, he had friends here and there along his route. But he and Ken McCoy often had lunch together in the pilothouse, and they spelled each other when one of them needed a break.

For the lowly crew, though, one of our favorite times aboard the ship was dinner, which we ate only after the last passenger had left the dining room. We didn't have the same menu, of course—no rack of lamb for us. Dormitory stuff all the way, but it was well prepared, and Chef Carlo's fettuccini was to die for.

Conversation at dinner depended on who was there. If

Quinton or Dianne ate with us, we kept things polite and light. If it was crew only, there was more gossip, more noise.

One thing I noticed was that we didn't talk much about our plans beyond the summer. Once in a while someone would mention that he was staying over when the fall cruises began or would be working for another line. We kept to the present—how many staterooms we'd been assigned to clean, where we could cash our checks, which bar might serve without checking your ID. There were a lot of stories about the past—getting stuck on a roller coaster at Kings Dominion or deep-sea fishing off Ocean City. It was understood, I guess, that this was time-out for whatever we might face in the fall.

At the start of the third week, Pamela and I were among the groggy ones who rose at five thirty to set the tables for breakfast and welcome the passengers, who began arriving at seven.

Breakfast, we discovered, was the most difficult meal of the day. Not only did people wander in at odd times, but each had her own routine—four prunes, not three; half a Belgian waffle and one strip of bacon, not sausage. At lunch people settled for a club sandwich and a bowl of soup; and at dinner either baked or scalloped potatoes would usually do. But at breakfast our order pads were full of instructions—coffee, no cream; toast, no butter; sunny-side up, not scrambled.

In the galley on Tuesday, Mitch was swearing under his breath as he fished out seven raisins from a bowl of oatmeal.

"You'd think they were bugs," he said. "She couldn't do this herself?"

"Don't forget to smile," I teased. But no sooner had we closed the dining room doors and vacuumed the rug then it was time to set the tables for lunch.

It was after three before we got our break, too late for any excursion, but at least we had it fairly easy the rest of the day. We did the bed turndowns during dinner, distributed the program for the following day, followed the chocolate-on-every-pillow routine.

Pamela and I usually went up on the observation deck after we'd finished, provided no passengers were up there and we could have it to ourselves. We stretched out on the lounge chairs or propped our feet on the railing. Pamela looked a little less harried this week, I thought.

"Things settling down on the mom front?" I asked, keeping it general.

She slowly turned her head in my direction and gave me a sardonic smile. "No, not really."

"Okayyyy," I said. "But I haven't heard your cell phone ringing so much."

"Because I don't bring it with me on breaks, and I keep it turned off in crew quarters, that's why. If Mom has a real emergency, she can call the main office and they'd get in touch with the ship."

"True," I said, and leaned my head back, enjoying the last rays of the sun that warmed without roasting.

But I'd left the conversation open, and Pamela was in a pensive mood: "It's all about *her*, you know? I finally figured that out the other day. *Her* car! *Her* doctor's appointment! *Her* schedule! It's like nobody else ever has problems!"

I followed the trail of a plane so high, I could barely see it—just a blinking dot of light across the ocean of sky. "I thought your mom was doing better for a while. What do you think—that things not working out with that guy started her off again?"

"That and the fact that Meredith's still in the picture."

"She and your dad ever going to get married?"

"I don't know. I wouldn't be surprised if she moves in with Dad after I leave for college. Meredith's good for him in a lot of ways. If they do ever marry, Mom will be the last person they'll tell."

"Well, *you* seem to be taking all this remarkably well," I told her.

"I made a deal with myself," Pamela said. "I'll check my cell phone twice a day to make sure there's no emergency, and I'll text Mom once a week, just to keep in touch. But that's it."

"Sounds good to me," I said.

Finally I got to Tangier Island. Quinton told us that if there was an excursion along the cruise that we really wanted to take, we could go if we found someone who'd trade jobs with us. Emily said she'd take my tables at breakfast and lunch if I'd take her galley duty that evening. So on Wednesday morning I stood in line at Crisfield with the *Seascape* tour group to board the ferry to the island, and I was pleasantly surprised to find Mitch waiting too.

"I figured this was the last port of call you'd want," I said.

He smiled down at me, the bill of his cap facing forward now to shield his eyes from the sun. He wore a nondescript T-shirt of an indeterminate color—khaki, perhaps—and cargo shorts and old deck shoes without socks. And he was perfectly put together.

"Why'd you think that?" he asked.

I shrugged. "I don't know. Just imagined you'd probably been here before."

"Five or six years ago. Wanted to see if it's changed."

"Good! Then you can show me around."

"Glad to." The smile again.

Mitch was one of those people who made you happy just by being there. I'm not sure what it was. He gave off a feeling of quiet acceptance. Whatever or whoever you were was okay with him. No agenda.

Stephanie, a sailor cap perched jauntily on her head, was handing out touristy maps of the seahorse-shaped island—Cod Harbor, Whale Point, the tidal flats. . . . . Except for a couple of the other male stewards, Mitch and I were the only crew members on the ferry.

We sat on the back bench in the little throng of passengers who were listening to Stephanie's introduction to the island. She was speaking at a higher pitch than normal, trying to be heard above the drumming of the engine as the ferry moved across the water.

"Tangier—the place where time stands still," she was saying, "the most unbelievable sunsets you'll ever see. No cars, no buses . . ."

I wasn't prepared, I guess, for how wide the bay was, now that I could really pay attention to it. Looking at it on a map, the bay looks like the trunk of a tree, with rivers forming its limbs, then creeks branching off into smaller and smaller streams beyond. You'd think you would see a shore—both shores, perhaps—wherever you were on the bay. But here we were in the widest part, and I couldn't see land ahead or behind us or on either side.

It was cool on the ferry when the sun went behind a cloud, and we were just far enough to one side of the boat's cabin that we got the wind from the bow. I wished I'd brought a jacket. Mitch noticed the way I was hugging myself and pointed wordlessly to the goose bumps on my arms, one eyebrow raised in a curious, bemused way.

"Feels good to be cold for a change," I lied, but I knew that the minute the boat stopped, we'd get the unrelenting heat of the summer sun.

Slowly, slowly, a few blurred objects came into view as I got my first glimpse of the island—the steeple of a church, a water tower. . . . The base of all the low buildings seemed to be level with the choppy gray water as we approached. There was scarcely a tree higher than the roof of a house. The ferryboat's engine noise dropped to a mutter as we entered a narrow channel, and a white egret, balancing on one leg, didn't even move as its yellow eye followed us over to the dock.

Islanders waited there for relatives returning from the main-land, with small wagons or shopping carts to haul purchases back to their homes. Already my ears picked up the remnants of Old English in their dialect. As we waited to disembark, I heard one woman ask another if she had been able to see all her grandchildren this trip, and the woman replied, "Ever' one of 'em, and theer mamas let them speak theer mooinds no matter what they say. But, Lor', live and let live. Day I cain't go across the sound to see 'em, I know I'll doie."

Mitch and I smiled at each other, and as we stepped off the ferry, he lifted the woman's heavy bundle for her and placed it in the waiting cart of a friend.

"Much obliged," the round-faced woman said.

"Good day for strollin'," the friend remarked, and probably saw us as a couple.

We followed the *Seascape*'s tour group through the line of crab shanties and boat sheds, stopping to let a golf cart pass, the island's method of transporting tourists around. But when we reached King Street, which served as the backbone of the island, Mitch put one hand on my shoulder and we set off in a different direction.

"Let's see it on our own," he said. "I'd like to mosey around the way I did six years ago when I was here."

"Okay, let's mosey," I said, liking the idea. "What were you here for then?"

"Came with my dad to see about a boat for sale. Didn't end up buying it, but I got to look around a bit."

There wasn't much of a breeze, strangely. You'd think that an island would always have one, and there wasn't much shade, either. But I liked the feeling that I was here on an island in the middle of the bay and that I couldn't see land in any direction.

We headed for the salt marsh, ambling over to where two young boys—maybe ten and twelve—sat in a rowboat untangling some fishing line, both of them barefoot.

"How ya doin'?" Mitch asked them.

They shielded their eyes against the sun and looked up, lips parted, showing adult teeth they hadn't quite grown into.

"Mornin'," one of them said while the other went back to work on the tangled line.

"Catch anything yet?" Mitch asked.

"Nary a one," said the first boy. His tousled blond hair hung loose almost to his shoulders, wind-blown and sun-bleached. He could have been Emily's cousin, he had so many freckles. But then he brightened. "This here's my boat," he said proudly. "I'll be savin' up for a motor, and then I can take her out beyond the flats!"

"Hey! Good for you!" Mitch said, and watched them some more. The two were working together now to untangle the line, so we moved on. I heard Mitch chuckle.

I looked up at him. "What?"

"That was the biggest day of my life so far, when I got my first boat," he said. "I know just what that kid's feeling."

"Sort of like getting your own car?"

"Exactly. There's no fence out there on the water. You can go wherever you like."

As we walked across a large piece of plywood the boys had constructed as a sort of bridge to get to the next little ridge, Mitch grabbed my hand to help me across, and when we stepped off the other end, we jauntily fell into step walking arm in arm as we started our tour of the island.

It really was a walk back in time—a decaying trawler beached on a spit of sand; a couple of leather-faced watermen mending their nets; and, as we made another turn, the weather-beaten clapboard houses, some with raised graves and headstones in the front yard to protect them from the sea.

A sun-bonneted woman on a bicycle rode by, taking her time, her bedroom-slippered feet pressing down on the pedals.

Miss Molly's Bed and Breakfast, Hilda Crockett's Chesapeake House, Shirley's Bay View Inn, Spanky's Ice Cream, Lorraine's Sandwich Shop . . . Everything, it seemed, was named for somebody. Some of the names—Pruitt, Crockett, Parks—appeared again and again, as though there were mainlanders, like me, and then there were the real settlers, who had watched sunsets from these houses forever.

"You hungry for a soft-shell crab sandwich?" Mitch asked me, reading a sign in a window.

"There is such a thing?"

"Yep."

"I'm game if you are," I said, and thought how much more

willing I was to try something new with him than I was with Ryan McGowan last spring—Ryan, who had tried to change me from the inside out.

I don't think we'd passed a single person who didn't say hello, and the same happened when Mitch opened the screen door and we went inside the shop.

"You Earl Park's youngest?" asked the sixtyish man at the deep fryer. The lenses of his glasses were spotted with grease and foggy with steam.

"No, sir, I'm up in Dorchester County," Mitch said.

"Oh. Murland, then," the man said, giving us a welcoming smile, and I remembered that Tangier belongs to Virginia. Strange, the invisible line that travels across bay waters.

"Yeah, I was here six years ago and just wanted to see if things had changed," Mitch said.

"Boot the same, but thar's less of it," the man said, wiping his hands on his thick apron and coming closer to the counter. "Ever' year the bay takes a bit more of the island. Some day, they say, it'll take a boite and swaller it down. What'll you folks have?"

We placed our order and sat down at one of the few small tables by the window. The spicy scent of seasonings filled the air and made me realize how hungry I was.

"Lucky we got a table. I expect some of the tour group will be in here after a while," I said.

"No, they've got reservations at Hilda Crockett's—that's part of the tour," Mitch said. "Walk in there, you come out two pounds heavier, your wallet a little lighter." He took off his cap and placed it on the empty chair beside us. "Hilda used to advertise, 'If you leave hungry, it will be your fault, not ours.' Probably still does."

I watched him settle back in his chair. "You look more contented here," I told him. "More relaxed."

"More contented than where?"

"Back on board."

"Expect I am. Always figured I could feel at home most anywhere, though, long as it was on the bay. You ever feel that way about Silver Spring?"

No one had ever asked me that before. I started to say, *It's a much bigger place,* then realized that—compared to the bay—it was a speck on a map.

"I know the major streets," I said, "and if you dropped me off someplace, I could get somewhere I recognized. But I wouldn't call that 'feeling at home.'"

"Well, that's what I mean by home," Mitch explained. "Bay's sort of like a big, spread-out family—the watermen part of it, anyway. I don't feel the same about Baltimore or Annapolis, but leave me on an island—Smith, Tangier—along the coast or in the marshes, it's pretty much home territory, whether I've been there before or not."

We sat smiling at each other, and I was about to ask about his family when the counterman appeared with a platter in each hand. He set one down in front of me—fries at one end, coleslaw at the other, and in the middle, two pieces of white bread with a crab in between, its spindly, golden-brown legs hanging out at each side.

"Ulp!" I said, looking from my sandwich to Mitch and back again.

"If you don't want it, I'll eat yours, too, and you can order something else," he said.

And that's all it took to make me try it. I imagined fried onion rings. I imagined crusty Popeye's chicken. I took a bite of bread and lettuce and mayonnaise and something crispy and delicious, and the second bite was even better.

As we finished lunch, I told him about going out with Ryan after the spring play and how he had introduced me to oysters on the half shell, as well as all the things he found wrong with me.

"I'm glad this time was different," Mitch said. "Having fun?"

"Yes. I'm glad you came along."

"Something new to tell the boyfriend," he said, and his eyes were laughing as he wiped his mouth.

"You going to tell your girlfriend?"

"I would if I had one."

"That's hard to believe—that there's no one to tell."

He kept his eyes on me as he took a long swallow of Coke, but he had the same amused expression on his face. "There are only three hundred people in Vienna, Maryland, where I live, and most of them are middle-aged."

"Where exactly is Vienna, by the way?"

Mitch put on his country-boy accent: "Wah, it's haafway 'tween the Nanticoke and the Chicamacomico Rivers," he said.

"And of the nine gals my age in town, two of them's my cousins."

I laughed. "Where do you go to meet people, then?"

"Salisbury. Quantico, if you want to watch a bunch of Marines get drunk. But every once in a while a friend knows a friend. . . . That's the best way."

"So now you're cruising a cruise ship?" I said, and watched his grin spread across his whole face.

"There are some nice girls on that ship," Mitch said. Then, checking his watch, "Want to see the rest of the island?"

"I do," I said, wiping the grease off my mouth and chin.

"What we *can't* do," Mitch said as he scooted away from the table, "is miss the ferry. Do that, and we'd have to hire one of the watermen to carry us back."

We set out again up King Street. We passed the town hall and the New Testament Church; passed a girl of maybe thirteen or fourteen, leaning against a gate, ankles crossed. She was toying with a locket around her neck, talking with a boy about the same age who straddled a motorbike. And we could tell by the look in their eyes as we passed that they'd be seeing each other again.

12
THE GUESTS

Sometimes we fell into the rhythm of ship life so completely that it was as though fall and college and classes and grades were off in the distant future, not just weeks away.

Gwen and I had long ago decided we'd be roommates when we entered the University of Maryland. Then she found out that pre-med students could room for half the cost at a big house near campus, donated by a wealthy alumnus, and it would be crazy for her not to stay there for her eight years. So I was in the market for a roommate.

I'd indicated on Facebook that I was looking for a roomie, but being at sea most of the summer, I didn't get a chance very often to check and see if there were any takers. Like many colleges, the U of Maryland assigns roommates for the first year, but if two people both request each other, the housing office usually okays it. I'd posted my cell phone number and e-mail address, though, and now and then I heard from girls wanting to know if I was going to pledge a sorority or if I was into sports. As I only had a short time each day to use my cell phone, and even less chance to check my e-mail, I answered some messages too late or not at all.

Then late one night in the dining room, when we were checking our e-mails, I got one from a Margaret Sanderson—"Meggie," she called herself—who said she was the niece of one of Dad's customers at the Melody Inn, and she'd heard all about me and was so excited that I was going to Maryland too. *I read on Facebook you were looking for a roommate, and so am I, she texted. My aunt loves your dad's store, and so do I. Haven't decided on a major yet, have you?*

The message was three days old, and I hadn't had a chance to answer yet, but Meggie seemed possible.

Right now I'm working on a cruise ship, I e-mailed back, *but let's introduce ourselves.*

Ten minutes later, she answered:

Great! I hope I don't sound like I'm bragging, but I've got a 3.98 GPA. I write novellas, but none have been published yet (who knows? you may be a character in one someday!!!), and I've had a crush on a guy who doesn't even know me for, like, forever. But I could write about myself all day, who couldn't? Why don't we each ask three friends to say what they like about us (or not!!!)? Here are mine.

I stared at my screen. She was serious!

Hi. I'm Paige, probably Meggie's best friend. If Meggie has a fault, it's that she's totally honest. She tells you just what she thinks whether you want to hear it or not. But when my cat died, she stayed with me all night just to make sure I was all right.

The next paragraph read:

I've been Margaret's friend for two years. She's perfect in every way except she reads your mail. Oops! Meggie's trying to take the laptop out of my hands. . . .

"I don't believe this!" I said aloud.
"What?" asked Liz.
I scanned down to the third paragraph.

Okay, we're serious now. Meggie is one of the nicest girls I know. We went to camp together once and she gave every girl in our cabin a pedicure. We had a lot of fun together. She was into hypnotism at one point and claims she can hypnotize a chicken. Really. She can! She'll talk about almost anything, but she hates potatoes. Especially potato salad made with vinegar.

"Oh . . . my . . . God!" I said.

"Who's e-mailing you?" asked Lauren.

"You guys have got to help me!" I said in answer. "How am I going to get out of rooming with the niece of one of my dad's best customers? This girl would drive me crazy."

"Just tell her you found somebody else to room with," said Emily. "Simple."

"Just ten minutes ago I e-mailed her that I was interested!" I said.

Rachel stretched out on her bunk and examined the blister on one heel. "Well, then, in the last ten minutes you've found someone else," she said.

"But I'm still looking on Facebook! She'll know that. And I've got to find someone soon or the university will decide for me!"

"Let me see that," said Pamela, reaching for my laptop and reading the messages. Her face broke into a smile.

"O-kaay!" she cried. "Meggie wants the recommendations of three of *your* friends!"

"Now, wait, Pamela, it's got to sound real. I don't want to offend one of my dad's customers."

"Oh, we'll make it real, all right," said Pamela. She placed my laptop squarely in front of her, hit reply, and started typing.:

I've known Alice since sixth grade. I guess I'd call her a friend, but she humiliated me once onstage in a school play. . . .

"Pamela!" I laughed.

*She's nice, but she's got this streak of jealousy. If you can
put up with that, however, she's great.*

Pamela J.

"Tell her Alice is a compulsive eater," said Rachel. "That she
hides snacks all over the room."

"Let me have that," said Liz, and Pamela slid the laptop
across the table. Liz began typing:

*Alice will be your friend forever, but you need to know
that she has to have a light on when she sleeps, with music
playing. And she won't wear earbuds at night because she
says they hurt her ears.*

Liz

We clapped. Then Gwen took over.

*I've been Alice's friend since eighth grade. She'll give you
the shirt off her back, literally, but she'll also take yours
without asking. She has the feeling that once you room
together, all possessions are mutually owned. We were
camp counselors together, and I can't tell you how many
shirts of mine she ruined with grease stains and tomato
sauce. If you can put up with this, Alice is your friend
for life.*

Not-Quite-a-Friend

I didn't hear from Margaret for almost a week. Then I got a short e-mail saying that she thought she had someone else lined up and hoped to see me around campus.

So I was still minus a roomie come September.

We were all changing for our evening jobs the following afternoon—some in dress shirts and bow ties, some in their rattiest clothes for galley duty—when Pamela rushed in, all excited.

"Guess what!" she said. "Dad and Meredith signed up for this cruise next week!"

"Whaaaat?" I said. "Here? With us?"

"Dad just said that Meredith had gone online to see what the *Seascape* looked like, and she saw an ad for this huge discount—five hundred dollars off per passenger for immediate booking the second week of July."

"Wow!" I said. "That should be interesting!" I glanced over at her as I pulled on my shoes. "Will you like having them here, watching your every move?"

"I think so," she said. "They're not like that, and I get along with Meredith okay. It will be fun to show them around—let them see what we do."

And would you believe, I really *did* feel a tinge of jealousy, thinking how much fun it would be if Dad and Sylvia came on one of our cruises. Or Les! But I rose to the challenge: "It's only a week off. I'll trade shifts with you if you ever want to go on an excursion with them or something," I said.

"Me too, Pam," said Gwen. "Perfect chance to get in good with your new stepmom if they ever get hitched."

There was enough excitement even without that announcement, because it was the Fourth of July, and Chef Carlo was hosting a happy hour on the observation deck. Crew members who stayed aboard that afternoon to decorate got to mingle with passengers and chase down the red, white, and blue napkins that the breeze blew off the tables. But since I was on galley duty that night, I only got to emerge long enough to whisk away another tray of dirty dishes and pick up the strains of some band playing "God Bless America." My mouth watered when I glimpsed the appetizers Barry had just delivered. Every shrimp had a red, white, or blue toothpick in it; every hors d'oeuvre was topped with either a cherry tomato, a pearl onion, or a blueberry. I wished I'd eaten something before I went on duty.

Mitch had it worse, though—he was rinsing plates and filling the dishwasher by himself.

Since it was a Wednesday, we were docked at Crisfield as usual, and a waterman from Tangier had been invited onboard. After giving a short talk about the generations of Pruitts who had lived on the island before him and how the crab industry supported the local economy, he demonstrated how you crack open a steamed crab—what you eat and what you throw away. I heard only bits and pieces, desperately hoping each time I went on deck that there would be nothing more to carry below, but there always was.

It *would* have to be a night I had galley duty, because Captain Haggerty appeared at dinner and invited all passengers back up to the observation deck at dusk. He would be piloting the ship around the islands—Tangier and Smith and Tilghman—and along the coast, so they could enjoy the small local fireworks going off here and there while we cruised.

Mitch and I heard the announcement as we dealt with the reeking piles of crab carcasses waiting for the garbage bins.

"See what we're missing?" I told him.

He only grinned. "I liked our tour better," he said.

We finished up around ten thirty and went to the top deck to eat with the rest of the crew. Quinton had set up a long table and folding chairs at one end, and we devoured the biggest, fattest burgers Carlo could make, plus some of the leftover hors d'oeuvres from the cocktail party.

There was still an occasional rocket going off now and then, and we could see the sparklers along shore where there were campers. Sometimes we caught a whiff of gunpowder on the breeze from a short-lived fireworks display.

The *Seascape* was turning again and heading south when suddenly there was a muffled whump, and the whole ship jarred and shook.

I slid sideways on my chair for a moment, and someone's drink tipped over the edge of the table.

"What the . . . ?" Curtis said.

For a moment it seemed as though the ship's engine had

stalled. Silence. Then the sound of running feet on the deck below. We heard profanity from the pilothouse that mistakenly came over the loudspeaker, and Curtis headed for the stairs.

We went to the rail.

"Look!" Mitch pointed.

The ship's searchlight was swooping back and forth on the port side of the ship—back and forth, straight ahead, then to the side again. Then the grinding noise of the bow thruster—a shudder—and finally the ship moved sideways and on up the bay. We looked at Josh.

"Sandbar," he said, and smiled a little. "Captain grazed a sandbar. That's mud on *his* face."

"Doesn't he know where they are?" Liz asked.

"Supposed to, but this first-time cowboy thought he could cruise around at night."

"Really? First time?" I said. "This is his first ship or what?"

"No. First time piloting on the Chesapeake Bay. Not that it means anything in particular. Until now, anyway."

What the captain should do, Rachel told us, was get on the PA system and reassure the passengers—some of them, in their nightclothes, had come up to ask us what was happening.

"Not to worry," Josh told them. "Just scraped a sandbar. No big deal."

Finally Ken McCoy's voice came out of the speakers on both sides of the deck: "Ladies and gentlemen, we hope you have enjoyed Fourth of July on the bay, the very first for the *Seascape* . . ."

"Yeah, in its present form," Barry murmured.

". . . and we hope you had a most pleasant evening. The noise you heard a little while ago was simply the bow thruster, pushing us away from a sandbar. From all the officers and crew on the *Seascape*, we wish you pleasant dreams.'"

"Talk about smooth!" Rachel said.

"'The noise you heard was the bow thruster,' ha!" said Barry. "Notice how the big man passed the buck?"

"Maybe it was Ken who was piloting," Liz suggested.

"That's true," said Josh. "But I doubt you'll see the captain's face at breakfast."

We were all waiting for Frank to come up from below, and a little before midnight, he slipped onto one of the deck chairs, coffee in hand. He started to say something, then rubbed his jaw instead and burrowed down a little farther in his chair.

Josh's smile was more a smirk. "We got any damage?"

"Don't think so. Can't really tell unless I suit up and go down there, but the pressure's holding steady. Wish that were my biggest problem."

"What else?" asked Barry.

"Nothing yet. But as far as I can tell, the only 'new' things about this ship are the paint and the name."

"You want to know something else?" Rachel said, and we all listened, because as a lounge attendant she was in a position to pick up a lot of gossip we'd never hear. "It wasn't weather that delayed the start of our second cruise. The way I heard it from Stephanie, our major food supplier was about to pull the plug on our credit 'cause they still hadn't been paid for the first week. The front office probably had to put the ship up for collateral before they'd deliver the next order."

"Whaaaat?" said Barry.

"Okay, I'm exaggerating, but a pound of flesh, anyway."

"Well," said Frank, lifting the coffee mug again to his lips, "we're moving now. That's what counts. Let's don't go borrowing trouble. I mean, any more than we've got."

We took down the Fourth of July decorations from the dining room on Thursday, and that evening all the girls sat around women's quarters, winding each of the streamers into a tight little roll, to be used again next summer. Emily, who had worked in a craft store once, knew how to make rose petal wreaths out of crepe paper, and we decided to make one for our cabin door. Barefoot on our bunks, legs crossed—we folded, tucked, and stretched the little rectangles of crepe paper, turning them into roses.

"Reminds me of camp," Gwen said.

"What kind of camp was that?" asked Natalie.

"Disadvantaged kids," Liz explained. "It was the summer before our sophomore year. The four of us were junior counselors—Gwen and Pam and Alice and me."

"The summer Gwen broke up with Leo . . ." Yolanda added.

"Legs," I corrected.

". . . and started hanging out with Joe Ortega," Liz said.

"And *you* were dating Ross," I reminded her.

Emily threaded a needle through the rose in her lap, held the needle out away from her body as she pushed the rose down the thread, and secured it in place. "How long have you guys known each other, anyway?"

"Forever," said Pamela. "Liz and I started kindergarten together, Alice came into the picture in sixth grade, and we met up with Gwen in eighth."

"I'm just a tagalong," said Yolanda.

"I had a tight-knit bunch of girlfriends in high school, but then we all scattered," said Emily. "I miss the long talks and the closeness . . . the drama, even."

I passed another handful of roses to her. "What do you suppose guys talk about when they're alone?" I wondered aloud. "Like right now, when we aren't around?"

"S-E-X," Natalie spelled out.

"They probably aren't talking at all—probably watching TV," said Gwen.

"Football . . . soccer . . . cars," Lauren guessed.

"They tell stories, that's what they do," I said, thinking of Mark and Brian and even Patrick. "All the crazy stuff they've ever done, trying to top each other."

"Feelings?" Natalie asked. "Do they ever discuss those?"

"Are you kidding?" Yolanda rolled her eyes. "Have you ever heard a guy talk to a buddy about feelings?"

"That's what women are for," said Emily. "To help men express their emotions."

"Urges, you mean," said Lauren.

"Feelings, too," said Liz. "But guys aren't the only ones who hold back."

We worked silently for a minute or two, just enjoying the rare chance to hang out together, all at the same time. Emily strung another flower on her thread, then held it up to estimate how many more we'd need.

"What I've discovered about life is that feelings can change," Liz said. "I mean, a complete turnaround. Well, sort of." She held another petal between her fingers and curled the edges over. And then she confided what I'd thought only her few closest friends would ever know about: "I was molested when I was seven . . . by a supposed friend of the family."

Natalie gasped, and everyone else looked up.

"My parents had known him for a long time," Liz continued, "and he used to take me on, quote, 'nature walks.' He was a scientist."

Gwen and Pamela and I watched her, admiring her courage.

"My God!" said Natalie, not moving a muscle.

"Yeah, 'our big secret,' you know," said Liz.

"Was he ever arrested?" asked Lauren.

"No. He died in a car accident, and even then I didn't tell my parents what had happened until . . ." Liz looked over at Pamela and me. "Until these friends of mine got on my case and made me. But for years I had nightmares about his coming to get me and take me away. About hiding in the house and hearing him coming closer."

Not even Pamela and I had known about that.

"Oh, Liz," Emily said sympathetically.

But Liz continued: "After that I got angry—not just at him, but at my parents for not guessing what had been going on. I'd fantasize about smashing him in the face and kicking him in the balls. Scratching his eyes out. How I'd like to hurt him."

"Naturally!" said Rachel.

"Yeah, no guilt there," said Liz. "But a few months ago . . . I can't quite explain it . . . instead of that fantasy, I imagined myself sitting down across from him and saying, 'Okay. Tell me why you did it. Tell me if you felt it was wrong. If you ever asked yourself how *I* was feeling.'"

The room was absolutely still.

"I discovered I was as curious as I was angry. I wanted to know the *why*—the makeup of that pervert. I'm not entirely sure what it means, if I'm really over it or not, or—" She stopped.

"Maybe you've just . . . moved beyond it," I offered.

"I sort of think so too. I guess once I started applying to colleges, I felt I was . . . Yeah, you're right. I felt I wasn't just moving away, I was moving on. Like I wasn't going to rent him room in my head anymore; he'd been there long enough."

Gwen and Pamela and I just sat there beaming at her, and then Gwen leaned way over and gave her a hug. "That's my girl," she said.

"The feel of freedom," said Liz. "That's what it is."

Maybe she was feeling some of what I'd felt at Tangier Island with Mitch: being someplace I'd never been before; being friends with a guy I'd known for only a few weeks; watching the gulls soaring free overhead, going wherever they wanted. Just a sudden surge of freedom from . . . What, exactly? Giving myself a push, I guess. Getting on with life.

As the current passengers departed on Sunday and we worked like crazy cleaning staterooms, Pamela found out where her dad and Meredith would be staying—room 218, lounge deck— and we made sure it was perfect.

Mitch appeared at the door with Barry, holding a work order. "This the room that requests a double?" he asked.

"Yes," said Pamela. "Quinton said there are some over-sized sheets and blankets in the linen hold."

Mitch and Barry pushed the twin beds together and tied the adjoining legs to anchor them, then placed a foam divider between the twins to convert them into a two-sleeper. The guys were smiling as they left, and I heard Barry say, "*Somebody's gonna have a good time this week.*" We didn't tell them who was coming.

I was glad I was on dining room service that week—Pamela, too—though we rotated again the week after. Mr. Jones and Meredith would see us in our starched shirts and black bow ties, not our baggy shorts and dirty T-shirts, carrying buckets.

Liz and I had never been on more than polite terms with Pamela's dad. He and Pamela's mom had been an attractive couple back when Pam was in middle school—cool, I guess you'd say. But once Sherry ran off with her fitness instructor,

Mr. Jones became a lonely, bitter man for a while. We didn't much like him, especially when he told Pamela that if she ever brought African-American friends home, he wouldn't let them in the house. He slowly eased up on that after he met Gwen, though he never said more than a few words to her. But once he started going out with a nurse named Meredith, he seemed to mellow.

Quinton made a final check of the ship around noon before we unlatched the line across the gangplank. Passengers had been getting out of cabs and wheeling their bags down to the dock, and deckhands were going up to help with the larger stuff. A few passengers, believe it or not, even came with small trunks, a different outfit for every hour of the day, it seemed.

Pamela and I stood at the rail of the Chesapeake deck, scouring the crowd gathered below.

"There they are!" she cried, pointing them out.

A tall, slim man in a dark brown sport shirt and tan pants, canvas bag over one shoulder, was pulling a suitcase, and walking beside him was a woman not much shorter, dark glasses beneath her sun visor, denim skirt, and tee.

Pamela was waving wildly. "Dad! Hi, Dad!" she called. "Meredith! Up here!"

The mustached man shielded his eyes and looked around, smiling, then focused on us and waved back, grinning.

"Hey, Pamela!" Meredith called, smiling broadly.

Pamela scrambled on down to meet them while I zipped to crew quarters for my camera.

"I'll get a picture of the three of you when we have a chance," I told Pamela later when we met on the main deck. "How do they like their room?"

"They like it, I think. I know Meredith does. It's smaller than Dad expected, but he likes the view. Curtis just delivered their bags, so they're putting stuff away right now."

"It's nice that they came, Pamela," I told her. "I mean, that they're interested in where you're working this summer, sort of including you in their lives, you know?"

"That's what I was thinking. And Dad's looking really relaxed. I think she's good for him. I hope they do get married."

We were heading up the stairs to the lounge deck when Pamela suddenly grabbed my arm to hold me back, her eyes huge.

"What?" I said, looking at her pale face. *"What?"*

Pamela's lips moved, but no sound came out. Her nails dug into my arm.

"Mom . . ." she said finally.

13
UNBELIEVABLE

It was definitely Mrs. Jones.

The petite woman in the white pants and silky aqua top, clunky bracelets along one arm, was having a lighthearted conversation with a portly man about ship terminology.

"Here's the way I remember," the gentleman was saying. "When you bow"—and he demonstrated—"you lean *forward*. Remember that, and you'll automatically remember that the stern is in the rear."

Mrs. Jones laughed her high, tinkly laugh and thanked him as she strolled on, straw bag slung over one shoulder, platform shoes encasing her red-painted toenails.

Pamela turned to me with an expression of complete helplessness. Her face had gone from pale to pink. "What is she *doing* here? What can she be *thinking*?"

"Do you figure she knew that your dad and Meredith had signed up for this cruise?" I asked her.

"Of *course* she knew. Why else would she have come and not told me? I can't *believe* this!"

"Wait a minute," I said, pulling Pamela back as she started forward. "It's a stretch, but isn't it possible that she looked up the cruise line on the Internet—just like Meredith did— to see the kind of ship you were working on and read about the big discount they were offering for July? That she jumped at the chance and signed up, just as they did?"

Pamela shook her head, eyes blazing now. "Not without telling me."

"You haven't been answering her calls. . . ."

"No, but I've been reading her texts and I text her back once a week. Alice, don't you remember how she embarrassed me back in tenth grade when she signed up as a chaperone on the class trip to New York? That's the real Mom, in all her glory, come to mess things up for Dad and Meredith."

"Girls?" Dianne frowned as she passed. "We have enough help up here. Would you go back to the gangway and direct passengers from there?"

"Sure," I said, and my hand still gripping Pamela's arm, I guided her back down the stairs.

Pamela's "welcome smile" was a little too fake, but boarding passengers were either so confused or so excited, they didn't seem to notice the artificiality. The first pause we had in the stream of guests, however, Pamela got a copy of the passenger list from the reception desk—the list that would appear in all the rooms that night so people could get acquainted—and we scanned it quickly for her mom's name. Common as the name "Jones" is, there was only one listing: *Bill Jones and Meredith Mercer, Silver Spring, Maryland.*

"Your mom's not listed!" I said. "What *is* she? A stowaway?"

Pamela started at the beginning again and slowly traced her finger down the page, stopping at *Sherry Conners, Silver Spring, Maryland.*

"Here she is—her maiden name," said Pamela. "What if they're on the same deck? Oh, my God, Alice, what am I going to do?"

"Why do you have to do anything, Pamela?" I asked her. "*You* aren't involved in the hostilities. *You* didn't sign them up. None of the other passengers know they used to be married to each other. What will be will be."

"Yeah, and it could be awful," said Pamela.

"That will be between them if it is."

"I just feel so sad for Dad and Meredith. This was supposed to be such a fun trip," Pamela said, and I saw her lips tremble.

I stayed close to her for the next hour. I didn't see Mrs. Jones again, but I saw Pamela's dad standing in the doorway of his stateroom as we escorted a passenger up to her room, and when he saw Pamela, he called, "Pamela, when you have a minute, would you step in here?"

I watched her go in his cabin, a sinking feeling in my chest.

* * *

I had only a few minutes to talk with Pamela when we went down to crew quarters to freshen up for dinner service. It was the first time some of us had waited tables at dinner, so Pamela and I were nervous enough as it was.

"What happened with your dad?" I asked.

"He said he'd seen Mom in the lounge and wanted to know what the hell was going on—whether I'd known she was coming, which of course I hadn't."

"He's blaming you?"

"Not really, but he's pissed, and he's got a right to be."

"How did your mom find out they'd signed up, do you suppose?"

Pamela unbuttoned her shirt, rubbed deodorant in her armpits, and buttoned up again. "She's got spies. One of her friends works in the same hospital as Meredith, and it isn't too hard to find out who's going where and when."

Gwen came in just then to put on her bow tie. She took one look at Pamela and me and said, "What's going on?"

"Mom's on board," Pamela told her.

Gwen looked confused for a moment, and then her eyes widened. "Your *mom*?"

"Yes. Under her maiden name, Sherry Conners. Dad just found out."

"You *saw* her here? Omigod!" Gwen gasped.

We heard the clattering of footsteps on the stairs down the hall, and Liz burst in, followed by Emily and Rachel. "Pamela, I just saw your mom!" Liz cried.

"I know." Pamela flopped down on the edge of her bunk. To Emily and Rachel she said, "My dad's on board with his long-time girlfriend, and somehow, for some reason, my mom's here too."

Emily could only stare. "They're . . . divorced?"

"Yes," Pamela said. "And just when things are starting to go well for Dad—after Mom left us a few years back . . ."

"I'm surprised he didn't leave the ship," I said, remembering some awful arguments they'd had in the past.

"Well, that was his first reaction, but Meredith talked him out of it. 'Are we going to let Sherry control our lives?' she asked him. She said they'd come on this cruise to relax and have fun, and that's what she intended to do. 'If Sherry wants to make a scene,' she said, 'she'll have to do it without any help from us.' And finally Dad simmered down." Pamela gritted her teeth. I could actually hear them grinding. "She is so darn, damned selfish!"

"Oh, man!" Emily said. "What a situation!"

"What a *mom!*" said Rachel. "And I don't even know her."

"Dining crew!" came Dianne's voice from the end of the hall.

"Coming!" I yelled.

"I just hope I don't get Mom's table," breathed Pamela. "I don't trust myself to keep my cool. But I can't pretend I don't know her."

When we reached the main deck, Dianne took Pamela and me aside and into her office across the hall.

"I have a feeling there's something I should know," she said. "And I'd like you to level with me before we leave port. You both look upset, and I'm going to need your full concentration in the dining room."

A horrible thought crossed my mind. Could we both get sacked because of Pamela's mother?

Pamela gave a little groan. "Well, my parents are divorced, and my dad and his girlfriend are on board, as you know . . ."

"Yes?" Dianne studied us.

". . . and so is my mom."

Dianne looked confused. "I don't remember another Jones on the passenger list."

"She's under her maiden name, Conners. They don't get along, to put it mildly, and I just don't know what will happen. No one knew she was coming."

Dianne got the picture. "What will happen as far as the staff goes, Pamela, is that we will treat all our guests with courtesy. If they have issues with each other, that's between them. If they're disruptive, Quinton will step in. Believe me, he's handled such things before. But you're not responsible for your parents' behavior. Do your job. That's all we ask of you."

Pamela was visibly relieved. I could tell just by the shift of her shoulders. "Thanks, Dianne," she said.

"What Quinton and I *will* do," Dianne continued, "is try to seat them far apart in the dining room whenever possible. For tonight, since some people have already arrived and others aren't wearing their name tags, we'll just hope for the best."

* * *

We stood at the side of the dining room looking pleasant, small towels draped over our arms, as guests filed in. There was open seating at all meals, but if a couple hesitated or a single person held back, Quinton or Dianne promptly suggested a table and escorted them to it.

I watched Dianne have a quick conversation with Quinton, saw him listen and nod. But my eyes kept drifting back to Pamela. What was it like to have a mom who acted so hurtfully? What mother in her right mind would get it in her head to follow her ex-husband onto a cruise ship, their daughter watching helplessly from the sidelines?

My other thought, the one that always followed this question like a shadow, was what was it like to have a mother at all? I'd certainly got the feel of it once Dad married Sylvia. We'd had some arguments, but we also had a few close conversations, and I really did love her. But because she'd come so late in my life, it wasn't the snuggle-up-sit-on-her-lap-stroke-my-hair kind of love, much as I wanted that, down deep. She treated me as she should have then, as a young teenage girl, and it took a while for me to realize that I couldn't recapture my five-year-old self and the mother I'd needed then. She was really more like an older sister than a mom—a tutor, a mentor, an aunt, definitely a friend—but not exactly a mom. Right now, though, looking at Pamela, I could tell she wished that Sherry was anything but.

Mr. Jones and Meredith entered the dining room, still wearing the same clothes they had on when they boarded, as were most of the passengers. The first night aboard ship was always casual—everyone getting unpacked and settled, finding their way around, introducing themselves to each other. I saw Dianne scan their name tags when they came in and direct them to a round table over by the window with three other couples already seated, which meant that Pamela's mom couldn't possibly sit with them this first night. Six more nights to go, plus breakfasts and lunches, too.

As the room filled up, the noise level grew louder and I began to wonder if Pamela's mom had already come in and I'd missed her. Then a small woman in black silk trousers and a red clingy top showing lots of cleavage appeared in the doorway, crystal globes at her ears, and she stood there poised, expectant.

Quinton bent slightly to read her name tag, greeted her with his usual trademark smile, and suggested a place on the opposite side of the room, where two couples were waiting for their table to fill. I heard Pamela exhale gratefully as she picked up a water pitcher and headed to one of her tables. I did the same. We were going to get through this meal okay, even if it was the first time we'd served at dinner.

"Good evening, and welcome to the *Seascape*," I said cheerfully as I filled the glasses. "I hope you're all feeling a little bit settled?"

"Getting there!" a red-faced man said jovially. "We'll let you know after dinner."

"As long as we don't get seasick," said his wife. "This is my first cruise, and I don't do very well on boats."

"I think you're going to find it smooth sailing," I said

reassuringly. "I'm Alice, and I have the pleasure of serving you tonight. Someone will be by shortly to take your wine order, and in the meantime, let me know if you'd prefer soup or salad."

Across the room I saw Mitch talking to Pamela's mom, taking her order.

"Oh, look!" someone said. "We're moving!"

Passengers on both sides of the dining room looked toward their windows as Baltimore's Inner Harbor passed slowly before our eyes and the scenery changed from shops and restaurants to trees and water. Still the ship went on turning, the bow thruster doing its job, and finally, as I took my order to the galley, all I could see out the port side of the ship was water and sky.

You'll never believe this, I e-mailed Patrick that night. *Pamela's dad and girlfriend are on this cruise, and guess who else turned up? Pamela's mom!*

It was like a time bomb, I'd told him. But, as Quinton keeps telling us, every day on a ship is a surprise.

I don't know where Pamela went after we cleaned the galley, but when she came up on the top deck around eleven, all the girls were waiting.

"Well, I confronted her," she said, pulling a chair over and sinking down in it, hands folded over her stomach. "It didn't take me long to learn what room she's in—311, Chesapeake deck. I wasn't going to go the whole trip pretending I didn't know her."

"What did she *say?*" Liz asked. "How did she explain herself?"

"She didn't, and I don't know what to think. I followed her to her stateroom and said, 'Mom, how could you *do* this?' and she said, 'Do what? Is it so awful I wanted to surprise you?'"

We all rolled our eyes.

"'You *know* Dad and Meredith are on this ship,' I told her, and she said, 'Then they must have seen the same advertisement I saw, for bargain rates.'"

Lauren shook her head. "No, that's not the reaction a normal person would have had. That was just too cool and premeditated. If she hadn't known, she'd be completely surprised."

We agreed. But Pamela looked torn. "Still . . . it's possible, I suppose. And I'd feel ashamed if she really did just want to surprise me and didn't know they were here. And instead of being happy, I'm treating her like a criminal."

"Well, then, take her at her word!" Emily said. "Treat her like all the other guests and assume she'll make new friends. At least they're not on the same deck. Maybe she and your dad will simply ignore each other the whole trip, and all this worry will be for nothing."

At Norfolk the next day, Mr. Jones and Meredith went off to see the shipyard, and Pamela's mom stretched out on the observation deck in shorts and a halter top, with a drink and a magazine.

When she came to the captain's reception that evening, she was the most mesmerizing of the guests, in a short sequined cocktail dress, shockingly tight around the bust, and silver stilettos that would have killed a man if she'd used them as a weapon.

"Oh . . . my . . . God!' gasped Natalie, who was replacing the steamed shrimp platter. She looked at Pamela. "Is that your mom?"

"Does it show?" Pamela said.

"I just meant . . . wow!" Natalie said.

Mrs. Jones—Sherry—didn't do anything out of line, exactly. She didn't strike a model's pose in the doorway, but she had timed her entrance so that she was one of the last to arrive and could linger a bit longer with the captain and first mate. People did take notice.

Lauren overheard her ask the captain if she would be able to see the pilothouse, and he responded that every cruise had a ship's tour sometime on the schedule, pilothouse included, and she could sign up with either Stephanie Bowers or Ken McCoy.

Once again, Quinton carefully seated Bill and Meredith many tables away from Sherry, and we were glad to see that Mr. Jones seemed to be enjoying a conversation with the men at his table while Meredith chatted with the woman next to her.

The subject of Pamela's mom had been confined so far to the girls, but it came up at the crew dinner later that night. We had taken our dinners up to the observation deck and were chowing down on Sloppy Joes and fries when Barry asked, "Anyone know when the tour of the ship will be? The broad in the Saran Wrap dress was asking, and I said I'd try to find out."

We girls frowned his way. "The *broad*?" said Gwen, reprimanding him. "That is *so* forties."

"Okay, the silver stiletto babe," Barry said, and then, realizing he'd done it again, "Sherry Conners."

"That happens to be Pamela's mom," said Emily.

Barry did a double take. "Whoa! Sorry! But . . . wow!"

"Yeah, that's what *I* said," Natalie told him. "Pamela comes from hot stock."

I didn't know if Pamela had wanted us to keep it secret or not, but once it was out, it seemed easier, even for her.

"We've got a problem here," Lauren said, and told the guys about how Pamela's dad and girlfriend were on this cruise and how, somehow, Pamela's mom had booked herself on the very same one; we were trying to see that Sherry Conners didn't ruin the trip for them.

"They should all have code names," said Curtis, the snake-and-flag tattoo on his left arm moving a little when he flexed a muscle. "I could get on my walkie-talkie and say, 'Decup three stern.'"

"Decup?" I said.

Curtis grinned as he bit into his sandwich and chewed a couple of times. "Bra size," he said. "Sherry approaching Chesapeake deck at the stern."

"Oh, God, you guys are so sexist," Yolanda said. "You want to be known by the size of your jock?"

"Ouch," said Curtis. "Okay, okay, you think of a code name, then."

I figured it was all in fun.

"Cougar?" I suggested.

"Too obvious," said Lauren.

"Drama Queen?" said Liz.

"Too long."

It was Pamela who suggested it: "Flotsam, because we never quite know what will turn up."

"Flotsam it is," said Barry. "As long as she has a label, we probably don't need one for the others."

The talk drifted to what we might do in Baltimore the coming week if we had time to go out, but when a light rain began to fall, we decided to call it a night. I hung around a little longer to see if Patrick had sent me a text message on my cell. He hadn't, but I sent him one about how the evening had gone. Then I started down the back stairway.

What if it really *had* been a coincidence that Pamela's mom took this cruise? I wondered as I passed the Chesapeake deck and kept going. What if she needed a vacation as much as anyone else, and we were treating her as a joke, a threat to everyone's happiness? She might be trying just as hard to avoid Bill and Meredith, once she found them on board, as we were to keep them apart.

But as I reached the lounge deck and made the turn, I saw her, drink in hand, standing at the railing outside Bill and Meredith's stateroom. It was no coincidence.

14
GHOST STORY

It was awkward, but the next day went fairly smoothly. I didn't
know what to call Pamela's mom when I passed her on deck or
in the dining room. I'd always called her "Mrs. Jones" before,
so how could I say, "Hello, Ms. Conners" now? And I certainly
wasn't about to call her "Sherry."

She'd just smile and say, "Hello, Alice. Nice day, isn't it?" or
something innocuous, and I went on by. I'm sure she noticed
that whenever I happened to see her, I was in a hurry.

Occasionally my walkie-talkie would buzz, and I'd hear a
male voice saying, "Flotsam to four, Flotsam to four." If one of
the crew was on the sundeck, and Bill and Meredith were also,
that crew member would make sure there were no empty chairs
near the couple. If Pamela's mom was having a drink in the

lounge, Rachel might go back in the supply closet, click on her walkie-talkie, and say, "Flotsam served on second."

To us, it was a game, but it wasn't to Pamela. The fact that her mom behaved herself, more or less, made Pamela feel all the more guilty for suspecting the worst, and I saw her wince once or twice when she heard the reference to "Flotsam." That didn't last long, though, because Quinton caught on and put a stop to it. But we couldn't help noticing that Pamela's mom was usually first at the bar when happy hour began, and her laughter got a little louder as she started her second or third drink.

Patrick's e-mails were full of the sights and sounds of Barcelona—one of the few places, it seemed, that his diplomat dad had never taken the family. They were more like essays, really. Sometimes he'd write something in Spanish and see if I could figure it out. *¿Cómo está pasando el crucero?*

He'd tell me about Gaudi's architectural wonders, "more like sand castles," he described them. Or he'd start his e-mail with *Greetings from the Iberian Peninsula* and tell me about the dark cavernous church off the Plaza del Rey, with its metal cages, lit by candlelight, and the plastic body parts that hung on the metal gates, asking a saint's help in healing an affliction.

My e-mails were mostly about people—about Pamela's parents on board and the beach in Yorktown, about the breeze up here on the top deck and the gulls that circled overhead.

As we set the tables for dinner that night, Barry said, "You girls want to do something this evening, late?"

"Other than sleep?" Emily said.

"Hey, you can always make up on sleep," said Flavian.

"What did you have in mind?" Gwen slowly lowered a tray of glass goblets from her shoulder to a rack.

"Ever see the York battlefield at night? Entirely different from how it looks in the daytime," Barry said.

"How do you know so much about Yorktown?" Liz asked.

"Eighth-grade civics class," said Barry. "Big field trip of the year."

"So how do we see anything at night?" I wanted to know.

"Full moon," said Flavian.

Gwen laughed. "You guys are so full of it! There was only a half-moon last night."

"Ah!" Flavian grabbed a steak knife off the table and held it like a foil in a fencing pose. "'The moon was a ghostly galleon tossed upon cloudy seas . . .'"

"Give me a break," said Pamela.

"What? You never had to memorize 'The Highwayman' back in junior high?"

"I just want to know how we're supposed to see a battlefield in the dark."

"Leave it to us," said Barry. "It's great weather for a change, and we can walk there from the ship."

"Okay, I'm in," I said.

"Me too," said Gwen and Pamela.

* * *

We got away around ten thirty, those of us who were going. Lauren and Emily opted out. Lauren said she'd seen enough of battlefields in the daytime, she didn't have to experience them at night, so it was just Gwen and Pamela, Yolanda and Natalie, Liz and me, along with Flavian and Barry.

I found myself disappointed that Mitch wasn't along, but Barry said that some of the deckhands had gone in search of a bar, so I guessed Mitch was with them.

We crossed the street from the dock, and Barry led us to a sort of grotto, where we could just make out a cave in the hillside with a closed metal gate across the entrance.

"And this is . . . ?" asked Gwen.

Barry put one finger to his lips. "The gate swings miraculously open at midnight, and all the tortured souls of British soldiers come out to walk the battlefield."

Natalie was trying to read a sign in the darkness. "Cornwallis' Cave?"

"That's it," said Barry. "The general who surrendered to George Washington. You're standing on hallowed ground."

"I'm so scared," Liz said.

"You can jump into our arms anytime," Barry said, but I noticed Gwen was already in Flavian's, and ghosts had nothing to do with it.

I had the feeling that the guys were taking the long way around to the battlefield, wherever it was, but I didn't care. It seemed as though we were the only ones in Yorktown. Once the tourists left for the day, the place was deserted.

We walked along the historic streets, Barry telling us how the battle was fought. And then, under a dim streetlight, he stopped and lowered his voice. "What I'm about to tell you is simply what people have reported, but there have been too many of these stories for them to be coincidence." We started walking again. "There was this man whose ancestors fought with Washington here at Yorktown, and his great-great-great-uncle had come across this dying British soldier who begged him for water. So he put his own flask to the soldier's lips and let him drink. But the guy was hurt really bad, and he flopped back down again, moaning with pain, a gaping wound in his chest. So this great-great-great-uncle took out his revolver and shot him in the head."

"Barry, that's horrible," said Liz.

"It was the most humane thing he could do," Barry continued. "And a few years ago one of his descendants was here visiting the battlefield—it was almost dark—and he was here with his wife and his wife's sister. The women had gone on ahead, back toward the parking lot, and to his right, he saw this . . . well, orb of light, I guess you'd call it—sort of like the top half of a luminous circle—on the ground about twenty yards away, slowly rising higher, until it was a full circle, about shoulder height . . ."

We stopped walking again.

". . . and then he saw that it was a man's head, a man's face, coming toward him in the moonlight."

I could feel goose bumps on my arms, and Liz grabbed me, both of us grinning but wanting to hear the rest of the story. We were barely moving, we were crowded so close to Barry, who was walking backward, facing us. His expression was serious in the shadows.

"The man said he stopped and stood perfectly still while the apparition came closer," Barry continued. "He didn't speak, and the expression on the orb didn't change. He described it as mostly sad-looking. And then, for just a moment, the man said, the ghost's upper torso was visible too—the uniform scruffy and wrinkled and stained with either mud or blood, he couldn't tell. But the ghost's hand was holding a flask—holding it out, sort of, like it was offering it to him. And then . . . it faded out—the face, the torso, the flask, everything."

"Arrrgggh!" I said. "That's all? That's the end? What did the guy do?"

Barry shrugged. "I don't know. I've heard two different versions of the story. One said he nodded to the apparition before it faded away, like he understood. The other version was that he told his wife and sister-in-law what he'd seen and they didn't believe him."

"Anybody got a flask?" Flavian joked. "Let's go."

I think the guys were taking us in the back way, because the park closed at dusk. We steered clear of the caretaker's house and bypassed the parking lot. The moon was little more than half full, but now and then the clouds moved across it, and we had to follow Barry single file so we wouldn't stumble over something or fall in one of the trenches. From what I could see of them, they were only a few feet deep and the sides had eroded so they were more like gullies, but you still had to be careful.

Flavian and Gwen were bringing up the rear. Every so often when the moon came out from behind a cloud, we could see the blurred outline of a cannon. But mostly the battlefield was just that—a huge open space with a gentle breeze blowing through.

It felt almost irreverent to be out here on a lark, at a place where the whole course of history had been changed. Weird to think that right where I was standing, maybe, a British soldier could have been struggling for breath and begging for a drink of water.

Suddenly I heard Liz gasp, and Pamela stifle a shriek. Then Yolanda gave an electrifying scream. Straight ahead, maybe twenty yards away, we saw what appeared to be a . . . an illuminated head . . . a face . . . there on the ground. And just as Barry had described it, the orb—the head, the face—seemed to be rising slowly up . . . a foot high . . . now higher . . . chest high . . . And then it was as tall as we were, coming right toward us. When a second head appeared, we were all clutching at Barry, trying to run, and then Yolanda screamed again and a light came on in the caretaker's cottage.

"Quiet, you guys!" came a familiar voice, laughing. "Now they'll turn the bloodhounds on us."

"Josh!" I cried.

He was close enough that we could see the flashlight he was holding under his chin as he'd climbed out of one of the trenches, and I heard Mitch's laughter behind him. The next thing I knew, they were pulling us down in a trench and warning us not to make a sound.

I found myself half sitting on Mitch's lap, leaning awkwardly back in his arms, my legs over Pamela, who was lying on her side.

"You dog!" she whispered, pounding on Josh's back.

"Shhhhh," he cautioned.

We all waited for the sound of footsteps. Finally Flavian inched up and peered over the edge of the trench. "Caretaker's on the back step, looking around," he said, ducking down again. "Got a high-beam flashlight."

Nobody moved.

Flavian rose up again, his eyes even with the grass. "I think he went back inside."

"Yeah, but he'll call the park police," said Josh. "He's not going to let a scream like that go unreported."

"Yeah, Yolanda. Anyone ever hire you for sound effects?" Mitch asked.

"Let's go and at least get back on the road," said Barry.

We climbed noiselessly up out of the trench and moved in a single row toward the tree line, following Barry, our dark silhouettes bent double as we crossed the field. We breathed easier once we were back on the road, and we pummeled Josh and Mitch for scaring the daylights out of us, then turned on Barry and Flavian.

But we hadn't gone more than a hundred yards when we

saw a patrol car turn onto the road ahead of us, lights flashing.

We staggered in the blinding light and stopped.

"We're fried," said Flavian.

"But who did we hurt?" I asked.

"Don't sweat it," Josh said.

The patrol car came slowly toward us. We waited as it stopped and a park officer got out.

"Where you folks headed?" he asked, stopping a few yards away.

"Going back to the *Seascape*, sir," Josh said, politeness in every syllable. "It's the only time we get a break, so we decided to look around."

"If you're from a cruise ship, then you know the park closes at dusk," the park ranger said. I couldn't see his face in the shadows, but his voice didn't sound friendly.

"Well, we know it now," Josh said. "We're sort of history buffs, and this was our only chance to see the battlefield. We sail out in a few hours."

The ranger studied us a bit longer. "Caretaker reported some noise out on the field."

"Yeah," put in Barry. "That would be Yolanda's scream. We told her to look out for trenches, and she almost fell in. That's why we realized we wouldn't get far trying to see anything tonight."

"You wouldn't know where we could get a map of the battle-field, would you?" Josh was really laying it on, but the officer wasn't impressed.

"Talk to your cruise director," he said. Then motioned us back toward the port.

The patrol car followed us to within a block of the ship before it turned off. And a half block from the ship, we saw a taxi unload its passengers. When the cab took off, we recognized Curtis, with one of the stewards leaning heavily on his shoulder.

"Looks like they found a bar," said Flavian. "Had to go to Williamsburg, I'll bet."

"Hey!" Barry called. "Curtis. What's up?"

Curtis stopped and turned his head, but he couldn't turn his body because the stew was sinking to his knees, and Curtis was trying to hold him up. It was Todd, one of the younger, skinnier guys, and he was obviously wasted.

"Oh, man!" Mitch said.

"Yeah. Got a situation here," Curtis said. "And it's my ass too if Quinton finds out."

"How many beers did he have?" Flavian asked.

"A couple more than he should have. I've never seen him this drunk." Curtis pulled Todd to his feet, but he wobbled unsteadily for a moment and began sinking again, carrying on a conversation with himself.

"It's going to be either Ken or Quinton checking off names when we reach the dock," Josh said. "And you can't get very much past Quinton."

"McCoy will go by the book, though. They'll leave Todd behind when we sail tonight," Barry said. "Turn him over to the park police. And if they didn't replace Shannon, you know darn well they won't replace Todd. We'll be working our butts off."

"What'll we do?" asked Mitch.

"We can't sober him up out here—curfew's in fifteen minutes," Curtis said. He gave Todd a little shake, but he only laughed, limp as a wet rag.

"I'll see who's on duty," Barry said, and was gone only a minute or so before he came back. "It's McCoy," he told us.

Josh was helping hold up Todd now, and it was obvious there was no way he was going to walk up the gangplank on his own. We moved on a little farther, Todd's feet dragging until we could see the ship.

"Okay, here's the deal," Curtis said. "We're having a race, see? I'm going to carry Todd piggyback, and Josh carries Flavian."

"Wait a minute!" said Flavian, but Curtis went on:

"The rest of you guys go on ahead. Laugh it up like we're all kidding around. Tell Ken you've got a bet on who reaches the ship first, and we'll do a little whooping back here on our own. Then I'll come galloping up to the ship, Todd on my back, and run up the gangplank, as Josh and Flavian follow close behind. You guys stop and talk with Ken while I get Todd down to his bunk and under the sheets. It's the best we can do."

The rest of us went on ahead, kidding among ourselves, letting our voices rise—swatting at one another. Ken smiled when he saw us coming. He checked off our names one at a time on his clipboard.

"You guys have a good time?" he asked.

"Oh, yeah. Any time on land's a good time," said Barry. And then, turning, "Okay, here they come. Let's see who wins the race. I've got five bucks on Curtis."

"Who's still out?" asked Ken, looking down the dock, then checking his clipboard.

"Two crazies," I told him as the shouts in the distance grew louder.

"They're all idiots," said Gwen as Curtis, with Todd on his back, came barreling onto the landing. He raced across the dock, and with a loud "Whoeeee!" went pounding up the gangplank, with Josh and Flavian not far behind.

"Hey! Keep it down!" Ken chided as Flavian slid off Josh's back and gave another yell. "Quiet down, you guys, or Quinton will have our necks."

We hushed immediately.

Ken checked off the last name on the list. "Anybody still out?" he asked.

"You got 'em all," said Mitch.

We were in. I was impressed.

We found out later that Todd threw up on Curtis about the time they reached crew quarters, and the guys put him under the shower, clothes and all. The next morning Todd was subdued, but sober, and Quinton, from whom no things are hidden, said simply, "You lucked out that time, Todd, but it can't happen again. Same for you, Curtis."

* * *

It was obvious what Pamela's mom was trying to do: simply be the most alluring, attractive passenger on the ship. Certainly to put a damper on her ex-husband's love life, if she could. And definitely to make him wonder if he had made a mistake about not taking her back. That was the way we saw it, anyway.

She usually skipped breakfast and had a roll and coffee up on the sundeck in her short shorts and halter tops. She signed up for nearly every excursion and, Rachel heard from Stephanie, asked frequent questions of the guides, more for their attention, it seemed, than for the information.

Every dinner, Pamela's mom was stunningly dressed in clothes that were one degree shy of too sexy, and by the fourth night of the cruise, she seemed to have caught on that Quinton always seated her on the opposite side of the room from Bill and Meredith.

"Oh," she said, pausing. "I think I see a seat over there I'd prefer."

What could Quinton say but, "Of course," and follow her to the table next to Pamela's dad, pulling out the chair for her.

"Did you see that? Did you *see* that?" Pamela whispered to me from the door of the galley.

Unfortunately, both of those tables were mine that evening, and as dinner progressed and wineglasses were refilled, Sherry's laughter grew a little louder and more frequent, while Pamela's dad, at the adjoining table, remained stone-faced and seemed to be eating faster than usual. He and Meredith were the first to excuse themselves after dessert and coffee had been served as Sherry lingered at her table, telling an impossibly long story.

"Oh, I wish this cruise were over," Pamela lamented later, as we got ready for bed.

"Only a few more nights and we'll have a whole new set of passengers," said Lauren. "Hang in there. None of the other passengers know they're related."

"I can see the tension in Dad's face, though," Pamela said. "Now he'll never take her ba—" She stopped, her eyes wide. "I can't believe what I think I was about to say!"

"Sort of the universal desire, isn't it?" said Emily. "After my parents split, even though they fought like tigers, I wanted us all under one roof."

"Maybe so," said Pamela, wrapping her arms around her knees. "I guess what I long for, really, is the family I *wanted* us to be."

The following day we were docked at Oxford, and Pamela's mom had gone on a tour of the ship for those who didn't go ashore. Somehow she had wrangled an invitation from the captain to dine at his table that night, one of the few evenings he was eating on board this week.

"I can't watch," Pamela told me when she saw them together. "How did she manage *that*?"

"Maybe this is just what she needs," Yolanda said. "Attention. From a guy in uniform, preferably."

Sherry Conners had dressed for the occasion in a white silk

dress, butt-enhancingly tight, with a deep neckline. Her finger-nails and toenails were painted pearl white, and she was easily the most attractive woman at the table. Captain Haggerty sat next to her, and Ken McCoy introduced her to the five other guests in their party.

What she didn't have, however, was the satisfaction of seeing her ex-husband watch her dine with the captain because, we found out from Pamela, he and Meredith had reservations that evening for the Robert Morris Inn. And as the dinner pro-gressed, we could see her eyes scanning the dining room for someone who wasn't there.

It was difficult to focus on my assigned tables. I found my eyes darting to the captain's table all night, where Mitch was serving, and I could tell that things were going from awkward to unpleasant. At one point, when Dianne approached the table with a new bottle of wine, I saw the almost imperceptible shake of the captain's head, and Dianne and the wine immediately disappeared.

I was taking dessert orders at the table next to the captain's when I heard Sherry say, "I'd think you'd be seated on the other side of the dining room, Captain. All the action seems to be over there, by the dock."

I saw the raised eyebrows of the other guests. Haggerty kept his composure but didn't smile: "I'm sorry you find this table disappointing," he said.

"On the contrary," one of the men said quickly, "the plea-sure is in the company."

Pamela had heard too, and her face turned a fiery red, beginning at the neck.

Instead of apologizing, Pamela's mom continued her now-raspy harping: "It doesn't seem as though there are as many people in the dining room tonight as usual. I'm surprised passengers dine off the ship; I'd think they'd want to enjoy what they paid for."

The captain smiled politely. "We hold no prisoners, Ms. Conners, I assure you. Oxford has many lovely restaurants, particularly the Robert Morris Inn, which is a landmark here, and many of our passengers book reservations well in advance."

You could almost see the light beginning to dawn on Sherry's face. Her big night with the captain, and her ex-husband and his girlfriend were living it up somewhere else. "Well, no one told *me* about it," she said, and weaved slightly in her chair. The wineglass in her hand tipped dangerously before the captain steadied it for her. "Maybe our dinner should have been held there."

The other guests at the table were too shocked to comment, but Haggerty had obviously had enough.

"Officer McCoy," he said, "I believe that Ms. Conners is having a rather unpleasant evening. Would you escort her to her stateroom, where I think she'll enjoy the quiet?"

Sherry Conners looked shocked. She began to protest, but then she collected herself enough to thank the captain for inviting her, said good night to the others, and, leaning on Ken's arm, walked slowly away from the table.

Pamela was in tears when we met in the galley. I gave her a hug, but she turned for a moment, swallowed a sob, then gamely picked up her coffeepot and headed for the dining room once more.

After dinner I stood at the bow of the ship in the darkness with Pamela and Gwen, waiting for Liz to finish galley duty. There was a big poker game going on in the dining room among the stewards and deckhands, but we wanted to talk among ourselves, just the four of us.

We watched Pamela's dad and Meredith strolling leisurely back from their dinner out. Bill had his arm around Meredith's waist, and they'd obviously had a good time.

"It was every bit as wonderful as they say," we heard Meredith tell Quinton as they boarded below. "It was a fantastic meal."

"So glad you enjoyed it. We're always happy to recommend the Robert Morris," Quinton said.

"Hey! I put some extra chocolates on your pillows," Pamela called down to them.

They looked up and waved.

"A perfect end to the evening," Meredith said. "There's always room for chocolate."

Liz came up at last with lemonade, and we went up to the top deck, sitting in a little circle near the bow, our bare toes touching on the end of Gwen's chaise longue. Some of the guys sprawled nearby, Curtis and Josh comparing the calluses on their hands. Bugs circled and buzzed around a dim deck lamp.

"Well, so the worst happened and you're still here, Pamela," Gwen said.

Pamela sighed. "Yeah. I sort of think Mom will behave now that she's made a total fool of herself. And she wasn't so drunk that she didn't realize it."

"Maybe it's good that it happened, then. Get the venom out of her system," Liz suggested.

"Just so Dad and Meredith have a good time," said Pamela. "I promised to go biking around St. Michaels with them tomorrow if they get up early enough. I think they'd like that. It'd be nice to do something with my dad for a change."

"Four more weeks!" I said. "And then . . . we start a whole new life."

I had just reached for my glass of lemonade on the deck beside me when suddenly the air was split with the shriek of the alarm, immediately followed by Captain Haggerty's voice over the PA system: "Man overboard, man overboard, this is NOT a drill."

15
MISSING

Curtis got up so fast, his chair tipped over.

The captain's voice continued: "Passenger over port side aft. Go immediately to stations."

We were all on our feet and running. Each of us had our own assignment, and Pamela was beside me, her face chalk white. Then I lost her.

The door to the pilothouse must have been open as I passed the Chesapeake deck on my way down because I heard loud squawks coming from a transmitter. Passengers were gathering port side, many in robes and pajamas, but I continued on to the lounge deck's fantail. Gwen got there momentarily.

"Anyone know who it was?" I asked Rachel, who was looking over the rail.

She didn't take her eyes off the water. "No. Quinton and Dianne are checking the staterooms."

We heard the microphone click on again, and then Haggerty's voice: "This is your captain. All passengers return to your staterooms to be counted. All passengers, to your staterooms."

Gwen and I focused on the water.

A few yards from the ship, a life preserver made a ring of bright orange, bobbing up and down on the dark water. The flashing beacon from a buoy bobbed next to it. They separated, came together again, then the space between them grew wider. And all the while, a searchlight scanned the surface.

By leaning out and looking down, I could see Frank on the main deck holding a Jacob's ladder. I'd seen it before—a plastic device that floats and looks like a ladder to assist someone getting back onto the ship. Curtis was beside him with a shepherd's hook. While the deckhands prepared for a rescue, the stewards' job was to locate the person in the water and never take our eyes off him or her. But the ominous thing was that we couldn't see anyone anywhere on the surface.

"At least we're still in port," Rachel said. "If the ship had been moving, we'd immediately have to stop and go into reverse, and we might lose sight of the passenger altogether."

Ken McCoy came up from below to talk with a man who stood barefoot, shirt unbuttoned. It looked as though he'd been undressing for bed.

"Are you the one who saw the passenger fall in?" Ken asked.

"Like I said," the man told him, "all I heard was this woman's scream. So I opened our cabin door, and some lady was running by saying somebody jumped and pointing out there." The passenger turned and pointed in the direction of the life preserver.

"I heard the scream too," another passenger said, coming over. "My wife thinks she heard the splash."

"The splash and then the scream?" Ken asked. And, into the walkie-talkie, "I'm talking with some passengers now. They all seem to agree it was port side aft."

"Uh . . . I guess it was the scream and then the splash," the second man said.

The beam of a searchlight swept the water again. On the dock a small crowd was gathering, despite the hour.

"Can you tell me who the woman was who told you someone had jumped?"

The barefoot man let out his breath. "Whew. Haven't a clue. I mean, you hear someone jumped overboard, you head for the rail, that's all."

A woman behind him spoke up: "I heard that all you could see were two arms going under. That's what the woman next to us said."

"Did she see it?"

"No, she was in bed like we were. That's what she heard."

"I heard someone pushed her!" another voice called.

Quinton's voice behind them all: "People, we have an emergency situation here, and we're checking the passenger list now. Please go back to your staterooms so we can tell who's missing."

Some began to leave, others lingered, then left. I heard the harbor police arriving on the deck below, and a minute later we saw Josh and Curtis out in a speedboat, slowly circling the life preserver in wider and wider arcs.

Someone edged in beside me at the railing. It was Pamela. I slipped my arm around her. None of us had to ask what she suspected. And when Dianne and Quinton had checked off every person on the passenger list, the only one missing was Pamela's mom.

In the water the speedboat circled again and again. The police boat joined the search. We took Pamela around and around the walkway, just to keep moving.

"What are they doing?" someone on dock called up to us.

And when we didn't answer, one of the passengers called back, "Rescue operation. A woman jumped."

"Recovery operation," someone murmured behind us.

I'm not sure how long we waited. Forty minutes, maybe. Pamela sat down on a bench, wrapped in Gwen's arms. Mr. Jones sat on the other side of them, arms on his knees, hands dangling. Meredith stood at the railing, looking down. There's a point at which you feel that not knowing is worse than knowing, even when the news is bad. That not knowing is a poison that makes you sick all over. You're physically ill, not just worried.

A sudden commotion below, and Mr. Jones stood up. He went down to the main deck, and it was a while before he came back. His face was gray and drawn.

"Did . . . they find her?" Pamela asked weakly.

He had something in his hands and sat down beside her. It was a scarf. "They found this floating on the water," he said. "Was it hers, do you know?"

Pamela broke into tears, nodding violently, and this time leaned against her father. He pulled her close. My own knees felt shaky. I crouched down where I was so I wouldn't fall, and grabbed Liz's hand.

Not another summer like last one! How could Pamela cope with this? How could we? We weren't even halfway over the shock of losing Mark Stedmeister last August.

And suddenly I heard Meredith say, "Sherry!"

I rose to my feet and stared as Pamela's mom came through the little crowd and looked around.

"What's going on?" she asked timidly.

There were stains on the front of her jacket, and her hair was disheveled, her face groggy.

"Mom!" Pamela cried, startled, but she didn't stand up. Bill Jones stared at his ex-wife in disbelief.

In moments Captain Haggerty and a police officer came up from below.

"She's here!" people told him. "Sherry Conners is here!"

Haggerty looked at her closely, relief and doubt on his face. "Ms. Conners, you've been reported missing," he said.

"Why . . . no! I just heard all the commotion and . . ." Sherry looked around.

"Can you tell us where you've been the last hour?" the policeman said.

"Well, I don't know . . . I was in the restroom downstairs for a while—"

"We checked there, several times," said Dianne.

The barefoot man worked his way through the crowd. "That's her!" he said. "That's the woman who told me someone had fallen in!"

"Ms. Conners, would you come down to the office please so we can clear things up and let our other guests go to bed?" Captain Haggerty said. "Our hotel manager needs to file an onboard incident report."

Ken called down on his walkie-talkie to bring the speedboat in, retract the buoy.

Pamela and her dad and Meredith stood with their arms around each other. No one, not even Pamela, had welcomed Sherry back.

It was after one when we finally got to bed, and even then, we sat around crew quarters, trying to put it together.

"Where do you suppose she was all that time? We checked everywhere!" Yolanda said. Six of us had crowded onto Pamela's bunk; the others sat on the beds across from us.

"She's small—she could hide anywhere," said Pamela. "Under a desk. Behind a sofa."

"But *why*?" Liz asked.

Pamela turned on her. "There doesn't have to be a why, Liz. It's Mom! It's the way she operates. Whatever brings the most attention."

"What do you think they'll do to her?" asked Natalie.

"Nothing," said Rachel. "She said she couldn't remember anything, and who could prove she couldn't? Haggerty's so relieved we didn't lose a passenger on his watch that he could have peed himself."

Pamela hugged her knees, her chin resting on top. "It's the first time in my life that I hope she was dead drunk. I can't stand the thought that she probably planned the whole thing—the scarf and all. One minute I'm so glad she didn't jump, and the next minute I . . ." Her voice wobbled. "I feel like I hate her guts."

"I think a lot of us are pretty mad at her," I said.

"Know what?" said Emily. "Tomorrow everyone will be touring St. Michaels and what happened tonight will be yesterday's news. Let's get some sleep."

I couldn't, though, for a long time. Inside I was seething at Pamela's mom and aching for Pamela. She must have been having trouble too, because some time later she crawled in my bunk with me, snuggled up against my back, and put one arm around me. I patted her hand to let her know it was okay, and when I felt her breathing more slowly, I fell asleep too.

When I came up on main deck early the next morning, I saw Pamela's mother wrapped in a yellow raincoat, wearing dark glasses and a scarf around her neck, sitting beside two suitcases near the gangway.

I knew Pamela had seen her too because she'd been watching from the lounge deck. I paused, wondering if I should say something to her. But a taxi pulled up in the parking lot, and Curtis removed the line across the gangway and carried the bags down.

Pamela's mom followed without looking back and climbed in the cab. I watched her leave without a wave, a hug, a good-bye to her daughter, even.

Pamela was going to spend some time in St. Michaels with her dad and Meredith, but I just wanted to stroll around and see more of the town—let myself unwind. Mitch and I decided to eat lunch somewhere onshore.

"Pamela okay?" he said as we left the dock to the flapping of sails on the boats anchored nearby.

"I think so. She's with her dad, anyway."

"Anyone know where her mom was while we were all look-ing for her?"

"Rachel said she was sitting in Stephanie's office in the dark, watching us search the ship. Dianne found her when she turned on the light." I sighed. "She was doing so well for a while. We thought she had turned a corner when she started working, got an apartment, and had a boyfriend. . . . And Pamela's supposed to leave for New York this fall. Got a partial scholarship to a theater school."

"Man, you hear of parents having trouble with their adult children, but sometimes it's the other way around."

We settled on the Crab Claw Restaurant and went inside.

"Let me treat this time," I said, remembering the last meal I'd enjoyed at his expense.

"Only if you insist," he said, smiling. "I heard paychecks are going to be late this time."

"Doesn't make a whole lot of difference, does it?"

"Well, some of the guys send their paychecks home. I know Curtis does. But if we're paid eventually, I won't complain too much," Mitch said. "I pay my folks room and board every month, but most of my salary goes in the bank."

"What are you saving for? A bigger boat?"

He folded his arms across his chest and grinned at me. "Naw, just want to fix up the one I have, put a cabin on her. All I've got now is a sunshade. Would sure appreciate a way to get in out of the weather when a storm hits on the bay."

I leaned my chin on my hand and studied him. "Where do you see yourself five years from now, Mitch? I love hearing about life plans."

"Life plans? You selling insurance on the side?"

I laughed. "No, it's interesting, that's all."

"Well, in five years I'd like to think I'd have an all-weather boat; like to have me a wife—a pretty one." His grin grew wider still. "Maybe even have the first of nine children."

"Nine!" I bolted back in my chair.

I loved the way he chuckled. "Okay, how about the first of three? That would make a nice number."

"So tell me about your phantom wife."

"My wife. Well now, let's see . . ." He stopped as a waitress came and took our order, then left again. "I think it would have to be a girl who had lived for a while in the city."

"Really? That's surprising."

"Why? I wouldn't want to marry a girl who was always dreaming of leaving the marshland and moving to Richmond or Baltimore or someplace. I'd want someone who really liked the waterman's life and the work that goes with it."

"You may have to extend your search a little beyond Vienna, Maryland," I said.

"Hey! I'm looking around, aren't I? Not working on the *Seascape* for nothing." Mitch tapped my ankle with the toe of his shoe. "Where do you see yourself in five years?"

"Well, graduated from college, hopefully with an MA in counseling. So I guess in five years I'll be looking around for a job, preferably in a high school or possibly a middle school."

"Any idea where?"

I gave a loud sigh. "That's the unknown. I'd like to be within an hour or so of my family—Dad and Sylvia and Les—but who knows where Lester will be then? He's got resumes out all over the place."

"And what about Patrick?"

I wasn't sure how to answer that. "He could be anywhere in the whole world by then, and . . . if we marry . . . I'll probably end up working wherever he is."

"Will you miss home?"

"Probably. But Patrick's worth it. I guess we always give up one thing to get another, don't we?"

"I don't know. It hasn't happened to me yet," Mitch said.

We walked all over St. Michaels after lunch. Once we sat

for a while, and I actually nodded off on a bench near the dock, I'd had so little sleep the night before. Mitch joked that I was boring company, so we went back to the ship and I slept for a half hour before Gwen woke me to change for dinner.

We had good weather the rest of the cruise. Pamela didn't mention her mom again, and Bill and Meredith seemed to enjoy themselves. By the time of the farewell dinner Saturday night, with the usual lobster and filet mignon, everyone seemed in a good mood, even Pamela. It was almost eleven the following morning, after the last passenger had disembarked, that the arguments started.

Quinton had assembled staff and crew in the dining room—minus the captain and first mate—and announced that our paychecks would be a week late. "If anyone has a critical situation and needs it immediately," he said, "see me afterward, and we'll work something out."

Obviously, no one was delighted with the news. The deckhands grumbled the loudest.

"It may not be a critical need, but I had plans for that paycheck," I heard Curtis say to Dianne.

"So did we all," Dianne told him.

You could see the difference in morale the following week, unless I only imagined it. Seemed as though people worked a little slower, a bit less cheerfully. Fewer smiles. We blamed it on a somewhat lackluster group of passengers this time, who weren't as enthused as the group before, but they probably picked up vibes from us.

Quinton had arranged for a local band to come aboard one evening and play dance music; a comedy team came another. There was one glorious afternoon when the wind was just right that we had a kite-flying contest on the top deck, and Stephanie was a surprisingly good cheerleader. Mitch and I flew one together, battling the yellow and orange kite that Gwen and Flavian had launched, until they tangled in midair and came spinning back down to the deck.

When the following Sunday arrived, however, and the passengers left, Quinton had to announce that, once again, there was a shortfall. But we would absolutely get our paychecks by the end of the month. This time there were open hostilities.

"I need mine now, Quinton," Frank said. "I've got bills to pay, and I've certainly been doing cruises longer than the captain. He getting a paycheck?" I could tell by the murmurs that went around that he spoke for all of us.

"Cruising's our profession, Frank," Quinton said. "We both know that part of this job is being able to roll with the punches. But I can guarantee that everyone here will get their paychecks before Dianne and I get ours."

But even Quinton couldn't have known what would happen next.

16
CHANGES

Up until now, summer on the bay, though hot, had days of respite, when the breeze picked up and the humidity went down. On these days passengers preferred being out on the decks, not in the air-conditioned lounge looking through travel magazines about what it was like every other place in the world. But now, as we started the last full week of July, the temperature shot up to the mid-nineties every day.

Whatever the weather in Barcelona, Patrick was obviously enjoying himself:

Students are just beginning to arrive for fall quarter. I'll be transferring to a dorm as soon as summer courses are over. Finished all the graphs for Professor Eagan's book.

*Just proofreading yet to do, so I'm free for most of the day
now. He sends me on errands and I explore the city. His
girlfriend's coming to stay with him middle of August. She's
teaching a course too. . . .*

The *Seascape* wasn't completely booked for the next cruise
either. In fact, I heard from Lauren that people were now offered
discounts of $800 for immediately booking in August. Dianne
even told us—jokingly, maybe—that if we had relatives who
were considering a vacation at sea, they might be able to get it
at half price.

What Frank told us one night, though—and he's practically
lived his life on cruise ships—is that in the heat of summer,
most people think about cruising the New England coast or the
St. Lawrence Seaway, or they fly out to Vancouver and take the
Inner Passage to Alaska.

Even the *Seascape* crew hunkered down in air-conditioning.
The only time we wanted to sit on the top deck was when the
ship was moving or after dark. Few of us opted to take excursions, even when we had the time. If we left the ship, it was to
find a bar or a pizza place, to go bowling in air-conditioned
comfort, or to take in a movie. Our paychecks finally came
through, as Quinton promised, but he said we would be paid
again in two weeks, not one.

When we did go out at night, for a couple hours after
the day crew finished up, I began to notice a change in Gwen
and Flavian's relationship. It had started out as a parody of

love—lots of one-liners and laughs—then a sort of affectionate joking around. But now . . .

Liz and Pamela and I were watching as Yolanda replaited the cornrows that decorated Gwen's head. "Cornrow rehab," we called it.

"Do you think I'm leading Flavian on?" Gwen asked no one in particular, staring straight ahead since she couldn't move her head.

I was trying to cut my toenails with fingernail scissors, which didn't work, and realized I'd have to buy a pair the next time we were in a drugstore.

"Does he think so?" I asked. If you don't know the answer, ask a question.

"I'm not sure. He's been kind of moody. Haven't you noticed?" Gwen said.

"A little."

"He says I've changed. I said, 'For the better, I hope.' 'No,' he said, 'That's not what I meant.'"

"NMI," said Yolanda.

"What does that mean?" asked Gwen.

"Need more information."

"I told him he seemed quieter, more uptight lately. Asked him what was wrong. And he said it was me who had changed. Okay, we were kissing—serious kissing, I mean—and I guess I pulled away. I like it more playful, the way it started out with Flavian . . . and he doesn't. He wants to take things up a notch."

"You don't like Flavian?" I asked.

"Sure, I like him, but I didn't sign on for another relationship. I thought he knew that. I mean—look! I've got eight years of medical school ahead of me. I just wanted to really cut loose this summer and have fun."

"Maybe you each have a different definition of 'really,'" I suggested.

"I just don't want any baggage when I start school. I don't want long text messages from Flavian about when we'll see each other again. On the outside, Flavian looks like a fun-loving, risk-taking Romeo, right? On the inside, he's . . . I think he just needs a woman to validate him."

"How do you know it isn't just you? I mean that he never really fell for someone until he met you?" I asked.

Gwen was quiet for a moment, and then she said, "That scares the hell out of me."

"Why?"

"Because I can't be anyone's 'all' right now. Not even Austin's. I can't have anyone that dependent on me. This is my one time to cut loose and enjoy myself and not take on anyone else's needs."

And listening to Gwen, I wondered if this was how Patrick felt about me. If, once I started college, I'd feel the same. But I decided this was a conversation we could have when I visited him at Christmas.

It was the start of our eighth week, and the humid weather hung on. It had reached 101 degrees the week before and then went down to 93 where it settled in. We'd known the forecast before we left Baltimore this time, and Stephanie planned a lot of onboard activities that the passengers could enjoy in air-conditioned comfort if they declined the open-air trolley in Yorktown or the unshaded walk around Tangier Island or hiking on St. Michaels.

There's not a whole lot you can do on ship without a pool, an orchestra, or a theater, however. Still, Stephanie tried her best. We had a make-your-own-sundae afternoon and a bubble-blowing contest; a crazy hat day and short films on sea chanties and "The Disappearing Islands on the Chesapeake."

For the most part, though, passengers seemed listless and lethargic, and the subtle changes in the menu didn't help either. The stewards knew funds were low when the caviar appetizer disappeared from the Captain's Dinner. There was no Chilean sea bass, no duck pâté or heirloom tomatoes. Raspberry ice cream replaced the molten chocolate cake with fresh raspberry sauce that had been so popular on the other cruises.

Quinton had been asked to save money by substituting some clearly inferior wine at dinner, Rachel told us, but he chose to raise the price of premium liquors at cocktail hour instead. "Let's try to keep some shred of dignity," she heard him tell Carlo.

The third night, after we'd left Yorktown and were en route to Crisfield, we were getting ready for bed, listening to Emily's account of a guy she used to date who made his own beer, when the lights flickered a time or two.

I had just taken off my shorts when the lights went off completely.

"Awwk!" I said. "I can't find my sleep shirt."

"Listen," said Gwen.

"What?" We were quiet a moment.

"The air just went off too," Gwen said.

In fact, there was no noise at all. No hum of the fan, no drone of the engine. I felt around for my shorts and put them on again, then fished about with one foot for my sandals.

"I can't tell if we're still moving," said Emily.

"We're not," said Lauren.

"The passengers are probably freaking out," Pamela said. "I hope most of them are asleep."

"They won't be if the air doesn't come on pretty soon," said Lauren. "It was only down to eighty-six degrees outside at dinnertime."

"Shouldn't somebody be announcing something on the PA?" I asked.

"If the electricity's off, so is the PA. So is everything," Rachel said.

The only light we had was from the small, dim EXIT sign above our door, not much better than a tiny night-light.

"Let's go up top and see what's happened," said Pamela. "Does anyone know where we are?"

"In the widest part of the bay, that's where," said Rachel. "I'll bet we're fifteen miles from land on either side."

"Well, it's not like we're lost at sea," said Lauren.

Some of the guys were already out in the hallway too, and we collided with semi-bare bodies as we groped our way to the stairs. We could hear clunks and clanks coming from the engine room, Frank's and Ken's voices, but the last thing they needed was us getting in the way.

"Blindman's bluff," Barry called out behind us. "Oops, sorry, ma'am."

"Watch it, Barry," I heard Natalie say.

"What do you think is wrong?" I asked the guys over my shoulder.

"Powers out, that's all I know" came Mitch's voice.

"Generator," said Josh. "Gotta be the generator."

"Is that bad?" asked Liz.

"That's everything," Josh answered.

It was a little easier to see once we reached a door on the main deck. There was enough of a moon that we could make out sizes and shapes, even if we still had to guess at who they were.

"Are we sinking?" an elderly voice asked, and as we strained to see through the darkness, a small figure emerged from a doorway.

"No, ma'am," said Mitch. "Just a little problem with the power. Engineer is working on it now."

She was unconvinced. "We don't need our life jackets or anything?"

"No, you can go back to bed. If there was any danger, we'd let you know."

Since we didn't have a clue what to tell people, we felt our way over to the outside staircase, and when we got up to the lounge deck, we found Quinton and Dianne. She was holding a flashlight and Quinton was rummaging around in a metal box.

"I can't believe that's all they've got," Quinton was saying. "There aren't even enough for each member of the crew, much less the passengers." He handed a flashlight to Dianne and then, hearing us, called us over. "Each of you take a flashlight and patrol the decks. I want one person at the top and one at the bottom of each stairway. The generator stopped working, and until we get power again, we're all on duty."

"What are we supposed to tell people?" I asked.

"Try to keep them in their staterooms. Help them prop their doors open if they're too hot, open their windows for them. Those with inside cabins can go to the lounge if they like; we're opening doors and windows in there."

"I'm going to put pitchers of iced tea and lemonade on the bar," Dianne told us. "Rachel and Lauren, come help."

I took the bottom of the third staircase, Josh said he'd take the top. I heard Quinton talking to one of the passengers.

"It happens sometimes," he was saying. "This has been an exceptionally brutal summer, as we all know. The equipment's had to work nonstop at maximum capacity, and sometimes it does break down. But we've got an expert engineer on board who's spent half his life on ships, so we have every reason to hope for the best."

Mitch and Liz were heading for their assigned stairways.

"I'm supposed to serve at breakfast," Liz said, stopping a moment, the beam of her flashlight aimed at my chin. "But refrigeration is gone too, right?"

"Refrigeration and everything else that's run by electricity," Mitch said, "including the toilets."

"We can't flush the toilets?" Liz yelped. "I mean, not even once, not even at all?"

"They all operate on electricity," Mitch told her.

Trust Liz to worry about toilets.

In the dark hallway of the main deck, it was sort of like playing Marco Polo out of the water. Passengers were coming out of their stifling cabins, aware that all vent noise had stopped, and were bumping into each other.

"Has this ever happened before?" people asked us.

"How long before the air comes back on?"

"Do we get a refund?"

It was the toilets that bothered them most. It was hard to convince people that toilets at sea are not like the ones at home.

It was going on three o'clock, and some of the crew's flashlights that had been dim to begin with were going out. Quinton swore at himself for not checking on them at the start of the season, even though it fell under Ken McCoy's list of duties. Passengers were clamoring for flashlights for themselves.

As I was leading another group of passengers upstairs to the lounge, I heard Quinton ask Stephanie, "What have we got in the gift shop? Any flashlights at all?"

"Small pen-type things on an anchor key chain," she said.

"We're giving them away," Quinton told her.

"How many?"

"The whole stock. To anyone who asks."

Natalie took over my post at the stairs, and Stephanie and I walked the decks giving out pen-size flashlights and helping people move their bedding to their open doorways, where they might catch some semblance of a breeze. I was sweaty from the back of my neck to the soles of my feet. Perspiration trickled down my spine and between my breasts. Stephanie must have been miserable too, but you wouldn't hear it from her.

At about four o'clock, a few of us made our way toward crew quarters to use the bathrooms. We could hear Haggerty's muffled voice coming from below, and we squatted on the steps listening. Only scraps of conversation came from the engine room.

". . . only one more thing to try, and the chances are next to nothing." Frank.

"So try, damn it!" Haggerty. "Do what you have to do. The last thing I want is to tell the front office I can't even get this thing into port."

We turned around and headed back up, not wanting to be caught eavesdropping. We stood to one side at the top of the stairs as Haggerty and Quinton came up.

"Could I have some coffee up on the bridge?" the captain asked in irritation. Then, "Oh. Guess not. What are you doing about the passengers' breakfasts?"

"It will be a cold one, of course, but it's what we do after that that concerns me," Quinton said. "We can serve food for only a limited time after the refrigeration's off."

They went on up the next flight, and we ran down to use the restrooms while our flashlights still worked. Josh and Curtis were standing in the hallway. They shone their flashlights on our faces to see who we were and then went on talking.

"Doesn't look good, does it?" Barry asked.

"Worse than bad," Curtis replied. "That sorry thing isn't going to start again. Generator's shot and Frank knows it. He said it should have been replaced before the *Seascape* ever sailed."

"Are they going to send us a new one?" Liz asked.

We could barely see Curtis's face as he turned toward her.

"What? A helicopter drop or something?" he said, and we could tell he was laughing.

"I don't know. By ship, maybe," she said.

"This crate needs to be back at port. Takes at least a week to replace a generator," Curtis said.

"What the heck do we do?" asked Emily "People are going to wake up in a couple of hours if they haven't already."

"Be glad you're not the captain," said Josh. "He's the one who has to tell them they can't flush their toilets, can't turn on the lights, can't have coffee. That everything in the refrigerator is melting or defrosting. Some cruise, huh?"

I was embarrassed that one of my first thoughts was that I had something else exciting to tell Patrick.

17
UNDER A CLOUDLESS SKY

We'd been up all night—the whole crew—and looked it.

Any minute, we expected the captain to make an appearance and explain everything.

Wrong.

It was Quinton who faced the disheveled passengers at a breakfast of cold cereal, fruit juice, bananas, and yesterday's muffins, on paper plates. No toast, no eggs, no oatmeal, and—what caused the biggest uproar—no coffee.

"By now," he said, "you're all aware that the *Seascape* is experiencing a mechanical problem. Around midnight last night, our generator broke down, and when that happens, we are totally without power. This means no hot water, no toilets operating, no laundry, no cooking, no air-conditioning, fans, lights, or TV. We're doing everything we can to correct the situation and deeply regret the disappointment and inconvenience to our passengers. We do hope you'll understand that loss of electricity means that many accommodations have to be made."

That didn't satisfy anyone, and though some passengers joked ("Well, we wanted an adventure, didn't we?") and others took a stoical view and prepared to endure, most of them—by the looks on their faces—wanted more information *now*.

"We'll bring you updates at every meal," Quinton promised. "Sooner, if there are any new developments."

The stewards assigned to housekeeping were instructed to make beds without changing the linens and to ask passengers to please use their towels for one more day. And to keep the lids of their toilets closed.

Dianne told the stewards we could sleep in four-hour shifts, but it was stifling in crew quarters, so we strung ups sheets for shade among all the mechanical stuff on the "crew only" section of the main deck and piled blankets underneath to lie on. Some of us succeeded in a few hours' sleep until someone else came to take our place.

There was, of course, no excursion to Tangier Island, and lunch—served late—consisted of chef's salad, deli sandwiches, cookies, and soft ice cream. Quinton simply made an announcement that there was no word yet from the pilothouse, but he expected news of some kind by dinner. We would be eating at six o'clock, he told us, and choices were obviously limited.

"What's Haggerty waiting for?" we asked Josh after we'd seen him talking with Quinton.

"Wants to review his options," Josh said.

The restroom outside the dining room had a CLOSED sign on it. Understandably, passengers had been choosing to use that room rather than their own staterooms, since they couldn't flush.

We hated mingling with passengers. Sweltering, exhausted people were draped over chairs, over railings, like laundry, waiting for every little breeze. Every part of the body that touched a deck chair or railing soon grew too warm for comfort. Each time one of us crew members walked by, people called out to us, confronted us, asked how long we'd be here—stranded in the middle of the Chesapeake Bay—with no land in sight. They didn't believe us when we said we didn't know any more than they did. One woman asked if we were sure we hadn't drifted out into the Atlantic Ocean.

There was no cheerful steward walking through the ship ringing the dinner bell that evening. No welcoming scent of croissants fresh from the oven. Staff members were dressed in the same wrinkled shirts they'd worn the day before, even Quinton. There were no white cloths on the tables, no ice in the glasses, and the buffet was a repeat of what had been available at lunch, with applesauce and sliced beets added.

And there were few smiles. Voices were low, the mood grim. When the meal was over, both Quinton and Ken faced the passengers as promised, the rest of us standing at the back, listening. Quinton began:

"I know this has been a frustrating day for you, as it has for all of us. It's now evident to our engineer that the generator will have to be replaced, and that's not something we can do out here in the middle of the bay. While this is certainly a logistical problem for the company, our main concern is you, our passengers—your comfort and safety, as well as your expectations of a pleasant trip. The captain and first mate have been discussing our options, so I'll let Officer McCoy take it from here."

What was immediately evident was that First Mate McCoy would rather be anywhere else on the planet than here.

"Good evening, ladies and gentlemen," he said, and cleared his throat. "If I sound as if I haven't had any sleep, I haven't, but neither have most of you."

"Uh-uh, Kenny boy," I heard Curtis whisper behind me. "Don't whine."

Ken continued: "I guess it's pretty obvious that this ship is not going to make it back to Baltimore on its own, but that's our problem, not yours."

Curtis groaned again.

"All I can tell you at this point in time is that one of our options is to send our newly built sister ship, the *Spellbound*, down here and transfer you all to that—"

"Are they crazy?" Josh whispered, but the passengers perked up. The thought of a transfer at sea, a brand-new ship, air-conditioning, food . . .

"—but no decision has been made yet. And I want to assure you that we will remedy this situation as soon as possible. That's all I can tell you at this point in time, but if you have any questions . . ."

When did "this point in time" get so popular? I wondered. But yes, the passengers had questions.

"How is it you don't have the necessary parts with you?" a man called out.

"We have extra parts for many of the things we might need on the cruise, but a generator, unfortunately, is not one of them," Ken said. "Too big a job."

"I thought this was a 'completely refurbished ship,'" the man shot back. "Was that everything but the generator?"

"Bingo," Curtis murmured.

"I'm sure it was checked before we started our season, but there were some other malfunctions in connection with the generator," said Ken, and his face was slightly flushed.

"So we've got a whole damn engine room breaking down? Is that what you're saying?" the irate man shouted.

"No, sir. But sometimes, regardless, parts do give out, especially in the weather we've experienced," Ken said.

"How long can we go without fresh water?" asked a woman, clutching her half-filled glass.

"If we're careful to conserve what we have, there should be enough for drinking and brief washups at your sinks. Please, folks, no showers until the cruise starts up again."

"Can you give us any idea when that will be?" the man next to her asked. "We've already been sitting out here not going anywhere for eighteen hours."

"At this moment I cannot," Ken replied. And again, a murmur ran through the crowd. "But we're not in the middle of the ocean. The Coast Guard knows exactly where we are."

"What about food?" someone else called. But at that precise moment, Ken's walkie-talkie buzzed, and I even wondered if that was prearranged with Haggerty up in the pilothouse.

"If you'll excuse me, the captain needs me up on the bridge," Ken said. "I'm sure that Quinton can answer the rest of your questions."

For a brief moment I could see clear irritation on Quinton's face. He was already weary and looking more like Lincoln than Abe himself. But he stepped right up.

"Although we have plenty of food on board, we can't keep it refrigerated, so we've had to discard some," he said. "The food in the freezer will keep a few more days, but there's no way to cook it when it thaws. I don't think you will go hungry, but we have to conserve the ice that's left and will offer only those foods we know are safe. Remember, we're just fifteen miles from shore, so we can get a delivery if necessary, but first we need to know where we'll be tomorrow. As for sleeping, we will be glad to move mattresses to the upper deck for those of you who find your staterooms too uncomfortable. Right now we're going to feed our crew before it gets too dark to see. Then, if we can help you in any way, please speak to a crew member and we'll do our best."

The passengers began talking heatedly among themselves as they filed out of the dining room. We turned to one another.

"Is the captain insane?" asked Lauren. "They can't be serious about getting another ship. The *Spellbound* is up in Rhode Island."

Curtis found it funny. "The last I heard, they were three weeks behind in getting it furnished. Even if they just threw stuff together, stocked it, and brought it down, it would take a week. If we just want to transport one hundred and ten people fifteen miles, let's rent a ferry."

"Shoot," said Mitch, "I'll call my dad and tell him to hire some men in their oyster boats to carry us off. It's not all that complicated."

"Yeah, it is, actually," said Josh. "There's insurance, there's refunds, there's safety, there's all that luggage. The company is responsible for everything that happens to passengers until they disembark."

"It's even more than that," Lauren added. "It's saving face. If there's any rescuing to be done, the front office wants it done by the company—keep it all in the family, you know."

"How are they going to do that?" asked Barry. "There was already a WTOP helicopter circling this afternoon taking pictures. Probably covered on the evening news."

We had to patrol the lower decks from time to time to assist passengers who stayed in their rooms. The most we could see were the little pinheads of light from the tiny key chain flashlights we'd distributed earlier or an occasional beam from a crew flashlight. Some of the passengers had already holed up on the observation deck, using blankets and pillows to reserve the chaise longues. When I checked on them, I found only the slightest breeze fanning the humid air. We were too far from the mainland to see any lights. Not even a faint glow in the sky. All we had were stars and moon.

Mitch and I stood together at the railing.

"This will be the end of our summer jobs," he said.

"You think?"

"What else are we going to do? Say we get to Baltimore before this week is over. This particular cruise is kaput. So is the ninth cruise, because they'll be using that week to replace the generator. If we stick around for the last cruise of the season, who's going to put us up meanwhile? Our paychecks are already delayed."

"You could always go home and come back when the ship is ready," I said, considering.

"Don't think I haven't thought about it." He put an arm around my shoulder and gave me a playful hug. "You could come too. Sleep on the couch with the dog."

I laughed. "What's its name?"

"Rags."

"Rags?"

"Because when she was a pup, she tore everything to shreds. Grab hold of a shirt and you could pull it forever, she wouldn't let go. Springer spaniel."

"I'm sure your mom would appreciate having me there."

"Oh, she's used to it."

"Bringing girls home to sleep on the couch?"

"Bringing friends home—usually guys who are going out trapping with me the next day."

"What would you tell your mom about me?"

"I'd say, 'Mom, this is my friend Alice. She's sleeping with the dog,' and she'd say, 'Fine, she can set the table.' And you're in."

Why did I feel so comfortable around Mitch? I wondered. Why did I believe it would almost be that way if I took him up on it?

"We'll see what happens tomorrow," I said. "A mutiny might decide the whole thing."

The top deck was crowded with people now, like a beach on a summer day, except it was night and there were even a few mattresses. So Mitch and I and a few of the others took our pillows to the lounge deck fantail around one in the morning and crawled into the sleeping space the others had rigged up.

Sleepy as I was, I lay on my back and looked out between the gaps in the sheets strung over us, studying the stars. Every so often one seemed to wink at me, and I wondered how many light-years away it was and whether it even *was* any longer. I could hear Mitch's soft breathing on one side of me, Gwen's on the other. How special was it to be lying here between two friends, and when, if ever, had I had a male friend, other than my brother, whom I felt so close to and comfortable with, just staying friends? So far, at least.

* * *

222 • PHYLLIS REYNOLDS NAYLOR

I slept longer that I thought was allowed. No one woke me, anyway. I had to pee and desperately needed to stretch one leg, which was cramping. I managed to extricate myself from the tangle of bodies around me without nudging either Gwen or Mitch. I made my way down to crew quarters and could smell the toilets even before I got there. I took a deep breath, then zipped in and out.

No one else on the ship seemed to be up—not surprising since we were all exhausted, passengers and crew alike. But if there was a coolest part of the day, this was it—more breeze than we'd had for the last two days. I took the stairs to the Chesapeake deck, wanting to go around the walkway a few times to stretch my legs. When I turned at the bow, I saw a man leaning his arms on the rail, smoking, as dejected a figure as I'd ever seen.

The captain saw me, dropped his cigarette in the water, and turned his head away.

The breeze didn't last. When the sun rose, the shimmering orange ball seemed even more threatening than it had the day before, and its reflection on the water was like a warning arrow pointing directly at the ship. I rinsed my face in the crew washroom beside the others, brushed my teeth, tied my stringy, limp hair back away from my face, and went to the galley.

Quinton was there, dark circles under his eyes.

"Start filling trash bags," he was saying to Carlo and the assistant cook. "The sausage, the ham. If it wasn't frosted over when you took it out, it goes in the garbage. Eggs—out. Butter we'll use one more day. I'd rather have a hungry ship than a sick one."

"Any update from the front office?" Carlo asked.

"We're supposed to find out today if the Spellbound's coming down. There was talk of giving the passengers a free cruise on it later in the fall."

"Makes no bloody sense to me," Carlo said. "If the ship's not ready for a September launch, it's not ready now."

"I don't know, Carlo. We're taking one step at a time. Check the milk to see if we can offer cereal for breakfast. Cereal, cheese, and fruit. That's it."

An occasional fishing boat passed that morning, the watermen staring up at us talking among themselves. When two men came out in a speedboat and cut the engine, one of them yelled, "You guys having problems?"

And one of the passengers yelled back, "We're being held prisoner because the generator went out. Send food!"

The men laughed and the passenger did too.

"Can you give us a tow?" someone else shouted.

"Good luck with that," one of the men called, and they sped off again.

When Dianne found that a couple had taken a Magic Marker and printed SOS in huge letters on a sheet and hung it from the railing, she took it down. Quinton went through the ship with the megaphone and announced that the captain would speak to us in the dining room at noon.

Not even Ken McCoy was smiling this time.

When Haggerty came into the room at twelve, walking swiftly, like the president holding a press conference, he used "I," we noticed, when he talked about action taken, "we," when action was delayed.

"To all you good people who are sweltering along with the crew, I can tell you that I've been in contact with the front office almost continually since we lost power," he said, pausing as if for applause, but he got only silent stares from the crowd.

"It's certainly unfortunate that you have had to endure a disabled ship in the middle of your cruise, and the weather only adds to your discomfort. We had originally discussed the possibility that our sister ship, the *Spellbound*, could be launched immediately to pick you up, but that turns out to be not only impractical, but impossible. So without wanting to delay you any further, I am negotiating with a salvage company to tow us in."

"You mean they're going to junk this ship?" a woman asked in dismay.

"Why not?" a man yelled. "That's what it is."

Haggerty looked uneasy. "No, ma'am, I should have been clearer. Salvage companies offer many services, and one of them is providing tugs to pull or push a disabled vessel into port."

"So what's to negotiate?" another man asked. "We want to get off. We're all baking out here."

"I will definitely get you all off this ship, as soon and as safely as possible," Haggerty said. "But the front office has the final say on what the cost will be and where we'll be towed. They should reach a decision by the end of the day."

Now everyone began talking at once. One man even leaped to his feet. "That probably means we won't get towed till tomorrow! We're down to crackers and prunes, and this is one hell of a way to treat paying passengers. Pay whatever they damn want and get us *off* here!"

"Amen!" yelled someone else.

Haggerty was getting testy: "One of the things I learned in the navy is to expect the unexpected. Good sailors know there will be ups and downs."

Even I knew he was treading on thin ice—that is, if we had any ice.

"Well, this ain't the navy," yelled a man who needed a razor. "I'm a retiree with six years of combat in 'Nam, and I didn't sign on for ups and downs on a cruise ship."

"I understand and applaud you, sir," Haggerty said. "And I would be glad to talk with you longer, ladies and gentlemen, but I'm expecting some calls. And the sooner this is settled the better."

"After we're towed back, then what?" someone called after him. "Will the company pay our hotel bill?"

But Haggerty was out the door, heading for the bridge.

18
END OF THE LINE

The temperature climbed even higher the next morning, both in the air and in misery. Angry passengers gathered in the lounge and dining areas, watching the doorways for any sight of the captain or first mate.

"Probably abandoned ship," somebody joked, "Check the lifeboats—see if they're all here."

Quinton made a brief announcement: A decision had been made that we would be towed, but the question was whether it would be back to Norfolk or to Baltimore. When noon came, then one o'clock, and we still sat idled, tempers reached the boiling point.

The WTOP helicopter flew over again, and people yelled and waved, fruitlessly calling up to the crew. Someone had printed

WANTED: KFC on the floor of the top deck, probably five Magic Markers' worth of ink, and we could see the photographer on the passenger side of the copter, taking a photo.

"Just got a text from my dad," I told the others. "He said it was on the news last night. Wants to know if we're okay."

"Tell him to send a care package," Gwen said.

Most passengers didn't even want us to come into their staterooms because they were such a mess. We gave out the last of the clean towels. And Stephanie organized another Trivial Pursuit game in the lounge, with items from the gift shop as prizes.

Funny the way you can change your mind about a person. In all the trouble we were going through on the *Seascape*, I hadn't heard Stephanie complain once. I hadn't heard her gripe when our paychecks were late. Hadn't heard her grumble that it was damn hard to entertain 110 people in 100-degree weather on a stinking ship that was going nowhere.

Her clothes were wrinkled and sweat-stained, the same as ours, and her hair needed washing, too. Yet she helped carry pillows and blankets to the observation deck, same as us; and she tied up the plastic bags of used paper plates and napkins, same as us; she was as bone-tired as everyone else, yet she managed to look more optimistic and encouraging than we did.

Maybe it was all a sham and maybe she had a few more marriages to wreck in her future, but didn't she deserve a second chance? She sure rose up a few notches in my esteem.

"Is anything happening at all?" we asked Frank when he

surfaced in mid-afternoon for the slim lunch pickings offered to the crew. "What's holding things up?"

Frank looked even older than his sixty-some years. "The deal is that headquarters is sitting on its haunches because it doesn't want to pay what the salvage company is charging. And, not surprisingly, salvage wants the pay up front. Damned if I'll ever work for this line again."

It was almost four when I heard a huge cheer from the lounge deck. I dropped the stack of paper cups I was placing on the buffet table for dinner and ran upstairs. Passengers were crowded along the rail, waving at a large tug coming our way.

"What a relief," Dianne said beside us. "And they're towing us to Baltimore, saints be praised. More expensive because Norfolk is closer, but then the cruise line would have to pay travel expenses for all the passengers to get from Norfolk to Baltimore."

You'd think the seven men aboard the *Samuel Dawes* were heroes, the way passengers cheered when they pulled alongside us. Ken McCoy opened the side door on the main deck to let their pilot come aboard. Barry and Mitch were studying the tug.

"Can she pull a ship this big?" Barry wondered aloud.

"You watch," Mitch said.

Nothing is ever as simple as you imagine, though. The *Samuel Dawes* had brought fourteen cases of bottled water for the passengers, and these had to be carried aboard. Then there were papers to sign and a discussion between the towboat crew and Captain Haggerty, an inspection of the bow, another discussion with Frank, and two news helicopters this time to take pictures of the hookup. But once the cable was attached and we actually began to move, we caught a whiff of a breeze—the first in several days—and felt energized once again.

We were traveling at only half the normal speed, so I had no idea how long it would take to get to Baltimore. But when we passed Tangier Island in the early evening, another cheer went up as we slowly saw land appearing on first one side of us, then the other. There were more fishing boats, and of course we were the big attraction.

The company had arranged for a hastily prepared fried chicken dinner to be brought out to the ship from a restaurant on Tangier Island, and we watched as the food was transferred to us at the stern without our having to stop the tow—large plastic cartons of potato salad and cole slaw hauled up in a net. Fishermen seemed as delighted to deliver the food as we were to get it, broad smiles on their red, weathered faces.

After our "last supper," as Emily called it, passengers began packing up their things, and most opted to sleep in their staterooms with the doors open, now that we were manufacturing our own breeze.

The rumor was that the crew would stick around Baltimore for a week while the generator was replaced, then do the last and final cruise of the season, but who knew?

We bedded down after midnight wherever we could. Some of us sat on the floor at the bow of the lounge deck, our half-closed eyes focused on the lights of the tug, the chug of the motor lulling us to sleep.

Gulls woke us at dawn.

I found myself slumped with my head on Mitch's shoulder, knowing that my breath must be awesomely awful. It was comforting to feel his arm around me. I liked the way our feet splayed out in front of us, the sneakers and deck shoes that were scattered among the legs; liked the naturalness of the heads tipped this way and that, arms limp, all of us roommates on this crazy ship.

Liz and I got up eventually and went down to the "stink hole," as we'd taken to calling the crew toilets, to brush our teeth. We were on housekeeping duty this week, so we didn't need to help at breakfast, what breakfast there was. But we stopped at the dining room and picked up some oranges for our sleep mates.

I sat crossed-legged on the deck facing Mitch, pulling back the thick peel of my navel orange, lifting a segment and putting it in his mouth, then one for me. I didn't know when anything had tasted so delicious as the freshness of that orange with a breeze on my face from a ship that was moving at last.

It took the rest of the day to reach Baltimore, and everyone gathered on deck as the harbor came into view. We were greeted by two smaller tugs that helped nudge us into a berth, plus a Coast Guard cutter, there to be sure we did it safely.

We stewards did our best to look spiffy and act professionally as we commiserated with passengers in the lineup to get off.

"Well, you've certainly had an experience" was about all we could offer.

Captain Haggerty had shown up after dinner the night before—when stomachs were full, of course—and thanked the passengers for their patience. He explained that refunds would be mailed to them from the front office but made no promise to pay for a hotel once they disembarked. He also thanked the crew for their help and determination, but there was no promise of a hotel for us, either, and certainly no tip envelopes to pass out.

The gangplank was lowered to much cheering, and several reporters and photographers stood by to interview passengers about being "kept at bay" or "stranded at sea," as various passengers put it. I saw Dianne wince as one woman, eager to be interviewed, lifted her arms in the air in a victory pose and shouted, "I survived the worst cruise ever!"

Ken bravely shook hands with each passenger who left the ship, and so did Quinton. But Haggerty seemed to have slipped away unnoticed by us all. Finally it was just the silent ship and us, and we set to work stripping any beds we hadn't done yet, bagging the last of the trash, exchanging our white shirts for comfortable tees.

Most of us had contacted home by now, and I called Dad at the Melody Inn to tell him I was off the ship but would finish all ten weeks if I could.

"What an adventure, huh?" he said, laughing. "I wasn't worried about you, honey, but I knew it must by darn uncomfortable. Where are they putting you up tonight?"

"I don't know. Quinton is going to talk to us in an hour or so, but I'll be fine," I told him.

Sure enough, Quinton gathered us all on deck shortly after I'd talked to Dad. "The home office said they'll be caught up on bills by tomorrow, including paychecks. Let me know if you want to pick yours up in person or have us send it on to your home address. Your last paycheck, for this past week, will go out in about ten days."

"What about the final cruise of the summer?" Gwen asked.

"We won't know till tomorrow if they're canceling or not," Quinton said. "It's asking a lot of you, I know, to hang around for a week. If you'd rather go home now and come back for the final cruise, we'd be happy to have you. And if you decide to end your job today, we understand. I'll be at the branch office on Charles Street tomorrow after ten with more information."

Some of the deckhands had already taken off. Lauren and Emily went to stay with a friend, but six of us girls—Natalie, Gwen, Pamela, Liz, Yolanda, and me—plus Barry, Mitch, Josh, and Flavian, stood on the deck considering our options.

"Where you guys going to crash?" Flavian asked us. We had no idea.

Barry knew someone he thought would put the guys up for the night, but all we girls wanted was to find a motel and take a shower.

We sat down on some benches outside an ice-cream place while Josh looked up motels on his BlackBerry. We wanted a place we could walk to, if possible.

"The Renaissance?" Josh asked.

"Are you kidding?" Gwen said, looking at the expensive

place many of our passengers had stayed before boarding the *Seascape*.

"Pier 5 Hotel?"

"Get real," Pamela told him.

We finally settled on the Silver Motor Lodge and told the guys we'd meet them back on the dock at seven. Then we piled into a taxi van.

It was a crummy motel, a one-story building that had seen better days, and two of the letters on its neon sign were missing. They made the six of us take two rooms, so we divided up, three to a room. But a shower had never, ever felt so delicious. I shampooed three times just to feel that wonderful tingle and finally, reluctantly, let someone else have a turn.

We felt almost human again when we met the guys, then went to the Hard Rock Cafe. Despite our protests, they said they were paying, and we sat at two adjoining tables trading food back and forth, enjoying the huge fried onion that looked like a wig. It was great to be in a noisy place, with loud music and people laughing and *air-conditioning*. I felt that someone could lock me in a refrigerator, and even after an hour, it would still feel good.

We walked around Harborplace afterward, stopping to watch a mime, who pretended he was trapped in a box; danced a little outside a bar. Around midnight, when our sleep-deprived nights caught up with us, we looked for a cab back to the Silver Motor Lodge.

After the guys had put us in it, however, and waved good-bye, we noticed that they'd climbed into the cab behind us and were following along.

"They got the same motel?" asked Liz.

"I thought they were staying with a friend of Barry's," said Gwen.

We started giggling, bursting into laughter each time our cab made a turn and theirs followed. The driver was also laughing, and it came as no surprise when we reached the motel parking lot that the guys got out there too.

"Yeah?" Pamela said as they looked sheepishly in our direction. "And where are you guys sleeping?"

"On the floor?" said Mitch.

"Are you kidding?" I told them. "The rooms are doll-size."

"We're out of money," said Josh. "We spent it all on dinner. Honestly."

"We *said* we'd pay!" Natalie reminded them.

"That's when we thought we could stay with Barry's friend. Turns out he's not home," said Flavian.

"Listen, you guys," said Gwen. "They wouldn't even let the six of us stay in one room. 'Six girls, two rooms,' the woman told us."

"*Two* rooms? You've got two rooms?" said Mitch. "Come on! You've got to let us have one."

"How are we going to get you in there?" I said.

But it wasn't hard, actually. Our two adjoining rooms were along one corridor that ended at a door to the parking lot. No one could get in from outside without a key card, but it was easy for one of us to open the door from inside.

So the six of us girls came in the front entrance and said good night to the manager at the desk. She was a pink-haired, middle-aged woman in a thin nylon blouse with a black bra beneath and a cross around her neck. She had a tattoo of a guitar on her bicep, and her cherry-red nail polish was chipped.

"You have a nice evening?" she asked, not even taking her eyes from the reality show she was watching on TV.

"Yeah, the best," said Pamela.

"Checkout time's eleven," the woman said, and we passed her desk, made the turn, and walked all the way to the end. Yolanda opened the outside door, and the guys silently filed in.

This was almost too easy.

"Got to be bedbugs or something," Natalie said after we'd closed the door behind them.

"Shhhh. If we don't wake them, they won't bite," said Mitch.

"Hey! Adjoining rooms," said Flavian.

"And the door locks," said Gwen, giving him a look, and we laughed.

"Party time!" said Josh. "Who's going with me to get the brew? We passed a place just down the road."

"I'll go," Mitch offered. A half hour later they were back, both carrying a six-pack in each hand. They tapped on our window, and Liz went down the hall to let them in. We gathered in the guys' room.

"Bottle opener?" Natalie said.

Flavian produced the ship's flashlight key chain, whose anchor, we discovered, was also a bottle opener.

"To us," said Mitch, raising his bottle.

"To the *Seascape*. May she rest in peace," said Flavian.

"Aw, come on, she'll be good as new," Barry said. "She's *refurbished!*" And that got a laugh from all of us.

"Shhhh," Liz warned.

Someone suggested playing beer pong, but we didn't have enough beer for that, even though Liz and I wanted only one bottle. We were sprawled—all ten of us—on the two double beds and the floor.

So Barry opted for a game he called Truth or Fabrication.

"Drunk or sober?" asked Yolanda.

"That's up to you," said Barry. He dumped Natalie off the chair where she had been sitting.

"Okay," he said. "One at a time we have to sit in that chair and tell the others the most embarrassing thing that ever happened to us."

"Yeah, right. Like we'll tell the truth," said Liz.

"That's where the rest of us come in. If we decide you just made it up, or it's not embarrassing enough, you have to do whatever embarrassing thing we think of."

"Oh, no," I said. "We'll spill our guts and you'll still humiliate us."

"No, we won't. It'll be democratic. We'll vote," said Barry, and opened another beer.

What would I choose when it was my turn? I could practically remember every year of my life by my most embarrassing moments. Eating crayons in kindergarten? Asking Donald

Sheavers to play Tarzan and kiss me? Dinner at Patrick's parents' country club and bringing the napkin home in my bag? Bleeding through my white skirt at the dentist's office? Reciting the wrong poem in seventh-grade English? Falling down the stairs my first day of high school and wetting my pants?

Fortunately, the game started with someone else. Liz told the hilarious story of putting her push-up bra in the dryer and starting a fire. I knew it was true because I'd run across the street to comfort her and was there when the fire chief came out and warned her about putting rubberized products in a dryer. We gave Liz a thumbs-up.

Flavian was next, and it was hard to imagine that the guy with the movie-star looks would be embarrassed about anything. But then he told us about going to this fabulous water park with his friends when he was nine, and out of seven boys, he was the only one who wasn't tall enough to go down the huge slide.

"Awww," the girls all said in unison.

Then it was my turn. I sat in the chair, my back to the door.

"I don't remember where I was," I began. "Georgetown, I think. It was summer, I was wearing a tank top and full skirt. I'd used the restroom somewhere and was going back down the street when three guys walked past me from behind, and one of them said, 'Nice butterflies.' Then I discovered that in pulling up my underpants, I'd accidently tucked the hem of my skirt in the waistband and was exposing my bottom."

"Encore! Encore!" Mitch said, laughing. And they decided I

was telling the truth because my cheeks had flushed. There was a loud knock at the door, and I literally leaped out of the chair. The room fell silent.

"Who is it?" whispered Pamela.

I leaned over and peered out the peephole. The woman with the pink hair was looking right back at me. I turned to the others and pointed to my hair and then my bicep.

"Uh-oh," said Gwen.

People were sliding off the two beds, some heading for the next room, some the bathroom, but suddenly a key turned in the lock, and there she stood, taking in the whole situation.

"Well," she said as we froze in our tracks. "I didn't think that even six girls could make quite so much noise. We've had a complaint about the noise down here, and I see the population has doubled. Do you know what time it is?"

We looked at the bedside clock. Two forty-five, and our game was just beginning.

"We'll keep it low," Barry promised.

"The rate just doubled, due immediately, and you knock it off or you can pack up now—no refunds," Pink-Haired Woman said. "I don't like sneaks."

Josh got out his credit card. "Okay, you've got a right to be pissed. The truth is, we just got off that ship—"

"This is a seaport, buddy. People get off ships all the time."

"Well, we've been stranded out on the bay for three days without food or water."

The woman's face softened a little. "That seasick ship? That's what the newspaper called it. The one where the toilets wouldn't flush and the air-conditioning went out?"

"Yeah. You wouldn't believe . . ."

We thought of joining in, but Josh was doing a good enough job on his own.

"No lights, no hot water, food spoiling, passengers yelling at us, babies wailing, and we didn't even get paid for three weeks."

"The weather's been so hot and humid," Tattoo Lady said.

"Right. No breeze, not even on the water. We had to stand up all night at each stairway with flashlights to escort people up and down. Took two days to tow us in, the generator is shot, the cruise line defunct, and we're out of a job. We just wanted to have one more night together before we say good-bye."

The woman looked us over warily. "How do I know this isn't a bunch of bull?"

Barry picked up the flashlight key chain with *Seascape* printed on the little metallic anchor and handed it to her.

The pink-haired, black-bra lady studied it, and her forehead lit up. "Part of history," she said. "Okay, if you quietly sack up now, I'll keep the registration to six and you can say your good-byes at breakfast tomorrow."

"Deal," said Josh. "Thanks a lot. We appreciate it." She put her finger to her lips as she went out and closed the door softly behind her. We looked admiringly at Josh and Barry.

"Truth!" we said. "You win."

And so to bed. We girls headed to the next room. We were so tired, I'm not sure who slept where. It wasn't until the next morning that we discovered that Gwen and Flavian had spent the night wrapped in a blanket on our floor.

We managed to be out of the hotel by eleven thirty and had breakfast at a pancake place. We could have slept for five more hours, but we were hungry, too, and when we'd finished eating our strawberry-pecan-banana-chocolate-chip concoctions, we took cabs to the cruise line's branch office on Charles Street. We found Quinton and Frank talking in a small reception room with posters of ships on the walls and one-page information sheets with photos of both the *Seascape* and the *Spellbound*.

We gathered around as Quinton passed out our paychecks.

"So what's the word?" Mitch asked. "They going to make that final cruise?"

Quinton shook his head. "Afraid not."

We looked at Frank. "The generator won't be replaced by then?" I asked.

"Oh, the generator could be replaced, but they couldn't get it on credit. Their credit rating right now is about zero. By the time they send out those last checks and give refunds for cruises eight and nine, they'll have dug a hole so deep they can't get out."

"Wow," I said, and fingered one of the color brochures there on the desk.

"Yep. A shame," said Frank. "Big dreams, little cash. A small company trying to get going too soon. Should have waited till both ships could go out at once. But they just didn't have the cash to wait. Figured the summer cruises on the *Seascape* would pay the bills for fixing up the *Spellbound*, but things didn't turn out that way."

"So what are *you* going to do?" Josh asked him.

"Oh, I'll hang around Baltimore a day or two, talk to more shipping companies. See what's available. Something will turn up. Always does."

We looked at Quinton. "Dianne and I have a sailboat up in Maine. We just might take the autumn off. Sail around. Visit friends. Line up something for January. Frank knows he's welcome anytime."

I went back outside with the rest of the crew, and we sat on the steps of an office building, delaying our good-byes.

Liz called her dad, and he said he'd pick us up that afternoon. After a forty-seven-second kiss, Flavian said good-bye to Gwen and took a cab to the Amtrak station, and Josh and Natalie joined him. The rest of us wandered down to the harbor. We stood on the dock and looked at the *Seascape*, just as we had done the first day we came here in June.

It wasn't in the same berth, but farther down in a more out-of-the-way place where the mechanics could get at it. No crowd of people gathered on the dock, no activity. What would become of it? I wondered. All the planning, remodeling, the buying and hiring. All those dreams flying off like the swoop of a gull overhead.

Barry saw a friend of his and wandered off, and then it was time to say good-bye to Mitch.

"How do we do this?" he asked, smiling down at me. "Should we shake hands?"

"Not a chance," I said, and threw my arms around his neck for a long hug and then a kiss on the cheek and then another hug for good measure.

"Say hello to Patrick for me," he teased. And then he walked away.

19
HOUSEKEEPING

Yolanda had an aunt in Baltimore and had decided to visit her for a few days, so it was just Gwen and Pamela and me riding home with Liz and her dad.

Mr. Price was a willing listener to all the stories about the ship and its passengers. We didn't mention Pamela's mom—there were enough tales to tell without that.

"Everyone's a sailor at heart," he said. "And if he doesn't have his own boat, he likes to hear about people who do."

"So what's been happening in Silver Spring?" Liz asked him, leaning over to run her hand across his cheek. "Not thinking of growing a beard, are you?"

From the back, their hair color looked remarkably the same, except that we could see a spot on her dad's head where the scalp was beginning to show through.

"Just bumming around this weekend," he said. "And it's one way to get Nathan to bed—threaten to rub my grizzly cheek against his, and he goes screeching up the stairs." Liz laughed. "He's lost his first tooth. He'll want to tell you all about it."

Because we reached my street before the others, Mr. Price offered to let me off first, so we could at least dislodge some of the luggage. "Your dad know you're coming?" he asked.

"He knows the ship got in, but I'd thought I might be staying on for the final cruise."

"Yeah, that was a shame," Mr. Price said. "Messed up a lot of plans, I imagine." He got out and went to the trunk for my bag, then took Pamela and Gwen on home. I said I'd call them later.

I went up the steps to the porch, letting my duffel bang against my leg, thinking how much thicker the foliage seemed on the trees than when I left.

It was good to be home. I was thinking about Mitch and how he would be feeling walking into his house in Vienna, Maryland. I didn't know what it looked like. Didn't know a lot about his family at all. But I knew how much he liked the idea of home—the trees, the marsh, the muskrats, his boat. I couldn't identify with some of that, except that it was his idea of home, and that's what made it special.

I opened the door, then stopped and sniffed the air. What was that odor? I wondered. Something familiar. Closing the door behind me, I set my bag down and heard a noise upstairs. Voices. I had just started up when Sylvia appeared in the hallway above, her hair piled on top of her head, a paintbrush in one hand.

She stared. "Alice!" she cried.

"Yeah," I laughed. "I live here. I think."

"You're back!" She turned. "Alice is back," she called over her shoulder and Dad appeared behind her.

"Well, well!" he said, smiling and wiping his forehead. "Thought you were staying on! Cat's out of the bag, I guess, and here we wanted to surprise you."

"What?"

"We're painting your room," said Sylvia. "You said that it was time to get rid of the jungle look and that if you had a choice now, you would go with ocean blue, so . . ."

I ran up the stairs. "You remembered?" Sylvia and I had been looking at colors for the powder room last spring, and I'd fallen in love with a color called ocean blue, though she'd picked something else.

"We're not done yet. We still have two walls to go," Dad said as I whipped pass him.

"Oh my God!" I gasped. "I love it." I turned and looked at them bewildered. "But . . . I'm leaving for college."

"Well, we thought maybe this would lure you home from time to time," Sylvia said. "A new bedspread and curtains go with it. Crate and Barrel has some wonderful stuff, but we'll let you pick them out."

I started to throw my arms around her, but she held me off. There were paint spots all over her, so I hugged Dad from behind.

"Listen, kiddo," Sylvia said with a laugh, "the immediate problem is where you're going to sleep tonight."

I assumed Lester's old room, then realized they had moved all my stuff in there: headboard, mattress, dresser. A lightbulb went on. "Easy," I said. "Lester's. He still hasn't rented that room in his apartment, right?"

Dad chuckled. "He'll be delighted," he said.

"Yeah. Right. I've got a ton of laundry to do, so I'll do it there. He owes me one anyway."

"For . . . ?" Dad asked.

"On general principles," I said.

Dad gave me his car keys and I was off.

I called Les on my cell to tell him I was coming, but he didn't pick up, and I just drove on. If he wasn't home, I'd stay at Gwen's.

I decided I loved my home too—Silver Spring, I mean. The shady streets—that was something I'd missed this summer. Trees. Tall trees. The closer you get to the shore, the shorter the trees. Could I ever live on Tangier Island, without any really tall trees? I didn't think so.

As I drove, Silver Spring became Takoma Park, and the trees were even taller, the houses older, larger—relics of big families and bygone days. I pulled up to the yellow Victorian house with its wide porch and brown trim, the staircase at the side leading up to Lester's apartment. Lester's car was there and so was Paul's. I took my bag out of the backseat, went up the staircase, and rang the bell.

"Well, look who's back!" Les said when he opened the door. He was wearing an old pair of shorts and a torn tee and had a Dr

Pepper in one hand. "Thought for a while we'd have to call the Coast Guard." I grinned and walked on by him.

"Guess who's going to be sleeping in your spare room for the next week," I said.

"Whoa, whose idea was that?" he cried, but I think he was still smiling.

"Dad and Sylvia are painting my bedroom. They thought they still had two more weeks. Surprise, surprise."

"Well darn, there goes the girlfriend," said Les.

"What girlfriend?"

"There isn't one yet. Naw, it's okay. We'll put you to work. How are you, anyway? You're looking good. Got some sun, I see."

"What you see are freckles," I told him. "It was an experience and I'm glad I went. Got any more to drink?"

"Help yourself," he said.

I went to the fridge and got a 7UP. "I really will help around the place, " I said. "I'm not just here to crash."

"That's good, because Paul and I have a little project: girl bait."

"Girl bait? I'm supposed to be girl bait?"

"Not you. Come out and see." He led me back outside. We went down to the backyard, and there on cinder blocks was a sailboat. And Paul.

I stared. "You're serious? You guys bought this thing to attract women?"

"Actually, it belongs to Paul, but I get sailing rights if I help fix it up. A Flying Scot."

Paul beamed. "A nineteen-footer," he added.

It was in need of . . . well, everything. They had scraped off the paint about ten inches down all the way around, and I couldn't tell if some things needed tightening or replacing altogether. My tactless remark didn't seem to dampen their enthusiasm any. Paul ran his hand fondly over a smooth area.

"Well," I said, backpedaling as best I could, "I guess it would attract me. I mean, I'd be curious about the kind of guys who would put all that work into maintaining a sailboat. Like, it shows commitment, and if there's anything a woman loves—"

"Wasn't exactly what we had in mind," Paul said. "But, hey, welcome back, Alice. Heard you had quite a trip. Grab a sander there and a scraper, and we'll let you tell us all about your fateful adventure."

What was there about boats, anyway? Or was this just the month for painting, for refurnishing, for getting ready? Then I thought that I could invite the girls over here to help sand and paint, so I picked up a scraper and began.

Patrick: *So how does it feel to be home?*

Me: *Super terrific, except I'm not at home. Dad and Sylvia are painting my bedroom, so I'm crashing with some guys for a week.*

Patrick: *Twenty questions or what?*

Me: *Ha. I'm staying at Lester's. They don't have a third roommate yet. Paul bought an old sailboat, and I'm helping fix it up. Says he'll take me out in it sometime as payment.*

Patrick: *You haven't had enough of the sea?*

Me: *Hey, he's tall, handsome, has his MA . . .*

Patrick: *Uh-oh. She goes for older men.*

Me: *So what are the female students like so far in Barcelona?*

Patrick: *All babes.*

Me: *Any in particular?*

Patrick: *All of them.*

Me: *I'll think of you when I'm out on the bay with Paul, the wind blowing my hair.*

Patrick: *Gotta go. The lovelies await.*

Monday at Lester's was maybe the most beautiful day of the summer. It wasn't supposed to be. We were only days away from August, and August in the nation's capital, anywhere *near* the capital, is usually beastly—meaning that everything living, except at the zoo, takes off for the beach or the mountains. But on this day the humidity dropped along with the temperature, and I decided to play housewife while Les and Paul were at work. I started with the refrigerator.

I'd hung around Chef Carlo enough when I'd been on galley duty to see how he came up with the wonderful soups and stews he made for the crew dinners. He made them from whatever extra food he'd cooked for the passengers that never made it into the dining room. From these, he extracted meat and veggies, rice and noodles, and created these amazing concoctions, different every night.

I pulled out every leftover I could find and set it on the table: an ear of corn, some Wendy's fries, a dab of Popeye's red beans and rice, a McDonald's burger minus the bun. . . . I chopped and shredded, added two cans of V8, a chicken bouillon cube, some sautéed onion, a little minced garlic . . . *Stop! Stop!* I told myself, when I found a breaded pork chop in the back of the fridge and discovered it wasn't breaded at all, just moldy.

When the guys got home that evening with fish and chips, I had the beds made, a load of laundry done, the bathroom scrubbed, the table set, and a pot of soup on the stove.

They were clearly pleased.

"Maybe we should be looking for a live-in chef and butler, not a grad student," Paul said, his glasses fogging as he leaned over the soup pot to savor the smell. He strolled through the living room and looked around. "The apartment straightened up and—what's this? Laundry? Folded, no less?"

"Except that I didn't know what was whose, so you'll have to sort the underwear," I told him. "And I'm missing a yellow sock of my own, so if you find it clinging to your boxers, let me know."

"So they taught you to be useful?" Les said, opening a beer as we sat down to dinner.

"I'll say. Cracking crabs, man overboard, *Seascape* gripper . . ."

"What's that?" asked Paul. "Fishing tackle?"

"No. It's the way you grip a passenger's arm and he grips yours when he's going up or down a step, getting into a lifeboat and stuff—gives you a steadier grip."

"And 'man overboard,' what's that all about?"

I told them about the incident with Pamela's mom.

"Wow." Les leaned back in his chair. "She's done things like this before?"

"Not in front of an audience."

"Hardly got the reaction she expected," Paul guessed.

"No. Pamela thinks she thought her dad would be frantically looking for her, joining the rescue—"

"And hugging her to him when he discovered she'd been hiding somewhere, watching the whole thing?" Les asked incredulously.

"That he'd be so glad she was alive that his true feelings would come out and he'd drop Meredith and remarry her—I don't know," I said.

"Where is she now?" Paul asked. "Pamela doesn't live with her, does she?"

"No, fortunately. Mrs. Jones has an apartment in Glenmont, and Pamela will be going to school in New York this fall." I ate the last fry on the platter. "Would it be okay with you guys if I had the girls over here one night this week? It'd be great to have one last get-together before we all scatter."

"Sure," said Les, and for the first time, he didn't make some remark like, *Just let me know so I can be out for the evening*, as he usually did when I mentioned Pamela. But he added, "They could even help with the boat, if they wanted."

"They might," I told him.

Les made some coffee, and we sat around talking about what needed to be done to the sailboat. I couldn't help studying Paul. I'd always been attracted to him in a weird sort of way. Slim, bespectacled, introverted, and shy, he was a geology major; and for a long time that's the way I thought of him, as an intellectual type whose most intimate relationships were with rocks—billion-year-old rocks. And then I found out he was a ballroom dance instructor and a bluegrass musician in his spare time. I mean, go figure.

You can play with a band, though, and you're still the only one playing your particular instrument. You can be a dance instructor and still hold your partner out away from your body. I wondered if he was using his hobbies as a front, to make him appear far more social than he was.

But suddenly, with the purchase of the boat, he was like a

little kid. How fast it would probably sail, how he'd signed up for lessons this fall . . .

"What are you going to name her?" I asked.

He had an embarrassed smile on his face as he lowered his coffee cup. *"Fancy Pants,"* he said.

Les and I broke into laughter.

"Fancy Pants?" I cried.

"You're serious?" said Les.

"That's her name," said Paul.

"Uh . . . somebody you know?" I asked.

"My grandmother."

"Your *grandmother*?"

"Get's better by the minute," said Les.

I wondered what Mitch would say about this. But Paul explained: "Whenever she got really dressed up to go somewhere, my grandfather called her 'Fancy Pants.' But it was Grandma who loved the water, the sea. When I bought this boat, I kept thinking how much she would have loved sailing in it, so why not name it after her? Somehow 'Fancy Pants' sounds better than 'Ursula Birgit.'"

Couldn't argue with that.

"And you can tell each of your respective girlfriends you named it after her," I said.

"Now, that's an idea," said Paul.

Les and Paul cleaned up the kitchen while I got the TV all to myself. As he passed the living room, Les asked, "Any calls for me today, Alice?"

"No. Were you expecting one?"

"Probably not. But I sent out a new batch of resumes last week, and I listed our landline as well as my cell. I'm applying for some really nice spots, so . . . Well, if someone calls, be professional."

"Why me? I'm not applying for a job."

"You know what I mean. It might be a woman. Don't give her the third degree."

"You think I'd do that?"

"I'm just saying. If you know I'm waiting for an important call, you'll be ready."

"Of course I will."

"Good. I'm especially interested in a job at the Basswood Conference Center in West Virginia."

"Are you expecting any calls, Paul?" I asked when he came in to watch a program.

"No, I think I'll stay working where I am for a while," he said. "Now that I've got a boat, I'd like to be fairly close to the bay."

"Can't leave old *Fancy Pants*," said Les.

I was on Lester's computer most of the next day. I'd already told my friends that my room was being painted and I was staying at Lester's for a week until it was ready. Now I was desperately trying to catch up with Facebook and e-mail messages from potential roommates, and I found that many had given up on me. I hadn't responded fast enough or told them enough, or they had opted for the "experience" of letting the university pick a roommate for them.

A girl named Rainey said she hoped I wouldn't be offended, but she was really looking for someone more into the arts. Briana said she was Irish and wanted to know my "heritage." I didn't even answer. Kayla said her mom wanted her to room with a Christian.

For God's sake, I thought, *we're not getting married!* If I couldn't have Gwen for a roommate, I just wanted someone compatible. I finally agreed to room with a girl from Ohio named Amber because we looked at each other's pictures on Facebook, and she said she loved my freckles and I said I loved her tattoos.

On Wednesday morning I was about to call Pamela with the news when she called me.

"How you doing?" I said, not daring to ask if she'd visited her mom yet. She and her mom hadn't communicated since that awful man-overboard night. And when Pamela didn't answer right away, I asked, "Have you heard from your mom?"

"She just called," Pamela said. "She's been in the hospital. Wants me to come take her home."

20
BEING PROFESSIONAL

"What can I possibly do?" I asked.

Pamela had pulled up in Meredith's Honda, and I slid in beside her.

"Just help me get her back to her apartment. Moral support, if nothing else. I don't especially want to be in a car alone with her, and I'm not sure what to say."

"That makes two of us. Things got pretty weird the night she reported herself missing."

I was surprised at Pamela's response. "She didn't report herself missing! I wish people would quit using that term."

I glanced over at her, wondering, then faced forward again. I didn't know what to say to *Pamela*!

She exhaled, and her hands went slack for a moment on

the steering wheel. "All we really know is that she thinks she saw someone fall overboard and got emotional about it, then holed up somewhere for a while. She may have been confused, it may have been deliberate, it may not have been her at all who reported that someone fell—or whatever . . . People shouldn't jump to conclusions!"

What was happening here? I wondered.

"Okay," I said. "Point taken. What's the latest? Why has she been in the hospital?"

The sharpness went out of Pamela's voice. "She just called and said she'd been in an accident with her car—nothing serious, I guess—and was kept in the hospital overnight for observation. They wouldn't release her today unless she had someone to drive her home—said she couldn't take a taxi."

"All right."

I settled back in the seat, my eyes fixed on the white crocheted cross that dangled from Meredith's rearview mirror—a symbol of her faith and her nursing profession, I guessed. There was a tiny tissue holder attached to the dashboard and a collection of odds and ends in a console tray—lipstick, change, parking ticket, comb. . . .

"I'm totally freaked out," Pamela said finally. "Everything's happened so fast."

"I know."

"I mean, the cruise, Dad and Meredith being there, Mom showing up, the generator breaking down, getting ready for New York, and now this."

"Everything coming at you at once," I said.

"How am I supposed to deal with it all?"

"Just like you're doing, Pamela. One thing at a time."

"Thanks for coming with me," she said, glancing over.

At Holy Cross we had to go through a parking gate, and Pamela finally found a place in the visitors' lot. I went inside with her. Pamela's mom was sitting in the lobby in a wheelchair, an attendant on the bench next to her.

Mrs. Jones, or Sherry Conners, or whatever she was calling herself now, gave us an impatient smile. "I've been sitting here for thirty-five minutes," she immediately complained to Pamela. "It's a simple ride home, and I could have taken a taxi if they'd let me."

"Hospital rules," the attendant said.

"I just came along for the ride," I said, hoping to make it easier on Pamela.

Mrs. Jones ignored me completely. "You should have pulled up here in front, Pamela. Now I have to wait even longer while you get the car," she said.

Pamela turned on her heels. "I'll be right back," she said flatly, and headed for the entrance.

I stood awkwardly off to the side, wondering what I was supposed to do. Pamela certainly didn't need help getting the car she had just parked, but staying here with her mom . . .

I had no choice. The attendant looked at me impassively, took out her cell phone, checked caller ID, and slipped it back into the pocket of her smock.

What should I say to Mrs. Jones? Had I ever felt this awkward in my life? I wondered. Yes, plenty of times. But not in the same way. Not with an adult who, by all rights, should be the one feeling awkward.

"She had to park at the very end of the lot," I said finally. "But it shouldn't be long."

Silence. Another attendant appeared, pushing a young woman in a wheelchair. The patient, her brown hair pulled back away from her face and fastened with a rubber band, was holding a baby wrapped in a pink checkered blanket. All we could see of it was a pink knit cap peeking out and one tiny fist. The mother was smiling proudly.

It made me smile too, and Mrs. Jones's attendant looked over and cooed.

"The happiest place in the hospital—the maternity ward," she said. And to the young mother, "Let's see that fine baby."

The second attendant wheeled her over, and the young mother held her baby up. A little red, scrunched-up face. The mother beamed at her, then at us.

"What's her name?" I asked, grateful for this brief interlude.

"Rebecca Ann, named after my great-aunt," the young woman said, then looked expectantly toward the door where a car was pulling up. Her husband leaped out, grinning at everyone as he came through the door, and assisted his wife outside.

"I remember when Pamela was born, and I carried her out like that," Mrs. Jones said pensively.

"Did she have any hair?" I asked, glad I thought of something to say.

"A little—like corn silk," Mrs. Jones said, and fell silent again.

The Honda pulled up at last.

"That yours?" the attendant asked me, and I nodded.

She wheeled Mrs. Jones outside, and I held the passenger door open. Pamela's mom got inside. The attendant helped fasten her seat belt, shut the door, and took the wheelchair back inside. I got in the backseat.

Wordlessly, Pamela drove to the gate, paid the parking fee, and exited the lot, heading once more for the beltway.

Mrs. Jones reached up and fingered the crocheted cross. "Whose car is this?"

"Meredith's," Pamela said.

"Bill wouldn't let you use his car?"

"He's at work, Mom."

When we reached the ramp for 495, Pamela studied her driver's side mirror and, when she saw an opening, merged onto the beltway and into the middle lane.

"I'm sorry to cause you all this trouble," Mrs. Jones said at last. "I must have nodded off before I drifted into a ditch last night and got this big bump on my head—you can't see it under my hair. The hospital kept me overnight for observation."

Nodded off, my ass. I was sure Pamela and I were thinking the same thing. Neither of us said a word.

Mrs. Jones continued: "I called my friend Dorothy first, but she's in Towson today. She'll go with me tomorrow to get my car, though. It's impounded on some lot."

"Well, I'm glad I could help," Pamela said.

More silence.

"I'm such a bother to everyone," Mrs. Jones said finally, her voice shaky. "When you live alone, with no one to see or care that you get home okay, it's scary."

"I'm sure it is, Mom," Pamela said.

We reached the Georgia Avenue exit and went north toward Glenmont. When we reached her apartment complex, Mrs. Jones got out.

Pamela said, "Are you going to be all right now, Mom? Do you want us to come in and fix you breakfast or something?"

"I didn't get a blessed wink of sleep the whole night," her mom said. "I'll just make myself some tea and go to bed."

"We could come in if you want," Pamela repeated.

Mrs. Jones glanced toward me in the backseat. "Another time." She closed the door, turned, and started up the walk to the entrance.

When she was safely inside, I got out and climbed in front beside Pamela, uninvited. Was this part of the reason Pamela wanted me along? I wondered. So she wouldn't be invited in?

The car moved forward, Pamela reached over and turned on the radio, and she drove me back to Lester's without saying much at all.

* * *

Some of the sultriness of summer returned, and I could feel my helpfulness around the apartment eke away. Dad said the only thing left to paint in my room was the trim, and the paint smell should dissipate in a few days. If Les could come over on Sunday, he said, and help move my furniture back in, I'd have some time to enjoy my room before I left for college.

On Thursday, I made the beds, put a load in the washing machine, and made some deviled eggs, but by eleven, the humidity overcame me. Mr. Watts's old house had air-conditioning units in the windows of most of the rooms, but they weren't strong enough on the second story to keep us sufficiently cool. I stretched out on the sofa in my shorts and a cutoff T-shirt and fanned myself with an old *Sports Illustrated*.

There was the sound of the refrigerator's hum in the kitchen, the rhythmic churning of the washer going off and on, a couple of crows cawing back and forth somewhere in the distance.

I was in and out of sleep . . . that state of stupor where your arms and legs feel deliciously numb and weightless. I seemed to be talking with Mitch, and we were getting ready to go somewhere—to see Patrick, I think! Maybe I was going to call him first, but then he must have called me because the phone was ringing. As the *Sports Illustrated* slid to the floor, I realized that the phone really was ringing, and I was in Lester's apartment and I was supposed to be professional and . . . "Hello," I said, "Lester McKinley's . . ."

There was a pause at the other end of the line. Then a

woman's voice said, "This is the Basswood Conference Center. Is Mr. McKinley in?"

Awk! Wake up! Wake up! I told myself, and knew my voice sounded husky. "I'm sorry. Mr. McKinley is out right now," I told her, sounding as though I had just wakened, because I *had*. Maybe she thought I was a girlfriend and we were lazily sleeping away the day together.

"And you are?" the woman asked.

"Uh . . . Mr. McKinley's secretary," I said. "May I take a message?"

"Please," she said. "Would you ask him to call Rita in Mr. Burns's office?"

"Just a moment," I said, and dived for a pencil and the back of an envelope, my mind racing, my mouth dry.

She gave me the number and said that Mr. Burns had some questions about Lester's resume. I assured her that Mr. McKinley would get back to her as soon as possible.

"Actually, I'm leaving the office now for the afternoon, so tomorrow will be fine," she said.

When I hung up, my hand left a sweaty imprint on the phone.

What had I done? What had I said? Was I even awake enough to hold a coherent conversation? Why did Rita what's-her-name have to call here, anyway? Why hadn't she called Les on his cell? What would I tell him? That he'd received perhaps the most important call of his life, affecting his very future, and I'd answered it half asleep and said I was his *secretary*?

By the time the guys came home that evening, I had made chicken salad out of the rotisserie chicken that Paul had brought home the night before. I'd walked over to a farmer's market on Wayne Avenue for fresh tomatoes and sweet corn and had also baked a batch of brownies.

"Heeey!" said Les, and gave me a really appreciative smile—the kind that indicates honest-to-God gratitude and affection.

Paul, burnished bronze now by the sun, put it more bluntly: "I swear, Alice, if you were ten years older and could pass my genetics test, I'd propose," he said.

With a guy like Paul, you can never tell when he's joking, because he's usually so serious.

"And if you were a few years younger and didn't walk around with a genetics test in your pocket, I'd accept," I said, and that got a laugh. "What's it for, anyway? You're not a white supremacist, are you?"

"Oh, God no!" he said. "It just makes sense to be sure we're not carriers of the same diseases. I'm a big believer in the power of recessive genes."

"Oh, boy, I'll bet pillow talk with you is really exciting," I said, and he blushed a little. I guess he's not sure when I'm joking either.

"Oh, I wouldn't bring it up right away," Paul said, taking a seat at the dinner table. "But there are certain hereditary diseases more common to Scandinavians or Middle Eastern women, for example, than to other nationalities. It's fascinating, but I'd never use it to fall in love."

"I should hope not," I said. And then, because I had everyone in a good mood, I said casually, "You got a call from the Basswood Conference Center, Les." I handed the envelope to him with my scribbles on it.

"Yeah? Yeah?" Les grabbed the envelope excitedly and read the message. "Rita Ornosky. Did she say what her job was?"

"No. She just said that Mr. Burns had a few questions about your resume and that she'd be away from the office this afternoon, and you should call tomorrow." I motioned him to the table, where Paul was already buttering his ear of corn.

"Damn! What was I doing that I didn't answer my cell?" Les wondered aloud.

"It's okay. She said tomorrow would be fine."

Les was still trying to figure it out. "What time did she call?"

"Uh . . . about eleven forty-five, I think. Just before lunch."

"Arrrgh!" said Les. "I was in the restroom and left my cell phone on my desk. Why does this always happen to me?"

"Because you don't want to be one of those guys you hear sitting in a stall laughing and talking to himself?" said Paul.

Les sat down finally. "So tell me everything this Rita person said." He was looking directly at me. "Were you professional? What did you say?"

"I said you weren't here at the moment but you would call back as soon as possible."

"And did she ask who you were? Why you were answering my phone? I hope she doesn't think I still live at home with my mother."

"Oh, she doesn't," I said quickly.

"How do you know?"

"I told her I was your secretary."

"My *secretary*?"

"Well, she asked who I was, and you told me to sound professional, so . . ."

"Holy shit! What are we here? A corporation?"

At least Lester was on the defensive now, not me.

"Okay," I said. "I'll call her back and say I'm not your secretary."

"No!"

"Come on, Les, don't sweat it," Paul said. "Call tomorrow and say you'd be glad to answer whatever questions Mr. Burns has."

Lester settled down. "You're right," he said.

"Unless you *want* to be a corporation," I put in. "The Lester McKinley Institute of Female Studies."

"Center for the Advancement of Philosophy Majors," said Paul.

"Enough, enough," said Les, and dug into his food in earnest.

When the phone rang halfway through dinner, though, he almost knocked over his chair to get the landline.

It wasn't Rita Ornosky, however. It was Mr. Watts. He told Les he'd distinctly detected the scent of brownies baking this afternoon and what did he have to do? Beg? Les told him we'd bring some down.

I smiled. "Actually, I was planning to take him a whole meal," I said. "Chicken salad, deviled eggs, corn, the works. I'll put it together." I dug my fork into the chewy chocolate of a brownie, swished it through the glob of melting cream on top, and let them pleasure my tongue. Was there anything as delectable as this? I wondered.

Later, after I'd come back from a long chat with Mr. Watts, I sat down in the spare bedroom to e-mail Patrick. The day had gone so well, considering. Then I found Patrick had already e-mailed me:

Heard from Mom yesterday. They're doing okay. Seem to like living in Wisconsin. Big news! They're going to visit me in Barcelona for a month over Christmas.

21
BREAKING AWAY

I invited Gwen and Liz and Pamela to Lester's for a sailboat-scraping party on Saturday. It would probably be our last get-together before we left for college—two of us were leaving the second full week of August, two the week after that. There was *lots* of prep work to do.

When I told Les, he said he and Paul would bring us a kebab dinner and whatever else our hearts desired. *Deal!* I'd planned to just order pizza, but Greek food sounded a lot better.

The weather cooperated—it does that sometimes. You think you're a prisoner of summer, with the hygrometer stuck on "hot and soupy," and then a taste of fall rolls through. You wake up to drier air, something clean and crisp, and you go, *Yes!*

"I didn't think I ever wanted to see a ship again," Liz said when she got out of the car.

"You gals are looking good," Les said when I brought them around back, where he and Paul had already been at work for an hour. Sweat soaked through their tanks, glistening on their shoulders.

"So this is *Fancy Pants*," said Gwen, walking slowly around it. "How many does it hold?"

"Four, max," said Paul.

"Just right for us girls!" said Liz.

Les laughed. "Start scraping."

It was laborious, but it didn't seem so bad because we were part of a team, a crew—and the four of us knew a lot about crew work.

"I got an e-mail from Flavian," Gwen said. "He heard that the cruise line canceled the whole fall season for the *Spellbound*."

I stopped scraping. "Oh, man, sounds like they're going under."

"They're gone," said Gwen. "No backup, no reserves . . ."

"That's scary," said Les.

The four of us girls stopped working for a moment, like we were observing a moment of silence. "All those plans—the ads, the brochures, blueprints, and stuff—just, like, washed away. They took a big chance and didn't make it," I said.

"And you can't even go back to mama; you declare bankruptcy," said Liz.

I rubbed my hand over the place I'd just sanded. "It's bad

enough when it affects only you and your own bank account. What does it feel like to have a whole staff and crew go down with the ship?"

"Could we stop with the sinking ship analogy?" said Paul.

"Oops! Sorry, Paul," I said. "Don't worry, when you take *Fancy Pants* out for the first time, the rest of us will be safely watching from shore."

"You wonder, though, where the rest of the crew will go this fall, everyone drifting off—uh, sailing off, I mean—heading in different directions," Gwen said.

"Mitch will be trapping," I told them.

"Lauren was supposed to work the *Spellbound* cruises," Pamela said. "She told me she might move in with her boyfriend if that didn't happen. Curtis will probably get a job on a freighter."

"What about you, Les?" Gwen asked. "What's going on in your life these days?"

"I've got an interview at the Basswood Conference Center in West Virginia. Would be great if that came through."

"Doing what?" asked Pamela.

"Actually, as assistant director. Companies use the place for conferences and retreats, with a back-to-nature venue."

"Great!" said Liz. "And, Paul! What are you going to do with *Fancy Pants* when winter sets in? Don't people usually think about getting their boats ready in the spring?"

"That's why I got the boat so cheap," Paul said. "Nobody wanted to buy it and store it through the winter. Except me, maybe. After I complete my sailing course, I'd like to take a leave of absence and go cruising off the Florida coast."

"In *this*? With no cabin?" Liz asked.

"Well, I'd go solo to start."

"I can see the headlines now: 'Maryland Man Missing Among the Manatee,'" said Gwen.

"I'll become a modern-day Gauguin. Sail to some faraway island, marry a native or two, raise my own crew, and come back to see how the rest of you are doing."

Around seven, he and Les stopped to go get dinner laid out. When they called us in later, we found the table set, kebabs on a platter, rice in a bowl, pita bread, hummus, feta cheese, and olives.

"Paul, you've got it made," I told him. "First you take the woman of your dreams out for a sail on the *Fancy Pants*, then you bring her back for a Greek dinner, with candles, and to whatever you propose to do next, she'll say yes."

"Darn! Why didn't we think of this before?" said Les.

We couldn't believe that the breeze coming in the window actually made us chilly. For an end to a special evening, Les said he'd pull out the cast-iron grate he'd stored under the back steps since March and let us have an outdoor fire.

"Paul and I are going to clean up the kitchen, then some guys are coming over later for poker. The patio's yours for the evening, so enjoy!" he said.

Les set up the grate on a heavy wood table, where we propped our feet. Once the sun set, we watched the flames dance and spit, and the fire lit up our faces so that we could see each other in the dark.

I decided to get the bad news over with, so I said, flat out, "Patrick's parents are going to spend a month with him in Barcelona over Christmas."

"They'll love it! " said Gwen. "Their own personal guide to—" She stopped short. "Oh Alice! Weren't you planning a surprise visit then?"

"Yeah. I was going to tell him, of course. I was waiting for my final paycheck to see if I could swing it. Then I got a text from him. . . ."

"That really sucks!" said Liz. "Did you tell him?"

I shook my head. "No, and I'm not going to. He didn't know I was planning to come, and he's excited about showing his folks around."

"Maybe you could still go and . . . no, I guess not," said Pamela.

I sighed. "The Longs will naturally want him all to themselves, and so would I. He'd be pulled in two different directions. Maybe I'll go over spring break. We'll see."

We watched the shadows appear and disappear on our faces. All of us had a sort of reddish glow.

"That's a bummer," said Gwen. "And I get home from a cruise that's been canceled to find the battery's dead in the car I bought from my brother. But Austin gave it a jump start."

"Austin's back in the picture?" I asked.

She gave me a sheepish little smile. "Yeah, we went to a movie. I guess we just missed each other too much. Haven't heard yet what he was up to over the summer, though."

"Will you tell him about Flavian?" Liz asked.

"Sure. He has no worries there."

"No?" I was surprised. "You and Flavian were . . . well . . ."

"We were wrapped up in a blanket and that's all that happened," Gwen said. "I'm not crazy."

We were quiet awhile. Then Liz turned to me again. "Maybe you should just take that money you saved for Barcelona and do something else with it. Go spend Christmas with Mitch in the marsh."

We laughed.

Gwen bumped my foot with her own. "He'd like that."

"I may visit him sometime, we'll see," I said. "But it's also just really nice having a guy friend, you know? Right now I'm going to concentrate on settling in at Maryland and decorating my new bedroom at home. Les is coming by tomorrow to help move my furniture back in."

"Hey, I met my roommate at Bennington on Facebook," said Liz. "She seems nice. A music major."

"What does she play? The tuba?" Gwen kidded. "She'll practice in your room."

"Voice and piano," Liz said. "I'm so psyched to go and get started."

"All I know about Amber, besides her tattoos, is that she seems laid-back, casual," I told them. "Didn't send me a virtual questionnaire to fill out. After all the excitement of this past summer, I could do with a little take-life-as-it-comes."

Interesting how you never think of measuring your friends, but as we sat leaning back in our patio chairs, legs stretched out before us, I realized that Gwen had the shortest legs and Pamela had the longest. Liz's were about as long as Pamela's, mine were slightly longer than Gwen's. . . .

"When do you have to be in New York?" Gwen asked Pamela.

Pamela didn't answer right away, and I stopped measuring legs and looked over at her.

"I may not go," Pamela answered.

I jerked up so suddenly, my feet slid off the table.

"Pamela? Why?" I asked, just now realizing that she had been unusually quiet all day, that there hadn't been the back-and-forth banter with Les that usually went on between them.

"I think Mom needs me," she said, shrinking down into herself.

We couldn't believe what we were hearing and stared at each other, then back at Pamela.

"Pamela, what are you *thinking*?" said Gwen. "You haven't officially pulled out, have you?"

"Not yet."

"Then *talk to us*!" I pleaded.

Pamela wouldn't look any of us in the eye. She wrapped her arms more tightly around her body. "Mom's just . . . so vulnerable now."

I thought of the way her mom had criticized her when we

picked her up at the hospital the other day. *Vulnerable* is not the adjective I would have used.

"Pamela, you've got a scholarship! You may never have another chance like this!" Liz cried. "After all the grief your mom has put you through, I can't believe it!"

"I know." Pamela's voice was soft, like a kitten's mew. "There on the ship, the morning she disembarked, all wrapped up in her raincoat—I was watching from on deck. She just looked so pitiful and alone. Dad and Meredith have started a new life, and here I am—about to leave too—and . . . she has nobody."

"One of the first lessons of life is that we have to live with the consequences of our actions," Gwen said. "And when you consider all your mom has done—"

"I know, I know. She really hurt Dad and me when she left us that time, and she's behaved like a lunatic more than once. But still . . . she just doesn't have many friends, and I could take courses in theater arts here at Montgomery College. I could live with Mom, and . . . she got some brochures for me . . ."

We sat in stunned silence.

"It's your mom's idea, then," Gwen said finally.

"She wouldn't have suggested it if there wasn't a way I could get the same thing here."

It was as though Pam had been brainwashed. Where was our fiery, gutsy Pamela who had sat with her hands over her ears on the floor of her bedroom when her mom threw gravel at the window, the Pamela who refused to go down and open the door? Living at home with a manipulative mom and taking courses at Montgomery College was not the same as being on your own in New York City, studying theater arts.

"There's a side of her you don't even know," Pamela said to break the silence. "Remember how devastated I was when I found out I was pregnant? I didn't feel comfortable telling Meredith, and I certainly wasn't about to tell Dad. And remember how you insisted I tell Mom, Alice, and went with me to her apartment and she didn't jump all over me or anything?"

I remembered, and yes, I did give Mrs. Jones points for that.

"Well, what I didn't tell you is that later on, before I miscarried, when Mom discussed my options with me, she said whatever I decided was up to me. If I decided to have an abortion, she'd go with me and see that it was done right. If I wanted to have the baby and put it up for adoption, she'd help me through it. But she also said that I could move in with her, and she'd fix up the spare room for both me and the baby. She said she'd help me raise it so that I could still date and have a life and everything. . . . I mean, how many moms would willingly offer to do all that for their daughters? She even showed me the catalog of baby clothes and furniture, and she had them all picked out and a design of how to rearrange the room."

I was listening to Pamela, but different pictures were bobbing about in my head.

"Pamela," I said, "do you remember when she first moved back here from Colorado, after her boyfriend walked out on her? How she fixed up that spare bedroom then, without even telling you, and how you reacted to it then?"

Pamela gave me a quick glance and looked away again. "Yes . . ."

"Why didn't you do it?"

She looked a little startled. "Why didn't I move back in with her then?"

"Yes."

"Because she would've controlled my life! I already had a home and a room. But it's different, offering to take in a pregnant daughter and her baby. That's real sacrifice."

"Pamela, don't you see?" said Liz. "It's all about her! She's playing the sacrificial mother! The long-suffering woman who was going to sacrifice her life for her child and grandchild."

"And she's still the mom who was so concerned about you and her family's welfare that she rode off into the sunset with a guy she barely knew until it all fell apart," I said.

Pamela glared at us. "But now she needs me. She thinks she seriously hurt her shoulder when she ran her car off the road and said she can hardly lift a coffee cup. She needs someone to be there and—" Pamela stopped and closed her eyes. "I'm so damned mixed up."

So was I. There were so many layers here. Why would Mrs. Jones want to deny her daughter a chance to pursue her dreams in New York? Could she be envious? Was that part of it, along with her loneliness? Did she need someone to help her with her drinking problem?

"Pamela," I said, "if you really, truly want to help your mom, go to New York. If you don't, you're saying, 'I think you're too weak to handle things here on your own, Mom. You're so weak that your only child has to give up her career plans, her scholarship, and move in with you.'"

"But what if she really *has* hurt her shoulder?" Pamela said, facing me now. "She *does* need help."

"Yes, and before you leave, you'll find someone who can come by regularly to check up on her," I said. "You know her friends. You'll call them and tell them about her accident, and you'll get her to an AA program. You said she used to attend those meetings."

"Don't be an enabler, Pamela," said Gwen. "The sooner your mom knows that she can't go on disrupting other people's lives, the sooner she'll look for her own solutions. You'll do everything you can to help before you leave, but you'll still leave."

We sat for several minutes without speaking, watching the tongues of red and orange in the iron grate, listening to the occasional rise and fall of men's voices coming through the open windows above.

"It doesn't . . . seem selfish?" Pamela asked finally.

"What? For you to go to New York, the chance of a lifetime, or for your mom to ask you to give it up?" Gwen said.

Pamela already knew the answer, so she didn't respond right away. "Okay," she said. "I'll go."

Our collective sigh of relief was audible. I leaned back in my chair, limp.

"Pamela," Liz said, "how do we know that after all we've said here, you won't have another talk with your mom and let her change your mind?"

"Because," Pamela answered, "I'd already written a letter to New York, telling them I wasn't coming, and . . . just before I came over here this afternoon, I tore it up. I just . . . I needed additional reinforcements, that's all."

"The Enforcers, that's us," said Gwen, smiling at her.

"But do you *promise*?" Liz wanted to know.

"I promise," Pamela told her. "You can even come over tomorrow and help me pack."

Was it always this hard, I wondered—this breaking away? Always so painful to move from one place to the next? Always so exciting and wonderful and . . . yes, so scary to make a pact with life that no matter what it might throw your way, you would deal?

"Know what?" I said. "I think—right now—we ought to make plans to go to California together."

Three faces turned my way, staring.

"When we're through with college, I mean. Like we talked about once. After we graduate, we should take a couple of weeks and just *go*. Do everything we ever wanted to do."

"In a red convertible!" Pamela said.

"I'm serious," I told her.

"So am I," said Pamela, and I think she meant it.

Gwen looked from one of us to the next. "I'll be in med school, but if I can make it, I'd sure like to."

"Count me in," said Liz.

We grinned around the circle in the darkness. We actually had a plan. It was a time for taking chances.

"And I get to drive," said Pamela.